Beloved

P. M. HARDING

Oysterville, WA

Beloved

ISBN: 978-1-936009-09-1

Graphic design by Ellen Pickels

To my three girls: my daughter Leslie, my granddaughter Samantha, and my very sweet, great-granddaughter Tala. I wanted to leave you a book with my name on the front cover.

To my parents, who didn't live long enough to know about this, but who always told me I could do anything I set my mind on.

Acknowledgments

To LoryL: This story never would have been written had it not been for your encouragement of a very amateur writer.

To MAB (Maryanne) and Bonnie N. who deserve big thanks for all their work and patience on the first edit of this story back in 2007. (Gosh, was it that long ago?) Their help is greatly appreciated.

I'm very grateful to Ellen P. for her work on the front and back covers of *Beloved*, and to Debbie S. for her work on the final edit. It was a real pleasure to work with both ladies.

In my own edit, Gayle Lynn was able to help me through Chapter 11, and Gayle M. worked with me through the final Epilogue. I appreciate everything you ladies did.

Last, but certainly not least, to my wonderful friends — Lorie, Theresa, Casey, Crystal, Gayle Lynne, Linda and Lily. Thanks to all of you for your friendship and love, especially during this difficult time in my life.

Prologue

May 9, 1790

Jonathan Worthington stared down at the urgent message that lay open on his desk. Thomas Bennet, of Longbourn in Hertfordshire, requested his presence immediately. His long-time friend wrote that he had an emergency of such import that its solution could only be entrusted to his dearest, most reliable friend. Worthington sensed his desperation; he knew Bennet would not call on him lightly.

Worthington had planned to leave for his estate in Staffordshire the following morning, but to accommodate Bennet, he changed his plans. Within an hour of receiving the express, Worthington was in his carriage, rushing to the aid of his friend.

As he was leaving London, Worthington wondered what could cause such uncharacteristic behavior in the master of Longbourn. He had known Thomas Bennet since their Cambridge days although it had been a number of years since the two men had actually seen one another. Whatever the problem, he hoped it could be resolved quickly. He was anxious to return home and be with his wife, who was to deliver their first child at any moment.

Sighing, he leaned back against the soft cushions of his carriage and tried to relax the tension building in his body, born of his need to be in two places at the same time.

Chapter 1

Thomas Bennet paced his study, wringing his hands and wondering how much longer it would be before his friend would arrive. At intervals, he checked a small room off his study where a young girl and a newborn were hidden.

He returned and paced the length of the room, muttering repeatedly, "Where is he?"

He poured himself a glass of port and began pacing again. In the quiet of his room, he told himself not to dwell on what was happening, else he might lose the courage to proceed with his hastily thought-out plan. He must do what was best for the babe to keep her safe. Yes, her safety was paramount to any other consideration. Still, no amount of rationalizing would calm him.

It was midnight when Worthington arrived. Bennet was waiting outside for the first glimpse of a carriage. He had been walking up and down the drive in an agitated state for the past hour. He had sought the safety of the darkness outside, should he collapse into tears like a silly woman — like his stupid wife. Any fears he had about the success of his plans were relieved when his old friend stepped out of his carriage wearing an expression of concern mixed with friendship. Yes, this would work. Worthington would save her.

He rushed his friend into his study and locked the door. Pouring two glasses of port, Bennet downed his in one gulp and poured another. Worthington watched him closely while he sipped his drink slowly, and waited for the information that precipitated this strange reunion.

Bennet sat in the chair across from his guest and took a deep breath. "Jonathan, forgive me for sending such a desperate message to you. I am ashamed we have not kept in closer contact since our Cambridge days, but since then much has happened. After two years, since our two-year old daughter was born, my wife finally gave birth today to twins."

"Congratulations! That is wonderful, but what is the problem?"

Bennet closed his eyes before answering. When he finally opened them, they were full of pain. "The boy's cord was wrapped tightly around his neck, and he was born dead. The other child, a little girl, lives and seems to be healthy."

"I am so sorry for your loss, but—"

Bennet held up his hand. "I need your help. My little girl's life is in peril."

"I will do what I can, but why is it so?"

Instead of answering his friend's direct question, Bennet resumed telling the story his way. "When I heard the news of my son, I rushed out into the garden. The house felt suffocating to me, and I hoped the fresh air would soothe my wounded soul. My son died! My heir! I saw him, Jonathan. He was so handsome. He was everything I had hoped for in a son." Tears welled up in his eyes. He gasped for a breath and then continued. "I admit it; I was heartbroken. My world seemed lost. I sank down on a bench and cried until my head pounded and my eyes swelled shut."

Worthington waited the few minutes required for Bennet to calm himself.

"Suddenly, I heard whimpering, and I got up to investigate, thinking perhaps an animal was hurt and needed to be put out of his misery. I felt like killing something, and a wounded animal seemed fitting — but I was wrong. I found a young girl instead, badly beaten, lying half under a hedge. She held a newborn wrapped in a thin blanket. The child made no sound, no movement.

"'My God!' I cried out when I checked on it. Her child was dead too! What kind of evil trick was this? 'Help me,' she whispered. I knelt down beside the girl and inquired about the child and, more importantly, what had happened to her. I demanded to know who did this to her. She begged again, 'Help me, please. I need to hide.'

"She said her father had abused her and that she had delivered a daughter only the night before. Mercifully, her child had been stillborn. Her cruel father had not known she was carrying his child until then, and he beat her to near death and then threw her out of his house, fearful that she would speak of his monstrous deeds. He threatened to do away with her if she dared come back. She admitted that she was not a local girl but refused to tell me where her home had been. I know not how far she walked, but she must have traveled at least a day, hugging her dead baby next to her bruised and battered body. How she was able to walk so soon after delivering a child, I do not know." For a moment, Bennet's mind went blank. Too much had happened that day, and he was having trouble thinking clearly.

Worthington tapped his friend's hand. "Take your time."

"No, I cannot." Bennet took a deep breath and expelled it quickly. "Every second we lose is one too many."

"Go on then. What happened next?"

"I picked her up in my arms and carried her from the garden through a door leading to my study. From there, I slipped into another smaller room, behind one of my bookcases. I laid her on the floor where she stayed, whimpering, until I returned later with food and blankets. She looked horrible. She had taken quite a beating."

"What does your wife think?"

"She does not know. She was upstairs in her room, and I imagined the servants had retired after cleaning up the evening meal. I brought the girl into the house unseen, but I kept wondering what I was going to do with her. At first, I intended to give her work here, but my wife would never let her stay."

"Why?"

Bennet closed his eyes and shook his head. He let out a sob and then began to pace, gulping port as he moved across the room. "It was while I watched her caressing her dead baby that I came upon a solution. I told the girl I needed to leave again and that she must stay as quiet as possible while I was gone. She nodded that she would. I was somewhat certain we had not been seen by anyone when I brought her and, more importantly, her baby into the house; however, I had to discover if this was true. This was crucial to the plan, Jonathan."

Bennet refilled their glasses. He stared directly into his old friend's eyes. "Please let me explain what happened next without question or comment. I can only say it once."

Worthington nodded for him to continue.

"I left the girl gripping her bundle to her chest with one hand and nibbling the food with the other. I checked the kitchen, the hall, and any room where we could have been seen. The house was quiet. I then headed to the nursery. Luckily, the servant was asleep in the chair across the room. As quietly as possible, I picked up my beautiful little baby. She was awake and kicking her blankets off. She is an independent little miss. When you see her, you will agree she is special — very special. I pulled a blanket from a closet in the hallway and hurried back downstairs. Please, I beg you — do not judge me for what I will admit to next."

Bennet dropped into a chair and stared out into the room. "I took the dead baby from the girl's arms and replaced it with my own beautiful little girl. I put her child's body in my dead son's coffin and sealed it shut."

"My God! Why, Bennet? And what exactly do you expect of me?"

"The largest favor I could ever ask anyone. I wrote to you because no other acquaintance of mine has such a kind and loving nature as you." Bennet held up his hand. "Let me finish, please. When I returned to the anteroom, the young girl was cradling my daughter, whispering to her, tears rolling down her face. She kept her close to her chest while she rocked back and forth. She was so gentle and loving.

"I whispered to her that I must send my own child away, and if my friend agreed to take her too, would she—"

"Wait!" Worthington jumped up and stood over Bennet. "You want me to take your baby? This goes beyond anything I imagined. Do you hate the child so much because your son died and she lived? What kind of man are you?"

"No!" Bennet cried, "I would never give her away unless her life was in danger, and believe me, she is in the gravest danger. I do not believe she would survive one week here. I told the girl perhaps you could find a place for her in your house as a servant. I revealed that your wife will be giving birth to your child soon, and you will need a wet nurse. Without hesitation, she agreed to leave with my baby. Now it is up to you."

Bennet shamelessly begged his friend to take his child and raise her as his own and to take in the battered girl for her own protection.

Worthington began pacing the room, not stopping until Bennet grabbed his arm.

"Jonathan, I must do what is best for my child to keep her safe," he said and then added with tears streaming down his cheeks, "even if it means I have to give her away and never see her again for the rest of my life."

An obviously stunned Mr. Worthington said nothing at first. He stared into Bennet's eyes and then blurted out, "I cannot. I cannot raise another man's child. This does not make sense. You have not explained what would happen to your little girl if she stayed here."

Bennet pulled him over to the bookcase and opened the door where his daughter was hidden. He waved the girl to come into the study. She came in carrying a small bundle in her arms. Worthington flinched at the extent of her bruises. Bennet took the bundle, placed it in his friend's arms, and pulled back a corner of the blanket.

Gazing up at the men was a pair of bright, violet-colored eyes in a creamy white face, capped by a head full of dark hair that was just beginning to curl. The newborn child stared up at him, yawned, and then closed her eyes and went to sleep. Mr. Worthington felt a strong tug at his heart.

"Tell me why her life is in danger," Worthington whispered as he handed the baby back to the young girl.

Bennet led the girl back to the small room with the baby. As soon as the door closed, Worthington demanded more forcibly to know the reason why.

Bennet sighed heavily. "My wife has the insane idea that my daughter is evil — a demon child — and that she killed my son deliberately by wrapping the cord around the boy's neck before they were born. She will not hold the child or feed her, and she declares that she will do away with her the minute my back is turned."

"Are you positive she would do such a thing?"

"She has already made two attempts."

Worthington looked at him in horror. "Thomas, I cannot comprehend anyone, especially a mother, wanting to destroy this child. She is beautiful, and she deserves the chance to live. Since my wife is very close to delivering our first born, perhaps—"

"My child could be your child's companion."

Nothing was said for several minutes while Worthington considered the whole of it. He strode over to the bookcase door and touched it gently when a whimper sounded.

"Perhaps I can bring her into my home. This young girl must come along so she can feed her. I cannot care for the babe. Is the girl old enough? She seems young."

"She is but fourteen. Her name is Sarah."

"If I only had time to consider everything — but I understand why a decision has to be made tonight." Worthington ran his fingers through his hair, exhaled a long breath, and then nodded. "I agree, but I wish it could be some other way." He let his shoulders drop down. "I am so sorry this has happened, Thomas. You deserve better."

"I have one request — that you allow me to see her occasionally whenever you are in London."

"Do you think that wise?" Worthington asked. "I fear that may raise questions and cause problems if I am to guard her from the truth."

"Perhaps we could meet in a park so I can catch a glimpse of her?" Bennet asked hopefully.

Worthington shook his head. "My friend, I hate to bring more sorrow to your life, but if we are to protect this child, you must never have any claim to her. No record of this arrangement must ever be written down. It is with a heavy heart that I must reject your request."

Bennet lowered his head for several moments and, with a flat tone in his voice, agreed to his friend's terms. He hurried to gather the two and returned with Sarah dressed in a hooded cloak that concealed her face. She carried a satchel where the baby was hidden.

Worthington walked them out to the carriage where his valet, Spencer, was waiting. "Have you given the child a name?" he asked in a quiet voice.

Bennet shared it with him and Worthington smiled. "That is part of my wife's Christian name." He climbed inside and gave the order to drive on.

Thomas Bennet felt the tears well up in his eyes as he watched his beautiful daughter disappear from his life. He lifted his arm and waved, softly calling to the carriage pulling away, "I will always love you. Goodbye my sweetest, most beloved Elizabeth Anne."

THE FOLLOWING MORNING, MR. BENNET went to his wife's chambers and told her their daughter had died during the night. "I have put her body into the casket with her brother, and they will be buried today."

His wife wailed and carried on about not wanting that demon child in the same casket as her precious son. She insisted that he put her into another, but her husband told her that it was done and the casket had already been sealed.

He hurriedly left his wife's room to make arrangements for the funeral, knowing he would never again enter her chamber. There would be no more children.

Chapter 2

The carriage sped toward Rosehaven, Worthington's country estate in Staffordshire. The two men sat opposite the young girl, who was oblivious to their presence as she tenderly cuddled the tiny babe in her arms. The moon was full, and its light streamed into the carriage, illuminating the deep purple bruises on Sarah's face and neck.

"Hush, hush, my sweet little girl," she crooned and then placed her swollen lips on the infant's dark head and, with the gentlest of kisses, quieted the fussy child. She hummed and rocked slowly without regard to the jostling of the carriage as it lumbered over the rutted roads.

Spencer whispered to Mr. Worthington, "They were the reason for the journey?"

Worthington nodded slightly and used a familiar signal to his valet that they would speak about it at a later time. His eyes followed Sarah as she cooed and whispered to the child, lightly touching the infant's face with her bruised fingers.

"My pretty girl, my sweet, pretty girl, I shall keep you safe."

"Sarah, let me have Elizabeth Anne." She carefully handed the child to her new master, and smiled as he brought Elizabeth closer to his face. "She is very beautiful, is she not?" he asked, his eyes never leaving the babe's face. Sarah dipped her head in agreement.

Worthington stared at the child. *My beautiful daughter*, he thought with pride. *You are my daughter, and you will be loved and protected.* To Sarah he said, "I believe Elizabeth Anne will bring us much joy in the years to come. She will be our beloved daughter."

Sarah smiled. "Yes, Master. She is worthy of our love."

Worthington smiled as he returned the newborn to the waiting arms of the young girl. "Sarah," he said again and waited until she lifted her eyes, "when we arrive, I need to speak to Mrs. Worthington privately as to the nature of your duties."

She held her breath, her eyebrows raised upwards, and she instinctively drew Elizabeth close to her chest. Sarah leaned as far back into the cushioned seat as was possible.

"Now, now!" Her master reached over and lightly patted her hand, being careful not to frighten her. "I will explain everything to my wife. She is a kind mistress, I assure you. Do not worry. You are under my protection and care now." He smiled when her body relaxed, and she nodded her head although she kept the baby close to her chest.

The newborn began whimpering and moving her mouth against Sarah's breast, so she turned away from the men and draped a blanket over the babe to allow her to feed. Soon after the baby had her fill, the gentle jostling motion of the carriage lulled Sarah and Elizabeth to sleep, giving Mr. Worthington and his valet a chance to talk.

Spencer had been in his service for five and twenty years; he was his most trusted servant, often helping him to find reasonable solutions to the problems he faced. Worthington was confident that he, with Spencer's excellent objectivity, would be able to find answers to this dilemma.

Casting his gaze to the sleeping girls, he whispered to his valet. "We must get Sarah and Elizabeth Anne into my chambers without anyone being made aware of it."

"I can lead her through the servants' entrance without detection, especially if we use the satchel to hide the babe, but not until after the trunks are unloaded. But, sir, may I ask why the secrecy?"

"I have decided to raise this child as my own."

Spencer's brows lifted, and he questioned his master with a penetrating gaze, inviting further disclosure.

"I will explain later. For now, we must focus on getting the child to my bedchambers without being seen. The servants must not be any the wiser. Only a handful of people can know the truth and then, only what is necessary to perform their duties."

"All your servants are loyal to you and would never question your motive."

"In this particular situation, I do not feel as secure as you."

"In order to avoid detection, I will need to clear the way first."

Worthington tilted his head towards a soundly sleeping Sarah. "Very good.

She and the babe will wait in the carriage until you secure the passageway."

Spencer nodded and the two men devised a scheme they believed would be successful. They settled back into the comfortable seats, dozing until the coachman tapped on the carriage to announce their arrival.

When the carriage came to a stop, Sarah woke with a start. Holding Elizabeth close, she peered out the window, her mouth agape at the well-tended house that was three times the size of Longbourn with the tallest windows she had ever seen.

Worthington quickly called Sarah away from the window and back into the seat, insisting she wait in the carriage until his valet returned. He briefly explained their plans. She slithered as far back into the corner of the carriage as possible, whilst whispering comforting words in the ear of the infant snuggled in her arms. Recognizing the danger of premature exposure, she gently rocked Elizabeth as the footmen unloaded the trunks and carried them into the house. Worthington waited outside the carriage until the coachmen left and Spencer signaled him to come. He left Sarah and Elizabeth in the carriage, hurried into the house, and waited.

Spencer headed towards the carriage, walking nonchalantly as if he had merely forgotten something. No one was in sight by the time he reached the carriage door, at which time, Worthington rushed to his bedchambers.

Once Sarah and the baby were safely inside his room, Worthington ensured their comfort. Spencer brought Sarah something to eat and promised to stay with them. Worthington scurried off to his wife's chambers.

"Agggh!" Mrs. Worthington screamed, as her husband sought admittance to her room.

"You must leave, sir," the housekeeper said gently. "It is not proper for you to be here. Your child will be arriving today."

"I must speak to my wife about an urgent situation. Is she well? I heard her cry out."

"Sir, this is no place for a man, excepting for the doctor, and I have sent for him."

"I will sit with her and speak quickly. I insist! Please bring me a light meal. I am famished from my journey." He raised himself to his full height, his piercing blue eyes glaring at her. She nodded and left him alone with his wife.

"Margaret, are you well?" He approached his wife cautiously but felt his muscles relax at her happy expression.

"Yes, my dear. It is early yet, but I think our child will be born today. I am pleased you have returned."

"I need to speak with you on a pressing matter. I need your counsel and agreement. Should I return later?"

"No. The pain has eased a bit. I have some time. What is it that troubles you so, my dear?" She held out her hand to him, pulling him to sit by her on the bed.

He began the tale of the young girl and her unfortunate situation. He squeezed his wife's hand when he revealed that her baby died.

"What is your purpose in telling me this, especially at this time?" Mrs. Worthington grabbed her stomach with her free hand.

Worthington's eyes widened. He gently stroked her hand, whispering words of comfort.

"Do you wish for this young girl to be nursemaid to our child?"

"Dearest, the rest of my story is also sad, but perhaps I should wait to relate it." He stood quickly. "At present, I am more concerned about you."

"Nonsense. Please continue, but do make haste in your telling."

He explained the situation with Mr. Bennet and his wife. Margaret listened wordlessly until he said that he had brought Sarah and the newborn home with him.

"Here? You brought another woman's baby here into our home? You want me to be her mother?" she asked incredulously.

"Ah, my sweet, she is so beautiful! She will take your breath away and capture your heart immediately. Young Sarah can be the wet nurse for the babe."

"How old is this girl?"

"She is but fourteen."

Mrs. Worthington laughed. "Who will be nursemaid to her?" She waved her hand in the air. "If she is able to handle two babies, I suppose she can be the nursemaid. Now bring them here before the doctor comes. I will decide only after I see this girl and the babe. Hurry!"

Worthington returned with the baby in his arms, leaving Sarah in the connecting sitting room. Knowing the generous nature of his sweet wife, he assumed that once she beheld the baby, all would be well. He was not disappointed as he placed Elizabeth in her outstretched arms.

Elizabeth woke and opened her eyes.

"Jonathan, she is the most beautiful baby I have ever seen! Look at all that dark hair! And her eyes, her beautiful eyes! Someday this one will break many hearts." With tears in her eyes, she continued. "I cannot imagine any mother rejecting her. Where is the wet nurse, Jonathan? I would like to speak with her whilst we are alone."

"I need to tell you — she was badly beaten, my dear, and I do not want you upset."

"Bring her to me, Jonathan."

Mr. Worthington knew better than to argue with his wife, especially now, so he left and returned with Sarah. Upon seeing the young girl, Mrs. Worthington gave a gasp and held out her hand.

"Come here, child," she said in a soft, gentle voice. Sarah looked at Mr. Worthington who nodded his head, and the girl stepped closer to the bed.

"Who did this to you? Who was so cruel?" Anger flashed in Mrs. Worthington's eyes, and her lips were pressed into a tight line.

"Dear wife, calm yourself. This cannot be good for our own babe."

"Jonathan, when Dr. Harris arrives, I want him to examine this child. She needs to be treated immediately."

Turning once again to Sarah, Mrs. Worthington said kindly, "Will you not tell me who beat you?"

Sarah looked down at her feet and slowly shook her head. Mrs. Worthington sighed. "Never mind, child. I will not force an answer when it is obviously painful for you. Perhaps one day you will confide in me. In the meantime, you have a home with us for as long as you desire it."

Upon the arrival of Doctor Harris, the housekeeper led him into Mrs. Worthington's chambers where he was acquainted with the amazing story. Doctor Harris had served the Worthington family for many years and was a man to be trusted. The housekeeper, Mrs. Winters, had been with the family since Mr. Worthington was a child. Both the doctor and Mrs. Winters vowed never to reveal what they were told that day, and the Worthingtons felt secure. In order to ensure secrecy and the ultimate success of the plan, Elizabeth remained in Margaret Worthington's chambers, away from the eyes of any curious servants.

It was a long and difficult night for Margaret. While waiting for their babe to be born, Worthington directed Spencer to take hot water to his chambers for Sarah to bathe. Mrs. Winters carefully washed and treated her wounds with salve provided by the doctor, before dressing her in a cotton nightgown that she had located for Sarah's use.

There was a bed in the nursery, and after Elizabeth had been fed, Mrs. Winters led a clearly exhausted Sarah to it. The housekeeper had also sent for a tray of tea, soup, bread, and cheese. So great was Sarah's hunger that she eagerly consumed it all without hesitation. After eating her fill, she lay on the bed and was asleep as soon as her head touched the soft pillow. Throughout the night, dreams of her father intruded, waking her from her slumber. She would find herself trembling, sitting straight up in bed, and gasping for breath, until she remembered she was finally safe. Sighing, she snuggled back into the warm bed and slept again.

At three in the morning on May 11, a son with dark curly hair and blue eyes was born — Andrew David Worthington. Doctor Harris recorded the event as a twin birth, a son and a daughter. Word of the births was sent throughout the house.

Mrs. Worthington held her new babies in her arms. Her confinement and the birth had been very difficult, and Doctor Harris had told her that she would likely never conceive another child. The news, however, was not as devastating as it might have been, had they not been blessed with the miracle of Elizabeth Anne.

TIME PASSED AND THE SECRET held. Every servant saw the resemblance of Elizabeth to Mrs. Worthington. As the children grew older and began babbling, Andrew's attempt at "Elizabeth Anne" came out of his mouth as "Lizzy," and so she always remained to him. It was less of a mouthful than Elizabeth Anne was. The twins grew close, and even though it was unnecessary due to his love for her, Andrew was taught early on that he must always watch over his sister and protect her.

Sarah became the children's nurse, and while she loved Andrew dearly, her heart would always belong to Elizabeth.

THE WORTHINGTONS WERE FRIENDS OF long standing with the Fitzwilliams who had two sons of their own, Albert and Richard. They also claimed close friendship with the Darcys who had one son, Fitzwilliam, and many years later were blessed with a daughter, Georgiana.

Albert, Richard, and Fitzwilliam were the eldest of the children, and while Albert and his brother either teased or ignored the younger ones, Fitzwilliam never did. He and his parents visited the Worthingtons shortly after the twins were born, and young Fitzwilliam was fascinated with the babies, especially Elizabeth with her violet-colored eyes. He thought she was the most beautiful baby he had ever seen.

Fitzwilliam was eight years old when they were born, and he loved to sit and watch them. As they grew older, he observed how Andrew would sit quietly and examine an object as though it was a mystery to be solved, while Elizabeth was lively and loved to laugh. She was perpetual motion.

The adults, in turn, enjoyed watching the different expressions that played across Fitzwilliam's face when he was in company with the children. He would smile at their efforts to roll over and laugh at their clumsy attempts to grasp objects that eluded their chubby fists. As the twins grew and began making hesitant first steps, he would frown when they tried to walk and fell down. He would run to pick them up and set them on their feet again. Fitzwilliam was always ready to play with the children, and he became their favorite "cousin."

Georgiana's arrival, when Andrew and Elizabeth were four years old and Fitzwilliam twelve, was a joyous time. The only mark on the event was Lady Anne Darcy's near death giving birth to Georgiana. Sadly, she never fully regained her strength.

Andrew and Elizabeth joined Fitzwilliam in spoiling the little girl, and Elizabeth declared she would be Georgiana's big sister.

On the twins' fifth birthday, Worthington decided he had one important task that he must complete. Lady Anne's near passing reminded him of unfinished business. He would not let another day go by without doing what he must, so he and his family departed for London, Sarah attending them.

MR. WORTHINGTON LEFT HIS SOLICITOR'S office and headed to his club. He had a desire to hear about his old friend, Thomas Bennet. Once a week, whenever he was in London, he would meet for lunch with William Reid, a friend from his Cambridge days. Without much prodding, the latest news about the residents of Longbourn would come gushing out of his mouth. Reid was a frequent correspondent with Bennet, and they visited each other a few times a year, sometimes meeting in London, sometimes at Longbourn. Worthington hoped that today's meeting would provide the most recent reports.

"I have not heard from Thomas Bennet in some time. Do you have news?" Worthington struggled to keep his curiosity and discomfort at bay.

"I visited him recently at Longbourn and was in the company of his wife. Her behavior seems stranger each time I see her. I believe it is her condition that prompted him to confide in me. Have I ever told you her story?"

"Only in a general way. What happened to cause her to behave so peculiarly?"

"Five years ago she gave birth to twins. Both babies died the day they were born. The male child was stillborn, and the female died shortly after birth.

Mrs. Bennet insisted that the female child strangled her brother while still in her womb. Strangled him! Can you believe such nonsense?" Reid exclaimed.

"Indeed, that is hard to believe." Worthington hid his smile of relief behind his napkin. The truth remained a secret.

"She actually made that statement to me! I did not know what to say, so I only mumbled that I was sorry to hear of their loss. Later, Thomas and I retired to his study where he told me the entire story. Apparently, their friends think his wife eccentric and sometimes very difficult, but harmless. Thomas, however, says he believes she could be dangerous with provocation. She insists that the female child was a demon with devilish violet-colored eyes. He says she is obsessed, and he fears she could harm any young girl with such eyes."

"Let us pray, then, that she never meets a female of that description."

"Indeed! I confess, Jonathan, that being around the woman was most uncomfortable. They asked me to stay for supper, but I made an excuse about having a business meeting early the next morning in order to hasten my departure."

"I do not blame you!"

"Bennet has no hope of her ever recovering. He tries to hide her true condition from others as much as possible and restricts whom she sees for the good of their only daughter. Her family and neighbors pay little attention when she rambles on about the demon child."

The subject of the Bennets was then dropped, and they spoke of other matters.

WORTHINGTON HAD COME TO REALIZE that Sarah, with her fierce love for Elizabeth, could be trusted with all things relating to both his son and daughter. Upon returning to his townhouse, he called her to his study and told her of the disturbing conversation concerning the Bennets.

"You must be careful for Elizabeth's safety, Sarah, not only in our home, but when you venture out into town. Be especially watchful when you take the children to the park. I doubt that Elizabeth will ever come in contact with Mrs. Bennet, but strange things do happen. If Elizabeth should ever meet her, you will need to provide our girl with all the protection you have in your power."

"Master, I would die for that child. Rest assured that no harm from anyone will come to her or Andrew as long as I live."

"Thank you, Sarah. I know I can depend on you."

Thereafter, whenever Mr. Worthington met with Mr. Reid, he obtained an update on Mrs. Bennet's condition, information Worthington felt essential in his determination to keep his daughter safe.

BOTH WORTHINGTON CHILDREN WERE BRIGHT and friendly, with pleasing personalities. When at Rosehaven, Elizabeth loved being outdoors with the sun on her face and the wind in her hair. As she grew older and more independent, she sometimes eluded the servants in order to take long walks by herself. Even though this worried her parents, they did not try to restrain her. Instead, they had Sarah discreetly follow at a distance to make certain she remained safe. Whether the young girl knew she was being followed was uncertain, but it was unlikely that one as astute as Elizabeth did not know.

Elizabeth and Andrew also became excellent riders, and they were given their first horses when they were six years old. As they grew, they were highly competitive and loved to race each other over the hills of Rosehaven.

If the weather did not permit walking out or riding, Elizabeth could be found curled up on a window seat with a book or sketchpad. When she grew tired of those pursuits, she practiced the pianoforte to the delight of her parents. She was a loyal friend and very kind-hearted, but she also had a temper, and woe be to the person who angered her. Her best features were her ready smile and expressive eyes, which flashed with mischief.

Andrew was a handsome lad who loved books, as did Elizabeth, but he was a more serious child, always eager to learn everything he could about the estate that would one day belong to him. He did not have the temper that Elizabeth possessed. Instead, his nature was calm, and he preferred to use reason and logic while Elizabeth sometimes let her emotions rule her.

LIFE WAS GOOD FOR THE Worthington, Darcy, and Fitzwilliam families when, unexpectedly, Lady Anne Darcy passed away. She had appeared to be improving but, when she became with child again, she was still too frail, and both she and the child died.

Georgiana was but five years of age, and Fitzwilliam was seventeen at the time of their mother's death. Nine-year-old Elizabeth was saddened at Mrs. Darcy's passing, for she dearly loved and admired the mother of her two close friends. Over the years, she had spent many happy hours at Pemberley, the Darcys' estate, and she had fond memories of Lady Anne.

The Worthington family paid a call to the Darcy estate on the day of Lady Anne's burial, and Elizabeth noted how stoic Fitzwilliam looked. He had not a tear in his eyes as he stood so straight, one hand on his mother's coffin. Elizabeth thought his eyes were the saddest she had ever seen, and she wished to comfort him. On impulse, she walked up to him and jerked on his coat sleeve. He was startled but bent down to her.

"I am very sorry about your mother," she whispered, her eyes glistening with unshed tears.

He did not say anything for a moment, but a slight smile appeared on his lips. "Thank you, Miss Worthington. That is very kind of you."

She returned his smile and stood with him for a while, still holding onto his coat sleeve. She glanced around and looked for Georgiana. Seeing the child sitting alone, Elizabeth sat down on the settee beside her.

Fitzwilliam watched as she spoke with Georgiana. He saw his sister shake her head from side to side, then smile and nod her head in agreement.

Elizabeth put out her hand for Georgiana, and the girls walked out of the room. Fitzwilliam was curious as to the destination of the two, so he discreetly followed them.

The girls stopped in the kitchen, and when they emerged, they had their arms filled with bread. Wanting to make certain they would be safe, Fitzwilliam watched them run to the pond and begin feeding the ducks. Sarah appeared at his side, and they smiled at each other, realizing the little girl had taken Georgiana from the weeping and sadness inside the house.

Without warning, the son of Pemberley's steward, twelve-year-old George Wickham, came bounding out of nowhere and pushed Georgiana to the ground, causing her to scrape her hands and knees. He grabbed the bread away from her and threw it all in the pond. Georgiana began crying, while George stood over her laughing.

Fitzwilliam and Sarah started running toward them, but before they could take more than a few steps, Elizabeth balled up her fist, hit George in the stomach, and then kicked him in the shins. While he was bent over gasping for breath, Elizabeth jumped on his back and started beating him over the head with her fist and yelling, "Take that, you old Sticky Wicky."

By the time Fitzwilliam and Sarah reached them, George was crying and yelling for her to get off. Sarah went immediately to Georgiana and enfolded her into her arms, while Fitzwilliam went directly to George Wickham.

"That is enough," Fitzwilliam said, as he lifted Elizabeth off of George. Then he turned to Wickham. "Are you not a little old to be tormenting two little girls?"

"I am not a little girl, and I can take care of myself. I beat *him*, did I not?" Elizabeth stood there huffing with her arms crossed over her chest. Fitzwilliam, amused at the fury of this little spitfire, laughed for the first time in days.

"George, I think you had better leave before Miss Worthington skins your hide."

George whirled around to Elizabeth and hissed, "Just you wait, you little brat! I will have my revenge against you."

Elizabeth laughed at him, "You and the Royal Army, George Wickham!"

Fitzwilliam grabbed George's arm and issued a strong warning. "If you ever attempt to hurt Miss Worthington, you will have to deal with me, Wickham."

As George Wickham stalked off, Fitzwilliam turned to Elizabeth. He knew he should scold her for unladylike behavior, but he did not have the heart to do so. Her anger and behavior had stemmed from Wickham making Georgiana cry, so Fitzwilliam smiled at her instead. Elizabeth looked up at him through long, dark lashes and returned his smile.

For as long as she could remember, Elizabeth had centered her romantic notions on Fitzwilliam Darcy. She began keeping a diary as soon as she could write, and most of her entries were of Fitzwilliam, his activities, their conversations, and her admiration of him.

"Mr. Darcy," she said, her hands on her hips and one eyebrow raised, "you had better not marry before I grow up to be a lady."

"And why is that, Miss Worthington?" Darcy could not hide the hint of amusement in his voice.

Grinning at him with a look of mischief in her beautiful eyes, she said, "Because I am going to marry you when I am grown." She grabbed Georgiana's hand, and they happily skipped back to the house.

Fitzwilliam Darcy laughed and shook his head as he watched the girls. Elizabeth had always been a favorite of his because of her lively spirit.

Aye, she is a little spitfire, that one, and I hope she never changes. When she marries, she will lead her husband around by his nose. Life will never be dull when Elizabeth is around.

No one noticed that Sarah had slipped away and followed Wickham. She would teach him to leave Miss Darcy and her beloved charge alone. It would be a lesson he would never forget, for George Wickham came close to losing his manhood that day. He never bothered the children again.

TWO DAYS AFTER THE WORTHINGTONS returned to Rosehaven, Sarah and the children were in the library searching for a book of plays. All three enjoyed putting on theatricals and went to a great deal of trouble with costumes and scenery. Their merriment was interrupted, however, when a servant brought a message to Sarah from her master, requesting her immediate presence in his study. Sarah's heart was pounding as she hurried down the hallway.

Chapter 3

Sarah knocked softly on the study door and tried to appear calm. When her master called for her to enter, she opened the door slowly and peeked around.

Mr. Worthington looked up and waved her in, then pointed to a chair in front of his desk. When she was seated, he looked at her intently and began. "Sarah, tell me about George Wickham."

"What would you like to know, Master?"

He sighed. "I understand he bullied Elizabeth and Georgiana before we left Pemberley. Indeed, it was said he caused scrapes and bruising on Georgiana's knees and hands."

Sarah did not try to avoid his eyes. "That is true, sir."

Mr. Worthington's lips briefly curled into a small smile. "I also understand that Elizabeth began fighting him in the defense of her little friend."

"Yes, sir, that is also true. And a fine job she was doing, too, if I may be permitted to say so. Mr. Fitzwilliam saved Wickham by lifting Elizabeth off of him." Sarah put her hand over her mouth in an effort to try to hide her giggle.

"And, what happened after that? Did you follow Wickham and punish him?" Worthington waited quietly for her to speak.

"Yes, Master," Sarah said in a soft voice, her eyes focused on her lap.

Worthington ran his hand across his face. "Fortunately, Wickham's father was angry with his son's behavior and not so much with yours. He determined that the manner in which you cut his son seemed to be more of a warning than an attempt to cause permanent damage."

"I admit that was my plan, Master."

"Now, Sarah, I have been giving much thought to you and considering my immediate course of action."

Sarah was certain her heart had stopped beating. She was unable to breathe while she awaited the punishment she knew had to be forthcoming.

Please, please, do not dismiss me. How would I live without my babies, especially Elizabeth? She felt a tear rolling down her cheek.

To her surprise, Worthington patted her shoulder. "Now, now, do not be distressed. I want only to ask a few questions and then inform you of my plans."

She exhaled heavily, relief evident on her face. "Then you will not dismiss me?"

"No, no, nothing of that sort. There has always been a mystery surrounding your background, and I wish you to tell me about your life before Mr. Bennet found you."

Sarah's eyes were wide with fear as she struggled with what and how much to reveal to him. If he knew the complete truth — all that she had done to her father — would he ever trust her to care for his children again?

"Please, Master, do not force me to tell you this. I am afraid you will hate me and send me away from your home." Sarah covered her eyes with her hands and sobbed uncontrollably like a child.

Mr. Worthington took a clean handkerchief from his desk and handed it to her. "Never mind, child. If the thought of telling upsets you to this degree, you need not speak of it."

Sarah looked out the window, but then turned her head back so she could face him. "I will tell you some of my story — enough for you to understand." She sighed. "My father was away from home when the child was born, but when he returned later that night, he feared I would tell the magistrate what he had done, so he savagely beat my mother and me.

"He was drunk. He was always meaner when he was drunk. His eyes were…wild. He lunged for me, but I evaded his grasp, making him angrier still. I ran out of the house into the woods, attempting to escape him, and he followed me relentlessly. Later, as he lay asleep on the ground, I searched his pockets and found a purse filled with gold coins and some bank notes. I did not count it, but I knew it would be enough for my mother to live in comfort for the rest of her life."

"How did he come by such a sum?"

"I know not, but I will tell you this — he never worked an honest day in his life. I believe you know the rest of my story from Mr. Bennet."

Worthington sat stroking his chin for some time, as though attempting to piece together the information Sarah had shared. She could tell from the expression on his face that her master knew there was more she had not told him. She hoped he would not force her to reveal what she had tried so hard to forget.

She grew pale and began trembling all over. Quickly, he poured her a cup of tea and put a generous dash of brandy in it. "Sip this, child. When you have calmed, we will speak of this further."

After some time, Sarah finished her drink and set her cup on his desk. Her color had begun to return, and she had ceased to tremble.

"Now, Sarah, you know that the care and protection of my children is uppermost in my mind. I would do anything to ensure their safety, and I trust that you feel the same. I wish to bring in masters who will teach you how to defend yourself and the children in case danger presents itself again. First, you will have fencing lessons until you perfect the art."

Sarah's eyes grew wide again. "But, sir, it is not proper for a woman to fence."

Mr. Worthington smiled. "I will decide what is proper for you, and what is best for the safety of my children, so do not be concerned with the propriety of this matter. Now, there is a man living in London who is from China, and he gives private lessons in the Asian art of self-defense. I will commission him and the fencing instructor that I have selected to come to Rosehaven so that you will be taught well, but in privacy. Mastery of these two skills will be the first and most important of the lessons you will learn."

Sarah looked at Worthington with shining eyes. It was unspoken between them; she had killed her father and he knew. "Then you still wish for me to care for your children and to live in the same house with you and Mrs. Worthington?"

"Yes, I am quite certain you would never bring harm to any of us. My wife and I trust you completely."

She jumped up, grabbed his hands and began to kiss them. "Oh, Master, thank you, thank you! I vow you will never have any cause to doubt or mistrust me. I will follow your orders and do all in my power not to betray your trust."

Sarah kept her vow until the day she died.

THE YEARS WENT BY, AND for the Worthingtons, they were happy. Sarah kept a close watch over her young mistress although no other incident of harm was attempted by Wickham or anyone else.

The Worthingtons made another sad trip to Derbyshire when Elizabeth was fifteen. The elder Mr. Darcy had passed away. Upon their arrival at Pemberley, Elizabeth went from room to room, searching for Georgiana. She knew how close her friend had been to her father since Lady Anne's death, and she wanted to make certain the younger girl was not alone at this terrible time.

As she was leaving the drawing room, she encountered Georgiana's brother, Fitzwilliam. They had seen little of each other while he was away at Cambridge and each immediately noted changes in the other.

My stars, she thought, struggling to breathe, *he is more handsome than I remembered. Look at those broad shoulders, and he has grown so tall!*

He seemed to be assessing her appearance with a critical look in his eyes at one moment, then his features shifted, and he looked to be in great pain.

Of course, he is in pain, she chided herself. *His father has just passed away.*

She watched as he took several deep breaths to calm himself. Finally, he was able to address her properly. "May I help you, Miss Worthington?"

Clearing her throat and wetting her lips, which had gone suddenly dry, Elizabeth responded. "I am looking for Georgiana, Mr. Darcy. Do you know where I might find her, sir?"

"She is in her chambers. I am certain she would welcome your company. Georgiana is having a most difficult time accepting the death of our father."

Elizabeth knew that she should bid him good day, but she did not want to leave him. "And you, sir, are you well?"

His dark eyes betrayed his grief, and his voice trembled ever so slightly. "I will be, with time, but it is difficult to comprehend that now only Georgiana and I are left. I feel quite adrift at the moment."

Acting on impulse, Elizabeth took his large hands in her small ones and held them for a few moments, wanting so much to bring him solace. She looked at their joined hands and then up into his eyes, fixed on hers. "I will find Georgiana now," she said in a soft voice.

Darcy squeezed her hands and then lifted them to his lips, placing a light kiss on each one. "Thank you, Miss Worthington. I am glad you are here with us today."

As Elizabeth turned and walked away, she had no way of knowing that Fitzwilliam, discomfited by his unwelcome state of arousal, had been frantically trying to think of something — anything — that would divert his attention from the desire coursing through his body. His face turned red from embarrassment due to his unexpectedly strong physical reaction to her. It would have pleased her to know that as Darcy stood watching until she was out of his sight, he had irrevocably decided to ask her to marry him as soon as she came out.

Finally, he understood why no woman of the *ton* had ever interested him;

he had been waiting for Elizabeth to grow into the beautiful woman she was now. He was in love, and the next two years would be sweet torture!

As she moved down the hall, Elizabeth appeared calm, but her heart raced all the way to Georgiana's chambers. She was excited by the way he had looked at her and the tenderness in his voice. It was a feeling unlike anything she had experienced before, and she had to admit that it delighted her.

She had no doubts that she would marry him. Elizabeth had overheard talk among her older friends and their mothers about how aloof Fitzwilliam was at society events. Some even thought he was haughty and proud. Although the matchmaking mamas continually pressed their daughters towards him, he seldom, if ever, danced with anyone, so Elizabeth was fairly certain she need not worry about competition from other women, however aggressive they might be. He would not be attracted by such behavior. She knew in her heart he was interested in her alone. His eyes clearly spoke his intentions, and her hands still tingled from his kisses.

AFTER MR. DARCY'S UNEXPECTED DEATH, Worthington spent even more time with his son, showing him in greater detail how an estate should be run. Andrew would be master of Rosehaven one day, and the death of Mr. Darcy had been a cruel but effective reminder to Worthington that life was fleeting. It was important that Andrew be prepared for every contingency.

A month later, the Worthingtons received a message from Darcy requesting the presence of Elizabeth and Sarah at Pemberley. He was deeply concerned about Georgiana, as that young lady was experiencing melancholy beyond what would be expected under such sad circumstances. He hoped Elizabeth could help her find the joy of living again.

The Worthingtons wished to be of help to Georgiana in any way that they could, but Margaret wondered if it would be best for her to visit with Elizabeth at Rosehaven instead.

"Jonathan, I would not wish for Elizabeth and Fitzwilliam to provoke gossip. I am certain he is thinking only of his sister, and it has not occurred to him that Elizabeth's good name might be compromised."

Jonathan nodded. "Fitzwilliam said that he will be in London the first week of Elizabeth's proposed visit, but I agree with you. It would be best if we invite Georgiana to Rosehaven for as long as she wishes to stay and invite Fitzwilliam to visit after he returns from London."

Worthington sent a reply to Darcy the following morning and was happy to receive his acceptance of their plans that evening. It was decided between the two families that Darcy would bring his sister in a week's time and travel on to London from Rosehaven. Upon the completion of his business, he would return to Rosehaven and visit the Worthingtons for three additional weeks.

Elizabeth was excited about having first Georgiana's company and then that of Mr. Darcy. Mr. Worthington promised Andrew time away from estate duties so that he might also enjoy their company.

ELIZABETH WAS WAITING ANXIOUSLY AT the window when the Darcy carriage appeared. She flew out of the house as soon as Georgiana stepped down.

"I am glad you are come, Georgiana. I have so anticipated your arrival. We shall have such a pleasant time together."

"Thank you for inviting me, Lizzy. I dreaded being alone while Brother was in London. I know I would have Mrs. Annesley for company, but she cannot ride, and she does not care for walking."

Elizabeth turned her attention to Darcy, who was talking quietly with her parents. "And you, sir, will you stay for dinner and resume your journey tomorrow morning?"

"Thank you for the kind invitation but, regretfully, I must be on my way immediately in order to reach London before nightfall. I shall return next week, and I look forward to spending time with you and your family."

Elizabeth's parents could not fail to notice the way Darcy's eyes lit up or the smile that appeared on his lips when he looked at their daughter. Suddenly, they were very glad Georgiana would be at Rosehaven. They approved of Darcy as a suitor for Elizabeth when the time was right; however, she was but fifteen, and Darcy would have to wait to declare himself until she had taken her place in society.

ELIZABETH AND SARAH KEPT GEORGIANA very busy that first week. They went for long walks to all of Elizabeth's favorite spots, relishing the freedom of the outdoors and enjoying the beauty of their surroundings.

One afternoon after a particularly challenging climb, they sat down to rest, whereupon Georgiana began speaking of her father and how much she missed him. Elizabeth held the girl in her arms for a long time as she sobbed out her long-suppressed grief and loneliness. The tears that soaked Elizabeth's shoulder were drops of healing to Georgiana's troubled heart, marking a turning point for her. After that, with Elizabeth's encouragement, Georgiana slowly began to regain some of her liveliness, and her previous melancholy began to dissipate.

Darcy returned after a week, and the four young people, with Sarah always in attendance, spent the next three weeks engaged in their favorite activities: riding, walking about, and going on picnics. In the evenings, they played cards or had lively debates about books they had read. Elizabeth and Georgiana entertained them by playing the pianoforte, and Elizabeth often sang.

Darcy always found a seat allowing him an unobstructed view of his beautiful Elizabeth as her clear soprano soothed his soul. He was able, for a brief moment, to forget the weight of responsibility that awaited him on his return to Pemberley.

Some might think it strange for a young man of three and twenty to enjoy the company of a younger sister, and two fifteen-year-olds, but Darcy was close to his sister, and Elizabeth's brother had always seemed to admire and look up to him as an experienced master of a great estate. Darcy had long been amused by Andrew's contemplative nature, so much like his own. He saw his friend as a serious, mature young man. They enjoyed spending time together, having many common interests, including a love of books and fast horses.

Darcy's relationship with Elizabeth was more easily understood; she was the woman he loved, so he naturally sought out her company at every opportunity, spending as much time in her presence as propriety allowed.

Several of Andrew's friends visited during those three weeks, and Darcy was disturbed to see the way they openly flirted with Elizabeth. She seemed to return their attentions by teasing and laughing with them, and he felt stabs of jealously until he realized that she treated them as brothers. Her special smiles and specific attentions were directed toward him alone.

On the afternoon before the Darcys were to leave Rosehaven, Andrew had gone with his father to visit their tenants, and Georgiana was in the music room with Mrs. Worthington. Sarah accompanied Elizabeth and Darcy to a small sitting room.

"Thank you for your kindness to my sister, Miss Worthington. I can see a difference in her already. I am most grateful for your help. I was confident that she would respond to you and your affection for her."

"Time will help heal Georgiana. I am glad you have agreed to bring her back to Rosehaven for regular visits. I so enjoy her company…and yours, also."

Darcy looked at Elizabeth for a long moment. Impulsively, he took her hand in his, stroking it with his fingers before turning it to kiss her palm and then her wrist. She closed her eyes for a moment, until Sarah cleared her throat, and he immediately dropped her hand. Elizabeth smiled at him, and he smiled in return.

Both felt they had reached an agreement; no words were necessary.

AFTER ELIZABETH TURNED SIXTEEN, SHE and Mrs. Worthington began planning her presentation to the court and her coming out, which would occur the following year. Elizabeth's godmother, Lady Matlock, was excited to be included in the planning since she had only two sons. Elizabeth had always been a favorite of hers, and the Countess loved her as much as she loved her own niece, Georgiana.

Elizabeth and her mother were very close, and Mrs. Worthington knew of her daughter's intense feelings for Darcy. One day, when she caught her daughter staring out a window with her bottom lip caught between her teeth, she laughed and teased her.

"Lizzy Belle, are you thinking of that handsome Mr. Darcy again?"

Elizabeth looked down at the floor, smiled slightly and said, "Perhaps."

"Well child, come here then and help me with the household accounts. You must know how to balance your accounts if you are to be a great mistress of Pemberley."

Elizabeth rolled her eyes. "Oh, Mama, I do not plan to marry so soon. I have ample time to master boring old accounts. It is a beautiful day, much too beautiful to stay inside poring over ledgers. Leave them and join me for a walk. Let us feel the sun on our faces and enjoy the pleasures nature sets before us."

Margaret Worthington happily closed her account books, tucked her arm into Elizabeth's, and gladly joined her daughter for a long walk, delighted to share the joy that was always Elizabeth.

THE FOLLOWING DAY, JONATHAN AND Margaret Worthington spent a pleasant dinner at the invitation of the Fitzwilliam family.

During the course of the evening, the wind began to gust and rain appeared to be coming, so their hosts urged them to stay overnight, but the Worthingtons were anxious to return home. Mr. Worthington had an important business meeting scheduled the following morning, and Mrs. Worthington was expecting her seamstress to call. So, braving the elements and ignoring the warnings, they left for Rosehaven.

It was an unfortunate decision. The wind soon howled even stronger and rain poured down in swirling sheets. They had almost reached the safety of

Rosehaven, when a vicious burst of wind snapped the tops of some trees, breaking the limbs and whipping them across the faces of the lead horses, causing them to panic and run wild. The driver valiantly tried to control them, but to no avail. The carriage careened wildly back and forth, until it ran off the road, turning over and tumbling down the embankment, spilling its precious cargo as it tore into pieces.

All were killed instantly, though none were found until the following afternoon. Due to the intensity of the storm, everyone at Rosehaven thought they had stayed with the Fitzwilliams, therefore, no alarm had been raised.

A somber message was sent to Mr. Worthington's brother, Henry Worthington, who rushed to Rosehaven to oversee the necessary arrangements. Andrew and Elizabeth were inconsolable.

"Andrew," Elizabeth sobbed, "what will we do without Mama and Papa? I cannot believe they are gone."

Andrew, struggling with his own grief, hardly knew how to answer his sister.

Sarah hugged them both close to her. She kissed Elizabeth on the forehead and then turned to Andrew. "Master Andrew, do not be ashamed to cry, for your grief must be expressed in some form."

Andrew only put his head on Sarah's shoulder. He was still in shock.

Sarah looked up as she tried to comfort the siblings and saw Spencer standing in the doorway. She nodded her head toward Andrew and Spencer said, his voice full of tenderness, "Come, Master Andrew, you must get some rest. Tomorrow your uncle will need your assistance. You must ready yourself."

Andrew kissed Elizabeth on her cheek and assured her that he would see her the following morning when they broke their fast.

After Andrew and Spencer left them, Sarah gently held Elizabeth's hand and led the young girl to her chambers where she helped settle Elizabeth into a warm bath. Exhausted from her grief, Elizabeth sat quietly in the tub with her eyes half-closed as Sarah bathed her. Sarah helped Elizabeth from the tub and dried her quickly, pulling a warm nightgown over her head. When she had settled her young mistress in bed, Sarah sat holding her hand, humming a melody until she fell asleep.

Only when she returned to her room could Sarah express her own overwhelming grief. She cried bitter tears, for she had dearly loved Mr. and Mrs. Worthington. She was especially grateful to Mr. Worthington for bringing her to Rosehaven. She shuddered to think what her future certainly would have held had Mr. Bennet, and then Mr. Worthington, not rescued her.

SHORTLY BEFORE HIS DEATH, MR. Worthington had called Sarah into his study, reiterating how important it was for her always to protect Elizabeth. She recalled well his warning to her.

"Sarah, you must always remember that Elizabeth is never to know the true circumstances of her birth. She will be in much danger if all is revealed. If something should happen to Mrs. Worthington or me, promise me that you will continue to protect her with your very life. In my will, I have left specific instructions for my brother to follow. You are to be responsible for the care of Elizabeth." His dark eyes implored her to reassure him of her commitment.

"Thank you, Master. You know Miss Elizabeth is as dear to me as my own child. You have no need to worry, for I will always willingly protect her, even at the cost of my own life."

"Promise me too, that you will help guide Elizabeth in her choice of husband. She will listen to you — she always has." Sarah allowed herself a small smile at the truth of his words. Mr. Worthington continued, "It is my wish that she will someday wed Fitzwilliam Darcy. He is a fine man and a match for her in every way. If they should marry, it will surely be for love, for neither need marry for money nor connections."

Sarah had long been aware of the faith and trust the Worthingtons had placed in her, and she vowed to do nothing to destroy it. In many ways, the Worthingtons had treated her as one of the family, although in public it was natural for her to retreat into the shadows, assuming the traditional role of a servant.

Few people were aware that Mr. Worthington had long ago had Sarah trained by masters so that she could protect both herself and his children. The skills she had been taught were the equal of any well trained gentleman. Eventually, she was also taught how to shoot with accuracy and how to wield a knife effectively, with the understanding that such knowledge would only be used as a last resort.

All this was accomplished to keep Elizabeth safe and in preparation for what had now sadly come to pass. Sarah was now Elizabeth's sole protector, and she alone had the responsibility of keeping from her the secret of her birth. Even Henry Worthington had never been told that Elizabeth was not the Worthingtons' true daughter.

DARCY AND GEORGIANA TRAVELED TO Rosehaven to join those who had come to pay their respects, all too aware of the sadness they would find there, having endured such profound grief themselves. Georgiana immediately sought out Elizabeth, and the two girls embraced, sharing the sorrow. Darcy was again amazed at their closeness, given the disparity in their ages. He was pleased, as always, for Elizabeth had helped Georgiana overcome her shyness and become the lively young girl he now saw before him. When his aunt, Lady Matlock, approached him, Darcy called her attention to the two girls.

"They treat each other as sisters, one comforting the other as necessary, do they not? I am so very thankful for the relationship they share."

It would have been difficult for Lady Matlock to overlook the tender expression on Darcy's face as he gazed lovingly at Elizabeth and his sister.

Lady Matlock smiled fondly at the two girls. "Elizabeth is one of the most kind-hearted young ladies of my acquaintance — as beautiful inside as out. Andrew will be a fine master for Rosehaven when the time comes for him to assume those duties. He has been trained well. Margaret and Jonathan were fortunate to have such children as Andrew and Elizabeth."

"Yes, indeed, they were."

"As soon as their mourning period is over, I will contact their uncle about continuing Margaret's plans for Elizabeth's coming out. Andrew will, of course, spend much of his time with his uncle here at Rosehaven before attending Cambridge. Now, let us go to Andrew and Elizabeth and offer them our condolences."

Lady Matlock went first to Elizabeth and embraced her, whispering words of comfort and reassurance in her ear as she gently stroked her back. After she turned to Andrew, Darcy approached Elizabeth with a grin on his face. She looked at him in confusion, wondering why he was smiling when she was in such intolerable pain.

"What do you find so humorous in this situation, sir? This is a time of great sadness for my brother and me," she said with a touch of anger in her voice.

Darcy immediately stopped smiling, realizing the impropriety of his expression. "Please forgive me, Miss Worthington. I do not mean to make light of your grief. When I saw you and Georgiana together, I suddenly remembered how you once came to my sister's rescue by fighting George Wickham. The memory of a little spitfire named Elizabeth Anne Worthington making Wickham cry warmed my heart. I suppose I smiled without realizing what I was doing."

Elizabeth looked ashamed of herself for her hasty conclusion. "No, I should be asking your forgiveness. As you well know, I have a quick temper, and once again, I have let it take control of me. I, too, remember that day and how George

Wickham cried like a baby."

Darcy smiled back, wondering if she remembered asking him not to marry before she grew up so that she could marry him. Her coming out could not come soon enough for him. He quite liked the idea of courting and winning the hand of this courageous young woman.

Chapter 4

*I*t was not until a month after her parents' funeral that Elizabeth returned to her first loves: riding and walking. She rode early in the mornings, often wildly, and jumped everything in sight. She knew she was being foolish and careless, but she felt unchained from the hurt and grief when she soared through the air over the highest obstacles.

In the afternoons, she walked for miles in the woods behind the house, only stopping in the shade under a now familiar large oak tree to sip a bit of warm tea from her father's flask. Sometimes she spent the time in contemplation, other times she slept. Before going home, she often picked wildflowers until her arms were full and then headed home to fill the quiet and empty rooms.

Her mother had preferred wildflowers and said so repeatedly. Her father had once joked that he should dismiss the gardener and let the grounds go uncultivated. He would use the money saved to purchase horses instead.

Elizabeth's sob caught in her throat at the memory of her father standing tall, his shoulder leaning against the doorframe, gazing at his wife with his eyes twinkling in mirth. Her mother would merely roll her eyes and groan.

One particular spring day, Elizabeth rushed home, no flowers in her hands. She ran to her private chambers without responding to anyone's kind inquiry. When Sarah found her, she was lying across the bed, sobbing. She did not respond when her longtime companion gathered her up in her arms, until the soft tones of a familiar lullaby calmed her into a deep sleep. The pattern repeated for several days, but stopped one morning when Darcy brought Georgiana to visit.

"Where is Andrew?" Darcy asked, after he and his sister had been shown into the sitting room to join Elizabeth.

"He is on the estate with Uncle Henry," Elizabeth said and then glanced at the window.

Her father's youngest brother, Henry Worthington, had inherited a small estate, Fulton Hall, also in Staffordshire, from an uncle who had died leaving no heir. Over the years, he had worked very hard to improve his estate and was rewarded with an annual income of 5,000 pounds. With her father now gone, Uncle Henry had left his estate in the capable hands of his long-time steward and temporarily moved into Rosehaven. He spent most of his time between the two estates, acting as Master of Rosehaven until Andrew was ready to assume that duty.

Elizabeth released a deep sigh. "Andrew works hard, and every evening he returns exhausted, eats dinner, and then retires for the night."

"Work is an excellent remedy for grief." Darcy stepped a little closer. "Do you have any such outlet?"

"I have roused myself by latching onto a number of projects — practicing on the pianoforte diligently, making screens, and painting tables — until one day I stumbled over the stack of both projects and fell, twisting my ankle." She walked over to the side table, and pulled out two screens and presented them to her guests. "The rest were carried to the attic, never to be seen again." Elizabeth was surprised at her chuckle. She had not laughed since her parents had been taken from her.

"And are you well?" he asked softly when their gazes locked.

"I admit that I have been melancholy for a while, but now you two have come." She attempted a smile, but bit her lip to hold back a sob.

Darcy took her hand. "We understand, Miss Worthington." He led her to a settee and tilted his head at Georgiana inviting her to sit beside Elizabeth. "You need someone to help you during this time," he said, and then directed his gaze at Georgiana.

"I would like to help, if I may stay," Georgiana whispered.

"I thank you. I could use the company." Elizabeth slid her arm around Georgiana. "You will make an excellent companion."

It was agreed. Georgiana would remain at Rosehaven. After a short visit, Darcy bid them farewell and returned to Pemberley.

The two girls continued to grow closer. They went for long walks accompanied by Sarah when weather permitted it, or they practiced on the pianoforte or read when it did not.

Elizabeth clung to her family and Georgiana, and Darcy kept his presence at Rosehaven to a minimum, respecting her need to grieve.

After some weeks, when Darcy traveled to Rosehaven to claim Georgiana, he found Elizabeth alone in the library.

Leaving the door open, he advanced into the room.

Elizabeth looked up from her book, startled. "Oh, Mr. Darcy, I did not hear you announced. Please, come in." She stood as he stepped further into the room. "I must thank you, sir, for allowing Georgiana to spend this time with me. She has been a joy and a comfort, and I believe my grieving was lessened with her presence."

"My aunt, Lady Catherine, insists that Georgiana and I visit Rosings. I have made many excuses, but the visit must take place to avoid an upset in the family."

"I see." Elizabeth would miss Georgiana, and she turned her head so that Darcy would not see the tears collecting in her eyes. He noticed, however and came at once to stand in front of her. Wanting to give comfort, he pushed aside propriety and embraced her, one hand bringing her head to his chest.

Elizabeth did not think of decorum; she was only aware of the beating of his heart, the warmth of his body, and the spicy scent she loved. She slipped her arms around his waist, and they stood together until they heard Sarah speak in a soft voice. Instantly, they sprang apart, both embarrassed at being caught embracing.

"Miss Georgiana is ready to leave, sir. Mistress, you may say goodbye to her while I speak with Mr. Darcy."

Blushing, Elizabeth flew out of the room. Sarah turned to Darcy, who was looking at the floor.

"You are fortunate that only I saw you and my mistress together. Promise me this will not happen again. I believe that Miss Elizabeth's uncle has spoken to you about the responsibility I hold in regard to her well-being. She will be out soon, and you can begin courting her. You are a gentleman, Mr. Darcy, and my mistress is a lady. Please remember that."

Darcy looked up and saw that Sarah was not angry. He nodded to her without comment.

"Come, sir, Miss Darcy will wonder why you are taking so long."

They walked out to Darcy's carriage where Georgiana and Elizabeth stood waiting. Darcy helped his sister inside and then turned to Elizabeth. Speaking in a low voice so only she could hear, he said, "I am sorry, Miss Worthington, for my lapse of good judgment. Please forgive me."

Her eyes were red, but she smiled, "There is nothing to forgive, sir. Please have a safe journey, and ask Georgiana to write when you arrive at Rosings."

They said their goodbyes, knowing it would be months before they would see each other again.

A NEW UNDERTAKING FILLED ELIZABETH'S days soon after Georgiana left, and it proved to be a whirlwind of activities. Lady Matlock had obtained permission to assist with her coming out. She brought her private seamstress, and the three of them decided on patterns and fabrics for her ball gowns and the one in which she would be presented at court. No expense would be spared. Everything done during the remaining mourning period would be kept secret, but when Elizabeth arrived in London, most arrangements would have been already made.

IT HAD BEEN MANY MONTHS since Georgiana's last visit when the Worthington family arrived in London. Uncle Henry and Andrew spent a great deal of time going between Rosehaven and Fulton Hall, while Elizabeth stayed in London with Sarah and the servants. She and Lady Matlock were finalizing their plans for her coming out.

One morning, Elizabeth received a message from Georgiana inviting her to tea, and she sent her acceptance immediately. She and Sarah left the Worthington townhouse the following afternoon and walked to Darcy House, which was a short distance from her own.

While they strolled, Elizabeth lifted her face to the sky, enjoying the warmth of the sunshine. Although she enjoyed the activities offered in London, she missed the long jaunts through the woods and rides on her horse at Rosehaven. Country air suited her much more than the stale air of London.

When they were shown inside, Sarah left to visit with the Darcy's housekeeper, Mrs. Bowers, while Elizabeth was directed to the music room.

She found Georgiana seated at the pianoforte, playing a lovely melody. Smiling, Elizabeth leaned against the door frame and closed her eyes, letting the music flow over her.

Georgiana looked up and, seeing the effect her music was having on her friend, continued playing.

When the last note sounded, Elizabeth opened her eyes and exclaimed, "That was beautiful, Georgiana! Who is the composer? I do not believe I have ever heard that music before today."

"I am glad you like it. It is one I wrote at Pemberley. I made a copy of the sheet music, and you are welcome to take it home with you, if you like."

"Oh, yes, I would like that very much!"

Although only fourteen, Georgiana Darcy was a prodigy when it came to music. As a small child, her father commissioned the finest piano master in London to give her lessons. She had secretly composed music since she was eleven years old, but had not shared this with anyone until the previous year, when she had confided in Elizabeth and, later, her brother. As she grew older, she created more intricate pieces.

Tea was ordered and the girls sat talking about music and Elizabeth's coming out, until they heard Darcy's knock on the door.

"May I join you, ladies?"

Georgiana and Elizabeth stood and waited for him to join them. "Come in, Brother. Tea will be served shortly, so you are just in time."

"Miss Worthington." Darcy smiled at her as he made his bow.

Elizabeth curtsied and returned his smile. "It is good to see you again, sir."

"And you also. Where are Andrew and Mr. Worthington? Are they in town at present?"

Before she could answer, they were interrupted by a voice at the front door. "Never mind, Bowers, I know my way."

Darcy cringed. "Richard is here!"

Like a whirlwind, Colonel Richard Fitzwilliam rushed into the room. Spying Elizabeth, he marched directly to her and lifted her hand to his lips.

"Miss Worthington, what a joy to see you again and, my, you do look stunning today! Tell me, when did you arrive in town? Are all your family well?"

Ignoring Georgiana and Darcy, he sat down beside Elizabeth and focused all of his attention on her.

"Richard, perhaps you would like to say hello to Georgiana?" Darcy glanced at his sister, rolling his eyes until she giggled.

"I am so sorry, sweetheart. It was very rude of me to ignore you."

The colonel jumped up and went to his cousin, kissing her on the forehead and then sat back down again by Elizabeth.

Elizabeth had noted Georgiana's confused expression and Darcy's angry eyes when Richard first arrived. Suspecting what the problem was but unable to do anything about it, she could only sit and answer the colonel's questions while smiling frequently at Darcy.

She had never been fond of Richard Fitzwilliam, primarily because of his harsh teasing while she was growing up. But even worse, she had learned from talks with her friends that he kept a mistress, which seemed disgusting to her.

"Did you have a purpose in coming here, Richard?" Darcy's voice was cold.

"The usual reason," the colonel answered. He glanced at Elizabeth and then back at Darcy. "I have not seized control of your mission, have I, Cousin?" His smirk widened.

The colonel had a bit of the devil in him, and Elizabeth knew he loved teasing his cousin. She was not interested in him — indeed, she was not certain she even liked him.

Mrs. Bowers interrupted by bringing in tea and cakes. As soon as she left, Georgiana began talking to Elizabeth about the latest fashions in gowns and shoes, not allowing either man a chance to interrupt. Darcy and Richard glared at each other.

Finally, unable to bear the tension between Darcy and his cousin any longer and wanting to get away from the settee she shared with Richard, Elizabeth stood. Both men jumped to their feet.

"Would you ring for Mrs. Bowers, Georgiana? I believe Sarah is with her." She then turned and whispered to Georgiana, "Will you take tea with me tomorrow?" Georgiana nodded. "Good, I will send Sarah for you."

The colonel insisted on accompanying Elizabeth home. She thanked him, but said she already had Sarah to escort her. He attempted to insist again, but Sarah entered the room and he stepped back.

Elizabeth said good-bye, and she and Sarah left for home.

Darcy turned to his cousin. "I demand to know the reason for your ill-mannered behavior toward Miss Worthington. Other than teasing her, you have never paid any attention to her until today. You rushed in here as though you owned the place, completely ignoring Georgiana, and acted as though you were courting the lady. For heaven's sake, Richard, she is not yet out."

"Are you jealous, Darcy? Very well, it was rude of me to ignore Georgiana, and I apologize. But I believe you are more upset with the attention I showed Miss Worthington than you are with my being rude. Do you fear me? Well, old man, you should, as I do intend to court her."

Darcy gave a harsh laugh. "Did you notice how uncomfortable she was with your forward behavior? She is not a fool. She knows you are looking for a rich heiress."

"Darcy, Darcy, you should leave the courting to a real man like me. You will never win a woman like Miss Worthington. You do not have enough fire in your body for her. She has passion, man, and you do not."

43

Before her brother could answer, Georgiana jumped up in tears. "I hate you, Richard! You ruined my day with Lizzy. I suppose that makes you very happy." She ran out of the room and up the stairs to her chambers.

Richard and Darcy had forgotten that Georgiana was still in the room while they had sparred, and both men were embarrassed.

During supper that evening, Darcy tried talking to Georgiana, but she only stared at her plate. Finally she said, "I am not happy with you, but I am most displeased with Richard. I have heard some bad things about him."

When he opened his mouth to reply, she responded, "Do not pretend with me, Brother. May I be excused? I do not wish to discuss it with you."

Darcy was not pleased that his sister had spoken to him in such a manner, but too tired to argue, he sent her away with a wave of his hand.

He retired to his chambers early, only to sit by the fire, drinking brandy while thinking of Richard and how correct he had been in his assumptions. Darcy loved Elizabeth and wanted her, just as his cousin had said. He had known he loved her from the moment he had seen her at Pemberley when his father died. Even though she was still too young for him to declare himself, he both hoped and believed that Elizabeth was as attracted to him as he was to her. Though the words had never been spoken between them, he was certain she knew his intentions and that she was in agreement.

He thought back to the remark Richard made about him not having enough fire in his body for Elizabeth, and he wanted to laugh aloud. If Richard only knew how he burned for her! It was true that he did not have the experience his cousin and other men had, but he was glad. Elizabeth did not deserve a man who had been with a great many women, especially a man who kept a mistress and whose goal in life was to marry for money. She would not want Richard, of that he was certain.

Chapter 5

Elizabeth was quiet on the way home from the Darcys. Sarah did not question her until they were in Elizabeth's sitting room where they would have privacy.

After listening to several long sighs from her mistress, Sarah asked, "What is wrong, lovey? Are you unwell?"

Elizabeth looked at her. "I was only thinking."

"Thinking of what?"

"Colonel Fitzwilliam came in while we were having tea, and Mr. Darcy became very angry."

"Oh? Do you know why he was angry?"

"The colonel paid a great deal of attention to me while ignoring Georgiana and Mr. Darcy, and that displeased him. However, I think he was more jealous of the colonel's attentions to me."

Sarah laughed. "Oh, I am certain you are right. Mr. Darcy is a jealous man when it comes to you, and he is protective of those he loves."

"I like the idea of Mr. Darcy being jealous and protective of me." She grinned.

"You like Mr. Darcy. I see that dreamy look in your eyes."

"Oh, do not tease me. You know that I do. I cannot remember a time when I did not love him. Sometimes he is very quiet and scowls, and other times he is an impossible snob, but when he laughs, the dimples show in his cheeks, and I want to lick them."

"Elizabeth Anne Worthington! I am mortified! Do you want me to turn you over my knees and spank you? Please, never say that to anyone else. That is a very unladylike statement, Missy."

Elizabeth giggled and hid her face behind her hands. "I cannot help myself,

45

Sarah. He looks so delicious when he laughs. Do not be surprised when I marry him."

"I think you must wait until he proposes. Perhaps he will ask another lady to marry him, and then what will you do? Perhaps he will marry Miss Bingley."

Elizabeth rolled her eyes at the idea of Mr. Darcy marrying another, especially Miss Caroline Bingley, a tall, attractive woman of five and twenty. She had mounted a determined effort to become Mistress of Pemberley as soon as her brother, Charles, had introduced her to Darcy. She had been certain she could convince him to marry her. Although Darcy had been aloof when in her company and never showed her special attention, she seemed unable to recognize his true feelings.

She instantly saw a rival in Elizabeth and turned her obsessive hatred on the young and vivacious Miss Worthington. Elizabeth was aware of Miss Bingley's dislike, but she usually ignored her. She pitied Caroline for her foolish and undignified behavior toward Mr. Darcy. Members of the *ton* laughed at her behind her back. Everyone but Miss Bingley knew that Mr. Darcy avoided her as much as possible.

"And perhaps he will *not* marry her!" Elizabeth replied defiantly. "I am not worried about that. I can tell by the way he looks at me that Mr. Darcy will make an offer for me. I have known his intentions for a long time."

Sarah stared at her for a long moment and said without requiring an answer, "And you want him too."

"Yes, very much! He shall be my husband. I will have his children and live with him until I die."

"My sweet girl, you and I must talk once again about proper decorum between men and women. Remember, I know how you and Mr. Darcy feel about each other, and you must be very careful in your manner and behavior toward him. You are no longer a child. He is a gentleman, and I hope he will remember that you are a lady."

"My stars, Sarah! Mr. Darcy does not act improperly with me but, if he tried, you know I would never allow it." Elizabeth paused, remembering that day in the library. "Well, perhaps we acted improper once — but that is all, Sarah, I promise you. I have to admit, however, that when he is close to me, I feel certain desires. Is it wicked of me to have those feelings?"

"No, lovey, it is not, but you must never act on them until you are married. When you are in your marriage bed, you and your husband may do or say whatever feels good to you both, but not until then."

They fell silent for a long moment, each with her own thoughts, until Sarah spoke.

"And the colonel? What are your feelings toward him?"

Elizabeth snorted and rolled her eyes. "Do you not remember how he teased me unmercifully when I was growing up? He teased me until I grew breasts, and then he smirked and leered at me."

She hesitated for a moment. What Elizabeth was about to ask was not proper for a single woman to speak of, but she knew Sarah would be truthful with her. "I heard some disturbing news from my friends about him. Do you know of what I am speaking?"

"That he has a mistress?"

"Yes, is it true? If so, how can he afford to keep one? He is a second son, and I do not believe his military pay would allow such a thing. He is quick to point out that he must marry for money but, if he can afford his mistress, why can he not afford a wife instead?"

"It is true. He has had a mistress for many years, and I doubt that a wife would cause him to give her up. He would only be more discreet, that is all. As for how he can afford her, not many know that old Mr. Darcy left him a tidy sum of money, and he has invested well."

"The entire affair is disgusting, and I would not want to be his wife. I will marry only for the deepest love."

Sarah grinned. "You mean Mr. Darcy?"

"Yes, of course!" Then with great disdain, Elizabeth exclaimed, "But, there are women who would turn a blind eye to a mistress just to have the colonel for a husband. After all, he is the son of an earl."

"That is true. Mr. Darcy is one who has no need of your dowry. He is far richer than anyone knows."

"Sarah, how do you know so much about everyone?"

She laughed and then said in a very sly tone of voice, "Sarah knows everything."

Elizabeth laughed and threw a cushion at her.

ON WEEKENDS, GEORGIANA AND ELIZABETH enjoyed walking in the park, and Darcy often joined them. One day as they rested on a bench, they heard a child's cry of distress coming from a nearby pond. Darcy jumped up immediately and ran toward the cry, the others following him as fast as they could. When the ladies reached the pond, they saw Darcy carrying a small boy in his arms who was bleeding from his leg. Two other children were hanging onto the dress of a beautiful, blond-haired young woman who walked behind Darcy.

"What has happened?" Elizabeth cried out as soon as she caught up to them.

"I believe he fell on some glass and cut himself." Turning to the lady, he asked, "Does this little fellow belong to you, madam?"

"Oh yes," she answered, holding out her arms to take the child.

"My home is nearby. Please, will you not allow us to take him there so that my housekeeper can treat his wound?"

"Thank you, sir, but if you would find a cab for us, I will take him back to his mother."

"Where do you live?" asked Elizabeth.

"On Gracechurch Street, in Cheapside."

"That is too far away. We need to clean the wound and stop the bleeding. If you will consent to let me carry the lad to my home, I will be happy to send you back to Gracechurch Street in my own carriage after he has been treated."

"Very well, sir, I thank you for your kindness."

It took no more than a few minutes for them to arrive at the Darcy townhouse where he turned the child over to Mrs. Bowers. Darcy led the others to a small sitting room and rang for tea, then excused himself to clean the blood from his hands and change clothes. When the maid appeared, Georgiana asked her to include sweets for the children.

Before long, the boy was brought back to the others, proudly showing off the bandage covering his wounds, and Darcy rejoined the group.

"We have been remiss in introducing ourselves, madam. My name is Fitzwilliam Darcy, and this is my sister, Miss Georgiana Darcy, and our friend, Miss Elizabeth Worthington."

"I am Miss Jane Bennet and these are my cousins, Jason, Michael, and Amanda Gardiner. We usually play in the park close to their home, but today the children wanted to see the swans. Our park has only ducks."

Miss Bennet was a soft-spoken young lady, probably in her early twenties. Elizabeth felt drawn to her, as she had a pleasing manner that Elizabeth liked, believing she would be a good friend. She decided she would like to know Miss Bennet better.

"Did you say your name is Miss Bennet?" Sarah asked. She had stationed herself in the corner of the room. "Is your family from London or the country?"

Elizabeth felt a shiver run down her back at the tone in Sarah's voice. But before Elizabeth could begin a conversation, there was a knock on the door and Mr. Bowers, Darcy's butler, announced Charles Bingley.

"Welcome Bingley, you are just in time to meet a few new guests. This is Miss Jane Bennet. Her cousin fell on some glass in the park, and we brought them home with us. Miss Bennet, allow me to introduce our good friend, Mr. Charles Bingley."

She gave a shy smile. "It is a pleasure to make your acquaintance, Mr. Bingley." She curtsied, but her eyes remained aimed at the gentleman now standing before her.

Bingley bowed. "The pleasure is mine, Miss Bennet. I trust that your cousin is well now?" His gaze locked with hers.

"Thank you for asking, sir. Yes, he is well. Mr. Darcy's housekeeper attended him."

Miss Bennet suddenly blushed and broke eye contact. She turned to find her host. "I thank you for your hospitality, Mr. Darcy, but I must return the children to their home."

"Certainly. Let me call for the carriage. By the way, Miss Bennet, is the uncle you spoke of Mr. Edward Gardiner?"

"Why, yes, he is."

"I ask because I know the gentleman. Please give him my regards."

"Thank you, sir, I will."

The carriage arrived, and Georgiana and Elizabeth expressed a desire to ride with Miss Bennet so they could become better acquainted. Darcy accompanied them, saying he wished to speak with Mr. Gardiner. Mr. Bingley then decided to join the party. He simply wanted to find out where Miss Bennet lived so he could call on her.

They were about to enter the carriage when Mr. Bingley's two sisters arrived. Bingley poked his head out the window when he heard his sister's voice.

"Caroline, I will be home later. We are seeing Miss Bennet to her home."

"Miss Bennet? I know of no Miss Bennet, Charles."

Darcy cleared his throat. "I am sure your brother will be happy to tell you the particulars later, but for now, we must be off." He stepped into the carriage and rapped on the ceiling.

"Louisa," Caroline frowned, "our brother has found himself in love again. Did you see his grin? And I will wager that Miss Eliza is behind this, whatever it is. Ohhh, I despise that little chit! I have hated her since Charles introduced us."

"Shh, she will hear you."

"I do not care if she does." Caroline stared at the carriage pulling away.

"Carrie, when will you admit defeat? Mr. Darcy is clearly not interested in you, and he never has been. Why should he marry you when Miss Worthington has more to offer? Her connections are excellent, and I hear she has a dowry of 60,000 pounds. You cannot compete with her. She has known Mr. Darcy all her life."

"Silence, Louisa!" Miss Bingley spat. "I mean to have him, and that is final."

Louisa Hurst rolled her eyes. "Your hatred of Miss Worthington will be your downfall. You must at least pretend to like her if you wish to be fully accepted by the *ton*! Miss Worthington is Lady Matlock's godchild, and you will get nowhere without that lady's approval. And, remember Pemberley — for you will never be invited there again if you treat Miss Worthington poorly. Make a fool of yourself if you must, but do not expect me to follow you in your senseless pursuit"

Miss Bingley scoffed. Her hatred of Elizabeth and her obsession with marrying Mr. Darcy had grown completely out of control. Elizabeth was a threat to her ambition of becoming wealthy and a leader in the *ton*. Mr. Darcy, with his estate, wealth, and rank, was her way to obtain all that she desired. A marriage to him would wipe away the stench of her father having earned his wealth in trade.

She did not love Mr. Darcy — she loved only what he could do for her. In turn, she hated Elizabeth because she had everything that Miss Bingley wanted: wealth, connections, and the attention of Mr. Darcy. The fact that her father had made his money as a tradesman highly irritated Miss Bingley, even though it did not irritate her enough to prevent her from spending his money. She ignored the truth and allowed her hatred to fester until it was like a poison spreading throughout her body and mind.

UPON ARRIVING AT THE GARDINER home, Miss Bennet invited her guests in to meet her aunt and uncle.

Darcy had gone with the others more out of curiosity than anything else, but he had invested money in Mr. Gardiner's business, and he wanted to see where the man lived. If Mr. Gardiner was home and Darcy could speak with him, so much the better.

The Gardiner home was modest but well kept, and the atmosphere inside was warm and inviting. Mr. Gardiner was very glad to see Darcy and called him into his study for a private meeting.

Mr. Gardiner handed his guest a brandy. "This is a pleasant surprise. I had planned on meeting with you in a day or two to let you know that the business is doing exceedingly well. You will be happy to know, sir, that your returns will be even greater than we had anticipated."

"That is good news! Do you still plan to open a tobacco shop on Bond Street? I am interested in investing in your new venture."

"Yes, indeed! In fact, I am expecting a large shipment of cigars, pipes, and pipe tobacco any day now. We will have everything needed to make the business a success. I have leased a shop and will open it as soon as the shipment arrives. I do not believe you can go wrong with this investment."

The two men spoke for a few moments about the current state of affairs affecting trade before joining the others. As they entered the room, Elizabeth had just invited Miss Bennet and Mrs. Gardiner to tea on the following Monday. Both ladies assured her they would be there.

AFTER ELIZABETH AND HER FRIENDS left, Jane reached into her basket and pulled out her needlework. Her head was down, and she had lapsed into silence. Mrs. Gardiner glanced at her niece several times. Anyone else would have seen only serenity gracing Miss Bennet's face, but Aunt Gardiner knew her niece well, and she knew when Jane was troubled.

"It was very kind of Mr. Darcy and his friends to bring you and the children home."

"Yes, it was, Aunt. And it was kind of Mr. Darcy's housekeeper to be so gentle when treating Michael's wounds. He did not cry even once. Miss Darcy ordered special sweets brought out for the children, which delighted them. We were treated very well."

"I was glad to see that Michael's wounds were minor."

"Yes, ma'am. The glass was not embedded deeply, yet his leg was cleaned well with warm water and soap. The housekeeper also used a salve that was prescribed for Miss Darcy by her doctor when she received a deep cut a few months ago."

The two ladies lapsed into silence until Mrs. Gardiner spoke again.

"Mr. Bingley seems an amiable sort of man."

A pink blush spread from Jane's face to her chest, and a small smile graced her lips. "Yes, he does."

"What think you of the Darcys and Miss Worthington?" Mrs. Gardiner sneaked a look at her niece from the corner of her eye.

Jane placed her needlework back in her basket. She knew her aunt would continue questioning her until she gave her the information she wanted.

"Miss Darcy is a lovely girl. Mr. Darcy seems pleasant enough, although he is more formal in his demeanor than Mr. Bingley. I liked Elizabeth — Miss Worthington — very much. We seemed to be drawn to each other at once. She confided that she wished for us to be friends."

Mrs. Gardiner moved to sit by her niece on the sofa. "What is troubling you, dearest Jane? You are unusually pensive for one who appears to have had a wonderful day."

"It *was* wonderful, Aunt. Yet, I am troubled about a friendship with Miss Worthington."

"How so?"

"What will happen if she has occasion to meet my mother? Did you notice her eyes? They are the color Mama looks for in every female. Would she try to harm my friend? And, Miss Worthington, would she be appalled at Mama's behavior? Would she turn her back on our friendship?"

Aunt Gardiner put her arms around Jane and pulled her close. "I do not know all the answers to your questions, dearest, but it is unlikely your mama and Miss Worthington will ever meet. Your papa does not allow her to leave Longbourn except for activities around Meryton, and it is doubtful your friend will visit Hertfordshire. When you return home, you may continue you friendship through letters, although you will no doubt see your friend when you visit us."

"I am sorry Mama lost the twins, for Papa says she has never been the same, and I do miss not having siblings. I understand that grief can change a person, but I wish..." She began to sob quietly.

"Shh, Jane, do not cry, my love. Too many years have passed for your mama to change. You have to accept her as she is. She loves you, and has always been kind and generous to you."

Jane sat up and wiped away her tears. "I know she does, and I feel the same for her. When I return home, I will be especially attentive and helpful, so she will know just how much I do love her."

"I believe that would be for the best, dearest. Love is a powerful force."

Jane smiled. "Yes, it is. Now, Aunt, what did *you* think of Mr. Bingley?"

Chapter 6

In the following weeks, Elizabeth had time to further her friendship with Jane Bennet and Mrs. Gardiner, even though Lady Matlock kept her busy with the final plans for her coming out. But it was the instant bond she felt when meeting Miss Bennet that drew her to her new friends. Strangely, Miss Bennet admitted she too felt a connection she could not explain.

Georgiana, who had indicated she liked their new friends very much and felt at ease with them, joined in visits as often as her brother allowed. He had expressed a different opinion on the growing friendships.

Regardless of his personal feelings about them, Mr. Gardiner was in trade and, therefore, his social inferior. He emphasized that it was acceptable to do business with the man, but not to socialize with him or his family. One afternoon when he informed Elizabeth of his opinion, she scoffed.

"You, sir, are a snob."

Georgiana glanced at her brother and waited while her neck muscles grew tight.

He chuckled and then nodded. "You must accept your position as above theirs, Miss Worthington. You are coming out soon, and whether you yield or not, those whom you choose as your friends will matter."

"I accept people for who they are, not based on their social status. Regardless, Miss Bennet's father owns a small estate in Hertfordshire."

A small gasp resounded from the corner of the room, and Sarah's hand flew to her mouth.

"Miss Bennet," Elizabeth continued, "is a gentleman's daughter. She is not beneath me." Her stare bore into his eyes, daring him to challenge her.

"Your father warned me once. He said you are like an energetic filly whose spirit could never be broken. I shall not try today." His dimples appeared, and Elizabeth fell speechless for a moment.

Nothing more was discussed about the Bennets. The rest of the conversation focused on her coming out. Darcy teased her about the event and how only the meanest members of the *ton* appeared at such affairs.

"They eat sweet little girls for breakfast and dine on intelligent ones. So you must learn to be empty-headed and silly if you wish to secure their blessing."

THAT EVENING AFTER DARCY AND Georgiana departed, Elizabeth sought out Sarah and demanded her opinion about what had been said about Miss Bennet. To Elizabeth's surprise, Sarah agreed with Darcy.

"But why? There is nothing wrong with them. The Gardiners are lovely people, and Miss Bennet is a gentleman's daughter."

"Mistress, you are too quick to accept people at face value. Your position in the *ton* is secure, but this could hurt you in other ways."

"I do not understand how a friendship with Miss Bennet could hurt me. You are being as much a snob as Mr. Darcy, and I do not like that. Regardless of how you or Mr. Darcy feel, I intend to continue being her friend. I like her very much."

Sarah knew from the stubborn set of Elizabeth's jaw and the tone of her voice that she might as well drop her objections. Elizabeth would do as she pleased, and all Sarah could do was stay close by her mistress. She would keep her eyes and ears open, however, in case the elder Bennets came to London. If nothing else, she would warn Mr. Bennet to stay away.

Relations were strained between Sarah and Elizabeth that evening but, by the following morning, Elizabeth appeared to have forgotten their disagreement and was her usual cheerful self.

Elizabeth and Georgiana hosted Jane Bennet and Mrs. Gardiner for tea several times, and they also were invited to the Gardiners' home. Although Sarah was on guard and listened to their conversations carefully, she was able to take some time to enjoy playing with the Gardiner children, who were well behaved and seemed to love her.

SEVERAL WEEKS BEFORE HER COMING out, an invitation to Elizabeth's ball arrived at the Gardiner home, generating much excitement, enhanced by the interest of Charles Bingley, who had been granted permission to call on Jane Bennet. She had been sent to London by her father in hopes of her finding a suitable husband. Being Mr. Darcy's friend and in possession of 5,000 pounds a year, Mr. Bingley was considered very suitable.

Jane and Mrs. Gardiner made several shopping trips with Lady Matlock, Georgiana, and Elizabeth. They would then retire to the Darcy townhouse for tea where Darcy and Bingley joined them.

It was plain to the others that Darcy and Elizabeth were in love. They spent a great deal of time staring and smiling at each other, and it was remarkable how many times their hands managed to touch, although they attempted to give the impression that it was an accident.

Sarah, who always accompanied Elizabeth, shook her head, rolled her eyes, and smirked at the lovebirds. The ladies thought it was as much fun watching Sarah tease Elizabeth as it was to watch Elizabeth and Darcy.

The only discord came from Caroline Bingley. One afternoon, while Elizabeth and Miss Bennet were having tea with Georgiana, Miss Bingley and Mrs. Hurst called and chatted for several minutes. It began pleasantly, but then Caroline directed her focus on Jane.

"Miss Bennet, perhaps you would like the name of my dressmaker. She has the most divine sense of fashion and would be happy to bring your clothes up to the current fashionable styles."

The others sat in stunned silence, although Mrs. Hurst gasped when Miss Bingley continued her rudeness.

"Miss Eliza, you must let me put you in touch with a French lady's maid who knows the latest styles in hair. She is wonderful with feathers. I think feathers are so stylish, do you not?"

"Miss Worthington's hair is beautiful, and she always looks elegant," Miss Bennet spoke softly. She held her head up, not in an arrogant manner, but coupled with such thoughtfulness in her voice that no one would mistake her for being anything but a sweet girl.

Georgiana reached for the teapot. "Miss Bennet uses the same dressmaker as does my aunt, Lady Matlock. She does not need another as she already has the best." Georgiana refilled Miss Bingley's cup, and with her glare aimed at her guest's eyes added, "And my brother often says how much he likes Lizzy's hair. He does not care for feathers and thinks Lizzy's hair styles are perfection."

Elizabeth smiled. "Thank you, Miss Bingley, but I am quite happy with Sarah."

Glancing in the corner where Sarah sat, Elizabeth was amused to see that her maid had trouble keeping her laughter under control. They both knew this would not be the last time Miss Bingley would speak out of turn. The lady was incapable of keeping her mouth closed.

THE NIGHT OF ELIZABETH'S COMING out ball, Darcy's valet dressed his master with extra care. Williamson had noted that Mr. Darcy seemed in a much better mood after spending time with Miss Worthington. He understood why his master looked on her with favor, for she was quite beautiful and had a pleasing manner. He, too, had known her since she was a child and thought she suited his master very well.

Darcy whistled softly between his teeth as he dressed, and Williamson struggled to suppress a smile. He was pleased that Mr. Darcy was in such good spirits, and he had high hopes that before long they would have a new mistress in the house. All the servants agreed that it was time their master settled down, and they liked Miss Worthington very much.

Darcy had confided in his valet that he was especially happy, for he had secured in advance two dances with Elizabeth. Her brother was to dance the first set with her, but Darcy had been promised the second and one other. The manner in which he fidgeted was an indication that he could hardly wait.

GEORGIANA MET HER BROTHER AS he was preparing to leave, and before hugging him goodbye, she said teasingly, "Lizzy will find you so handsome tonight that she will fling herself into your arms and beg you to marry her immediately."

He pretended to scowl. "When did you learn to tease your brother in such a manner, my dear sister? Who has been such a bad influence on you?"

Georgiana giggled and hugged him before pushing him toward the door. "Have a good time tonight, Fitzwilliam."

DARCY ENTERED THE BALLROOM, AND the matchmaking mamas, along with their daughters, descended upon him. He tried to be polite, all the while continuing to make his way toward his aunt. At last, he reached her.

"Good heavens, have you invited all the fortune hunters in London to Miss Worthington's ball tonight?" He had glanced at the crowd and noted the number of unmarried men milling about.

Darcy heard soft laughter behind him and, turning, he came face to face with Elizabeth. *Oh, my Lord*, he thought, as he drew in his breath, *she is the most beautiful woman I have ever seen.*

56

Elizabeth was wearing a silk gown the same color as her eyes, and in her hair Sarah had woven violet-colored flowers made from crystals with a small pearl in each center. Her jewelry was simple — she wore only a pair of pearl drop earrings that her father had given her. Her eyes shined and a smile played upon her lips.

"I see you had to run the gauntlet, Mr. Darcy. I am pleased that you made your way to us safely."

Darcy bowed and took her hand, brushing it lightly with his lips. His heart raced when a look of pleasure crossed her face.

"Miss Worthington, may I say how beautiful you look tonight?"

"You may say so anytime you wish," she teased, but there was a hint of passion in her voice that touched his heart.

"Nephew," Lady Matlock said, with a hint of bemusement in her eyes, "Miss Worthington had a similar experience tonight. I thought I would need a club to keep all the mamas and their fortune hunting sons from kidnapping her while she was in the receiving line."

"I am not surprised!" Darcy exclaimed. "And, I suspect your dance card is now full."

"Oh, yes," she answered. Then, teasing him again, she asked, "Mr. Darcy, how have you managed to stay unmarried with so many women clamoring for your attention?"

Before he could answer Lady Matlock said, "And here comes a most excellent example." Darcy did not have to be told of whom his aunt was speaking, as he heard her shrill voice in his ear.

"Mr. Darcy, I have been looking everywhere for you, and here you are." Caroline Bingley wrapped her arm tightly around his and hung on. "I am so looking forward to dancing tonight, sir." She batted her eyelashes at him as though expecting him to claim her for the first dance. He noticed Elizabeth turning away, her bottom lip caught between her teeth.

Darcy removed his arm and bowed. "Good evening, Miss Bingley. Has Charles arrived? I need to see him immediately on a matter of business." He looked around as though searching for her brother.

Miss Bingley rolled her eyes: "Oh, he has found a new angel. But surely you are not going to waste the evening talking business! I know that Charles will be busy dancing as you should be, Mr. Darcy."

Oh, good Lord, he thought, *I might as well make an end to this, but I will bloody well not dance the first set with her.* "Miss Bingley, if you are not engaged for the third set, perhaps you might consent to be my partner."

"I will be happy to grant you that set," she trilled, although her mouth drooped downwards. She glanced at Elizabeth and turned her most insincere smile at her.

Darcy bowed and left for a dark corner of the room where he could escape Miss Bingley and find a vantage point to observe Elizabeth.

When the music started, Andrew claimed his sister for the first dance, and Darcy settled back against the wall to watch. Several little curls on the back of her neck bounced when she walked or danced, and catching sight of them always aroused him. He imagined running his hands through her hair as it was spread out over his pillow.

Stop it, he scolded himself, *or you will soon embarrass yourself and have to leave to make an adjustment.*

He could not help but compare her to Miss Bingley, who was wearing another orange gown that looked even worse than her previous ones. He was not sure what she was wearing on her head — a turban perhaps with feathers. He shuddered as he made a mental note never to let Georgiana go shopping with Miss Bingley. Suddenly, he smiled to himself, realizing that thinking of Miss Bingley had solved his problem of dwelling on Elizabeth's enticing curls.

Darcy remembered that Elizabeth had asked how he remained single. The answer was simple. He had been very busy running Pemberley after his father died, but more than anything, once he knew he loved Elizabeth, no other woman crossed his mind. She was the only woman he wanted!

After their dance, Andrew led Elizabeth to Darcy. "I understand my sister has promised the next set to you. Here she is, sir. She is all yours."

When the music began again, he led her to the dance floor. They could not divert their eyes from one another. Not a word was spoken during the dance, and when he walked her back to Lady Matlock, his hand lingered a little too long on hers.

Colonel Richard Fitzwilliam claimed Elizabeth for the next dance, and when his cousin flirted with her, jealously ripped through Darcy. It subsided, somewhat, when she did not reciprocate. Occasionally, she smiled at something the colonel said, and there was conversation between them, but she definitely was not flirting with him. Darcy relaxed and waited for their next dance.

Elizabeth's dance partner after the colonel was a Mr. David Hemphill, and this time Darcy did not like his attitude toward Elizabeth at all. While the colonel may have flirted to make his cousin jealous, Mr. Hemphill's attentions were excessive, almost to the point of being improper. When he saw how uncomfortable the gentleman made Elizabeth, Darcy clinched his fists and had to control himself in order not to make a scene.

He knew Mr. Hemphill by reputation, and he did not like what he knew. Hemphill was a tall, pudgy man with greasy hair, sweaty hands, and a pompous air, but that was nothing to his habits. He had run up gambling debts that threatened his estate, and he was known to frequent houses of ill repute. He was certainly not someone Darcy wanted around his Elizabeth.

As soon as the music ended, Elizabeth did not wait for Mr. Hemphill to escort her off the floor. She turned quickly and almost ran to where Darcy stood. He saw that her color was high and that she was furious.

"Insufferable fool!" she exclaimed.

"Wait here," Darcy said, and went immediately to the refreshment table and brought back a glass of wine. Taking a sip, she smiled and thanked him for his kindness.

When it was time to dine, Lady Matlock sat Darcy to Elizabeth's right and her own son to her left. Seating herself across from them, she snickered while her younger son and her nephew vied for Elizabeth's attention.

"I pray you two boys do not kill or maim each other before Elizabeth is engaged."

"Mother, which man do you think will be successful?"

"I suspect Elizabeth has set her cap on someone, and hopefully it will not be long before I can plan a wedding." Her gaze drifted towards Darcy. "It shall be the event of the season." She hid her smile behind her glass of wine.

Jane Bennet and Charles Bingley were seated several seats to Elizabeth's right. Jane had come with her aunt and uncle, and Bingley had immediately claimed the first set. Many of the men in attendance were eager to dance with the beautiful blond woman who was new in town. There was much speculation about Miss Bennet. She smiled a great deal but spoke little.

Mr. and Mrs. Gardiner were acquainted with another family in attendance and were pleased to see them that evening — a Mr. and Mrs. Garnon, who had come with their daughter, Rose. Although the two men had been business associates for many years, their conversation focused on any subject but trade, and occasionally others joined in.

Darcy was relieved when he could claim Elizabeth for their other dance. It was the last one, which meant the evening would soon be over.

Elizabeth's eyes sparkled as they made their turns in the dance, but Miss

Bingley's eyes were dark with rage. Darcy had danced only once with her and then ignored her the rest of the evening.

"I believe we are out of favor with Miss Bingley," Elizabeth laughed softly. "I have just caught a glimpse of tiny little puffs of smoke coming from her ears. Perhaps you should have danced with her again." Elizabeth's eyes shone with mischief.

"Please, do not wish such a fate upon me," Darcy shuddered. "However, if you will notice, we are out of favor with quite a number of people tonight."

Elizabeth glanced around the room and saw that many of the men and women, along with their mothers, were frowning at them. Quite a number were whispering behind their hands. Darcy was the only man Elizabeth had danced with more than once, and they assumed this was her way of claiming him as hers. He, in turn, had ignored all the other women, except for dancing once with Miss Bingley and Mrs. Hurst. He would have ignored them as well, had it not been for his friendship with their brother.

"You know very well that I do not care what others think," Elizabeth said with a soft laugh. "Let us ignore them all and enjoy our dance."

When the ball came to a close, Darcy asked if he could call on her in two days. "I have neglected my business affairs, and now I must spend time on it. Besides, I predict that many suitors will be at your door tomorrow."

Elizabeth answered with dismay, "Oh, I do hope you are wrong, sir."

Darcy laughed. "I look forward to seeing you soon. Please do not forget me." He brought her hand to his lips as they said goodnight, and murmurs escalated around the room.

Chapter 7

"Oh, why do I have to endure this? They are wasting my time and theirs," Elizabeth complained while Sarah washed her hair.

She had many callers the day following her ball, including the particularly annoying Mr. Hemphill. She had been as polite as a well-trained butler. She nodded her head at his outlandish opinions and congratulated him on his ability to fill a room full of empty words. Each visitor seemed just as tedious, although a bit more sensible. At least no one lingered beyond the proper visit of a half-hour.

"Mr. Darcy was not one of your callers today." Sarah pulled her fingers through the wet hair. "Perhaps his not being here is the reason you are so ill-tempered."

Elizabeth sighed and thought while Sarah's strong fingers massaged her scalp. "Thank heaven he was not."

"Thank heaven? Do not tell me you are going to be fickle and cast your eyes toward one of those fortune hunters," Sarah teased.

Elizabeth laughed. "Oh, Sarah, stop! You know I like Mr. Darcy very much. He will call on me tomorrow. Business matters kept him away today. But, oh my goodness, those odious men, especially Mr. Hemphill, should have stayed away. I have no intention of choosing any of them as a husband. They want my dowry more than they want me."

"That may be true; however, I saw a few of them staring at your figure. They want more than money, my sweet girl. You must be careful."

Darcy was in a foul mood. He had witnessed the attention Elizabeth received at the ball, and the thought of those men calling on her today irritated him. "Blast," he exclaimed aloud while pouring another glass of brandy.

"Fitzwilliam?" Georgiana stared at him with questioning eyes.

"I am sorry. I was thinking of a problem at Pemberley."

"Pemberley? Bah! You have not heard from your steward lately, have you?" She paused. "You did not call on Lizzy today. Did last night not go well?"

"Pardon? Oh, yes...yes it went very well, indeed. I am to call on her tomorrow. I knew she would have many callers today, and I had business to conduct." He caught sight of her growing smile as she tried to hide her reaction.

Georgiana peeked up at him. "Perhaps you will arrive tomorrow before any other caller, and you can sweep her away for the entire day."

"You read too many romantic novels. I think I shall have a talk with Mrs. Annesley about your reading material."

Still, Georgiana knew her brother very well and understood that he was thinking along the same lines.

DARCY ARRIVED BEFORE ANYONE ELSE the following morning and convinced Elizabeth to leave the house for a walk in the park. Although Sarah accompanied them, he was pleased with the privacy she allowed them.

She stayed a little ahead while they walked, and when they stopped in a tearoom later, Sarah pulled a book from her reticule and began reading. Darcy's interest was piqued since few servants could read.

"Sarah, who taught you to read? Shakespeare's sonnets are quite a challenge!"

She put her index finger on the page to mark her place and looked up. "Mrs. Worthington taught me. She believed that I could serve the children much better if I could read to them. Many winter afternoons were spent with them while we snuggled together by the fire. After Master Andrew and my mistress began reading on their own, I continued for my own enjoyment. With the permission and encouragement of Mr. Worthington, I made extensive use of his library."

Sarah was a servant, but every one of his recollections of the Worthingtons suggested to Darcy that she was treated as a family member — almost. As long as he had known them, Sarah had gone everywhere with her mistress and appeared to be her protector and her friend. Although puzzled at this, Darcy accepted that if he wanted Elizabeth — and he did — then Sarah came along as a part of the arrangement.

Darcy had definite ideas regarding how servants were to be regarded, and it would not be as a friend. However, he would treat Sarah as such, but only in private, similar to his manner with Mrs. Reynolds, his housekeeper at Pemberley, who had been with him since he was four years of age. He considered her a family member, but he was careful not to show her special favor around the other servants.

Still, he had grown to think of Sarah as an ally, for he remembered how kind she was to him when she caught him embracing Elizabeth in the library at Rosehaven. But, he was decided, in public she would be treated as a servant.

They finished their walk, and Darcy, unhappily, left Elizabeth to deal with several men who had waited for her company.

Over time, he noticed that the number of callers decreased, for while she was polite, she gave none of the gentlemen encouragement. More times than not, she had already left with Darcy before the gentlemen arrived, so any rivals he might have had became discouraged and stayed away.

RUMORS SPREAD OF A WEDDING between Darcy and Elizabeth after members of the *ton* saw them as they attended the theater, the opera, and several balls together. Darcy always danced the first and supper dances with her. The tittle-tattle never hinted of scandal since they were never un-chaperoned. Sarah was always with them except for the affairs she could not attend, and then Andrew or Uncle Henry accompanied them.

One night, Mr. Bingley and Miss Bennet joined them at the theater in Darcy's private box. One person gawking and murmuring was Bingley's own sister, Caroline. She glared up at the box and nudged her sister.

"Charles should have invited me to join them, not that chit. One day, dear sister, I will be the one on Darcy's arm. One day!" She spent the intermission spreading falsehoods about Miss Worthington.

DESPITE THE OBJECTIONS OF MISS Bingley, speculation ran rampant as to when Darcy and Elizabeth would announce their engagement. They were obviously in love and did not attempt to conceal their feelings. Most everyone thought them a perfect match. Only the Miss Bingleys of the *ton* disagreed.

The only man not discouraged was Colonel Fitzwilliam, who desperately wanted Elizabeth's dowry. He continued calling on her, acting as if he had been granted permission to court her. Darcy was becoming increasingly irritated.

One morning shortly after Darcy had arrived, the colonel called upon Elizabeth and settled in for what appeared to be a long stay. When an hour had passed, Darcy grew tired of his cousin's nonsensical opinions on books and music, but when the colonel caressed Elizabeth's cheek with his fingers and pulled back a fallen curl, Darcy jumped up, a dark look on his face, and without a word, he stalked out of the house.

Elizabeth rubbed her temples and glared at Sarah.

"Mistress, has your headache returned?"

At Elizabeth's brief nod, Sarah turned to the gentleman. "I am sorry, Colonel Fitzwilliam, but Miss Worthington's headache has returned and she must rest in a darkened room."

The colonel stood and, after expressing his concern, left the house. Elizabeth began to stomp around the room in an agitated state.

"I am so angry with Mr. Darcy! How could he walk out without a word and leave me with that man? We had plans for the day!"

Sarah patted her mistress on the back. "Now, now, lovey, just you wait. Mr. Darcy will be back within the hour, and if he does not propose, my name is not Sarah."

"He is too late. If he proposes, I will refuse him now!" She picked up her embroidery and pushed the needle through the linen. "He has had opportunities to ask for my hand before now, and he should have taken advantage of them."

"When, my sweet girl? You have never been alone."

"The first time occurred during our walk when the rains came, and he slipped his coat over my shoulders. We were alone because you waited under a different tree. He was so worried for me. I was positive he would have spoken up then."

"A rainstorm does not seem like a proper place for a proposal."

"There was the time at the theater when you went to get some wine for me. Remember how I was coughing and could not stop?"

"I suspected it was your way to be alone with him. What did he do?"

"All he did was touch my hand. I dropped my program, and we both leaned down to reach for it. His hand lingered on mine, and he looked at me with such...desire. I waited, but still he said nothing."

"Perhaps he feared my return would interrupt him. He will propose, my dear. He will!

"There was one other instance. You were called away and left us alone in the parlor. He stood so very close I could feel his breath upon my neck. Instead of proposing, he merely asked me to walk in the park with him. So you see, Sarah, he has had opportunities, but apparently not the courage."

Sarah lowered her head and smiled.

"Why are you home so early, Brother? And why are you angry? Did you and Lizzy quarrel?" Georgiana rushed to him when he came stomping into the music room.

His anger was on the surface, and Darcy could not stop himself. "Richard arrived and simply settled in. He would not leave. He is, no doubt, still there, touching her face, sitting too close, and keeping her attention to himself. I would not be surprised if he has stolen a kiss by now."

"You could not outwait Richard? I suppose it is his military training. He knows how to seize opportunities, but do you?"

He turned toward the door and glared at the hallway. Darcy was already ashamed of his behavior and wanted to make things right with Elizabeth. Just as he was leaving, Georgiana called out, "While you are there, propose before she grows tired of waiting!"

Without a word, he hurried out the door and back down the street, arriving once more at the Worthington home, ready to do battle. However, after he gained admittance to the house, Darcy noted the colonel had gone, and Elizabeth was standing by the window with her back to him. He walked over to her and spoke her name, but she would not turn around or answer him.

He tried again, "Miss Worthington, I am sorry for the way I left. I am ashamed to admit I was jealous, and I let my temper get the best of me. If you will forgive me, I promise never to do it again."

Again, she did not answer or turn around.

"Please, Miss Worthington, will you not speak or look at me?"

Elizabeth shook her head.

"Can you not forgive me?"

She shrugged her shoulders.

"Elizabeth," he said softly, "I cannot bear for you to be angry with me."

She shrugged her shoulders again and then walked to the settee. Her bottom lip was caught between her teeth, and her eyes flashed with anger. She waved toward a chair. "Have a seat, Mr. Darcy."

Oh, the little spitfire is back. He knew, however, that she had reason to be angry with him, so Darcy determined he would let her punish him in any manner she wanted. He sat down and waited for her to speak.

"Mr. Darcy, you deserted me and left me to endure the company of Colonel Fitzwilliam, who is the biggest flirt and fortune hunter in England. How you could be jealous of him is beyond my comprehension! He has no intentions beyond trying to make you jealous. Apparently he succeeded!"

"It is true that I did not act as a gentleman today, and I am extremely embarrassed by my behavior. But, please, do not be angry with me. Say you will forgive me and relieve my suffering."

"*Your* suffering, sir? This is not only about you, Mr. Darcy! I was disappointed when the colonel appeared because I looked forward to spending the day with you. After you rushed out, I pled a headache and the colonel left. Your jealously has served no purpose but to make me angry and make you look foolish."

Realizing that he had better settle this now, Darcy went down on one knee in front of her. Taking her hands in his, he looked into her eyes.

"You have made it plain that you are angry with me, as well you should. My only excuse is that I love you passionately! I know I am a selfish being, especially where you are concerned! You should have a full season and meet other men, but it is agony to think of you having suitors and, perhaps, enjoying the attentions of others.

"Please, Elizabeth, say that you will marry me. I want more than anything for you to be my wife. I knew I loved and wanted to marry you that day at Pemberley when you were only fifteen. You are all I have thought about day and night. I have waited three years; I cannot wait any longer! Please say you love me enough to marry me."

Elizabeth looked at him, a smirk on her face. "This is a surprise! Oh, not that you proposed, but that it took you so long. What have you been waiting for, sir? I have been out six months. Please tell me why it has taken you so long to propose!"

"You do not know how many times I wanted to propose, but I did not want to hasten your decision. You are still young, and it is selfish of me to deny you a full season, but I cannot keep silent any longer. I love and want to marry you as soon as possible. Please say you will be my wife."

"I will have to think about this. May I give you my answer tomorrow?"

He could not believe she would make him wait for an answer! He knew she loved him, so why was she acting as though she did not care?

He would not wait another moment; she had to answer him now. Passionately, he cried, "No, Miss Worthington, I will not wait until tomorrow! You must give me your answer now! I thought you loved me and wanted to be my wife. If you do not, then tell me now. You cannot know the pain you are causing me."

He kept his gaze locked on her face, searching for some sort of signal. She finally smiled and he relaxed. When she put her hand on his cheek and gently caressed it, his heart beat rapidly. He held his breath.

"Fitzwilliam, I have loved you all my life, and it would be an honor to marry you."

He felt an explosion in his chest and yet it did not hurt. He had never before wanted anything so much and had thought it would be lost to him. And now she said yes! His hand trembled as he reached for her.

"But we need to have an understanding before we marry."

He pulled back. "An understanding? I do not know what you mean."

"It is very simple, Fitzwilliam. You thought only of yourself and your own feelings when you left me with the colonel. There was no thought of how I would feel when you stalked out.

"I have listened carefully to what you said, and you are correct, sir; you are a selfish man! You spoke of your feelings and desires, but I did not hear you ask what I felt or wanted. You have taken me for granted and shoved aside my feelings, and this must never happen again. In the future, if a matter concerns me, you must speak with me first before making a decision. Do we have an understanding, Fitzwilliam? I do not want to be ruled by you. I want to be your partner in this marriage — to be your equal."

Darcy took a deep breath and let it out in one fast release. "I should have expected this. You have always been spirited, and truly, I do not wish for you to change. Yes, we have an understanding! I promise you will be an equal partner in our marriage, although there may be times when you will need to remind me not to be selfish."

She threw back her head and laughed aloud. "Oh, Fitzwilliam, you may be sure that I will remind you."

"Elizabeth," he whispered and leaned forward to kiss her.

Sarah cleared her throat just as they heard the front door open, and footsteps coming toward them. Darcy quickly stood, and a moment later, Andrew and Henry Worthington walked into the room.

"Mr. Darcy, it is good to see you again, sir," Andrew exclaimed. After chatting a few moments, Darcy asked if he could speak to both men in private.

As they walked to Mr. Worthington's study, Darcy glanced back at Elizabeth and gave her such a brilliant smile that his cheeks hurt.

Chapter 8

Once inside his study with the door closed, Henry Worthington poured and handed each man a glass of brandy. After taking a sip, he looked at Darcy and asked, "Now, what can we do for you?"

Darcy cleared his throat, suddenly very nervous. "Mmm, I have asked Miss Worthington to be my wife, and she has agreed. I am here to ask you both for your consent and blessing."

A smile lit up Andrew's face, and he immediately stood and clasped Darcy by the shoulder. "This is delightful news, and I cannot express how pleased I am that you will be my brother. Are you aware it was the dearest wish of my father that you and Elizabeth would someday marry? He had the highest respect and regard for you."

This news was a welcome surprise to Darcy, and he could not suppress the huge smile covering his face. "Thank you, Andrew. I am honored that your father had such a high opinion of me."

"Darcy, you must know that I could not be more pleased if I had handpicked you myself." Mr. Worthington quieted and then fidgeted for a moment in his chair. "Lizzy has not been out long. Are you saying you wish to marry so soon after her debut?"

"Yes, sir, we love each other and would like to be married as soon as possible."

"Have you set a wedding date?" Mr. Worthington asked.

"We have not had the opportunity to discuss a date. I proposed to her only moments before you returned home."

"Shall we call Lizzy in and discuss this with her?" Without waiting for an answer, he walked to the door and called for his niece. When she and Sarah came into the room, she looked at Darcy and saw a smile on his face. Elizabeth immediately relaxed, knowing all was well.

Andrew grabbed his sister and hugged her. "I am so pleased, Lizzy. Fitzwilliam will make you a fine husband."

Mr. Worthington motioned for them to sit, and Darcy chose a chair next to his intended. They smiled at each other before turning their attention to her uncle.

"Lizzy, before we go any further, let me be sure of one thing. Are you certain you wish to marry after being out such a short time?"

When she stated an emphatic yes, he studied her closely. "Ah, well, you have always known your own mind. I only wanted to hear you say it. As you can tell, my dear, Andrew and I are happy about your plans to wed Darcy. Now, I am certain Lady Matlock will be thrilled to help you plan your wedding although Richard may be disappointed. He will need to look for another rich heiress, aye?" Henry cleared his throat. "What would be a good date for the wedding?"

The newly engaged couple glanced at each other, but Elizabeth spoke first. "I will ask Lady Matlock how long it will take to make the arrangements. Perhaps three months would be agreeable to her."

Darcy flinched. "Actually, I think tomorrow sounds better, but ... whatever you wish, my love. I cannot refuse you anything."

"Good, good," Mr. Worthington said. "We will contact Lady Matlock and set a time for her to meet with Lizzy."

LATER THAT EVENING, DARCY WAS telling Elizabeth goodnight when he raised her hand and kissed her palm, and then moved his lips to her wrist. She felt his warm breath on her skin, and this sensation, as well as the feel of his lips, made her weak in the knees.

"Fitzwilliam," she whispered, as she leaned closer to him and raised her arms to his neck.

"Mistress!" Sarah scolded

"Sarah," Darcy groaned, "We are betrothed. Just one kiss, please?"

"Very well, but make it short, and mistress, remove your arms from around Mr. Darcy's neck." Sarah then surprised the couple by turning her back to them.

Aware that Sarah would not give them much time, his lips brushed Elizabeth's lightly. As his kiss became more passionate, he felt her hands grip his arms. "Elizabeth, my love," he whispered, "Do you have any idea how happy you have made me?"

"I hope as happy as you have made me," she whispered back, and lifted her lips once more to his.

Darcy's arms grew tighter around her as he moved his lips to her face and neck. He could hardly believe that he was finally touching her in such a manner and felt himself becoming aroused from their kisses and the nearness of her body. Knowing he should not, but desperately wanting to, Darcy brought his hand to the side of her breast, brushing his thumb across her nipple. She gave a low moan that only he could hear, and he prayed that the next three months would pass quickly.

Just then, Sarah turned back around. Slowly, Elizabeth moved away from him. "We must stop, Fitzwilliam."

He dropped his arms but smiled at her before stepping away. "I know, my love. I will leave now and tell our news to Georgiana."

"Please tell her how happy I am that we are to be sisters."

"I will. Goodnight, my love," Darcy murmured in a low voice, as he leaned down and gave her a soft, tender kiss.

DARCY FORCED HIMSELF TO WALK calmly, though rapidly, to his home. As soon as Mr. Bowers opened the door, Darcy assumed that the fact he had asked Miss Worthington to marry him and that she had accepted was apparent to his butler. His wide smile was met with a "Very good, sir."

"Is Miss Darcy upstairs?"

"Yes, sir. She is in the music room, waiting impatiently."

He hurried and found Georgiana going through her sheet music. He presented the same smile, and by her reaction, he guessed what would happen next.

Rushing to hug him, she said gleefully, "You asked her and she said yes!"

"I did and she did. Elizabeth asked me to tell you how pleased she is that you will be her sister."

"May I go with you tomorrow to tell her how happy I am?"

"Certainly, and after supper tonight, we will plan a dinner party, which will include the Worthingtons, the Fitzwilliams, and the Bingleys."

"Oh, bloody hell!" Georgiana said half under her breath. "Will that include Miss Bingley and her sister?"

Her brother's mouth dropped open, and at first, he could not speak. "Georgiana, ladies do not say such words. Whoever taught you such language? Never mind, I feel sure Richard is the culprit. Do not let me hear you say that ever again! And, yes, it will include Bingley's sisters. He is my closest friend, and I cannot slight them."

"Oh, very well, but you know Miss Bingley will be rude. For myself, I promise to be polite and act like a lady." But he noticed that she rolled her eyes as she said it. "Will you also ask Miss Bennet and the Gardiners to come? I know they would appreciate an invitation."

"Georgiana, I am so happy that I will agree to anything you ask." But when he saw a gleam in her eyes, he reconsidered his statement.

"Well, anything within reason but, yes, we will include Miss Bennet and the Gardiners."

Later, as they were going in to dinner, Colonel Fitzwilliam's voice bellowed behind them. "I see that I am just in time for supper," he exclaimed, as he hugged Georgiana and kissed her on the cheek. "What happened to you this morning, Darcy? It was very rude of you to storm out of Miss Worthington's house in such a jealous manner."

"It was equally as rude of you to intrude on Miss Worthington. We had made plans, but you entrenched yourself as though you intended staying all day."

The colonel smirked. "I would have stayed all day, had she not come down with a headache. Ah, well, I will visit her again tomorrow. Perhaps she will be feeling better, and we can walk out together."

"Do not bother, Richard. Miss Worthington is now my betrothed, and your presence will not be welcome."

"Well, bloody hell, Darcy! When did that happen?"

"Richard! Watch your language around Georgiana. She has been imitating you in a most unladylike manner. And, for your information, I went back to Miss Worthington after you left and asked her to marry me. She said yes, and I obtained the blessing of her brother and her uncle. So find another rich woman and leave my intended alone."

The colonel shrugged. "You have all the luck, Cousin. It must be all that money you have. Ah, well, let us eat, for I am famished."

That night, Fitzwilliam Darcy lay in bed thinking of Elizabeth and her response when he kissed her goodnight. The moan that escaped her lips when he touched her breast reinforced his belief that she would be a passionate wife. He had no doubt that theirs would be a happy marriage!

Chapter 9

At Longbourn, Mr. Bennet folded his newspaper and, with a sigh, laid it on his desk. Over the years, he had made a point of reading the society news and gossip from London, looking for news of the Worthingtons. Six months before, he had read of Elizabeth's coming out. It had been difficult for him to accept that she was old enough to be out in society.

While he finished reading of her engagement to someone named Fitzwilliam Darcy, he took a sip of his customary afternoon port and contemplated the identity of the man who would become the husband of his beloved daughter. Mr. Bennet knew little about him other than he was master of a grand estate, Pemberley, in Derbyshire. He gulped the remnants of his drink down.

I hope they love each other and that theirs will not be a marriage of convenience.

Several times during Elizabeth's childhood, Mr. Bennet had disguised himself on his trips to London and stayed in the background away from Sarah's notice. He had caught glimpses of Elizabeth, but he had no contact with her. He knew that Jonathan would be angry if he discovered his old friend spying on his daughter in the park.

He contented himself with observations of her when she was young. He delighted in watching his little girl frolic with Sarah, laughing with a joy that only children seemed to have. She was happy, that had been clear to him, so he never regretted his decision. Usually, a young boy was with them, and he assumed him to be her brother. The two children were close as he thought siblings ought to be.

Once, he had seen a lovely doll with blond hair and blue eyes, the coloring and face of her true sister, Jane, and had decided to buy it. He had stood at the desk, waiting while the clerk filled out the receipt. Mr. Bennet had desperately wanted to give Elizabeth something of the Bennet family, if only her own sister in the form of a doll. He had planned to wait in the park to give it to her, thinking — no, hoping — that Sarah might have compassion on him and not tell her master. But he cancelled the purchase, gave the doll back to the clerk and left the shop, his heart feeling as empty as his arms. It would have been unfair to put Sarah in such a position, and after all, he had given Jonathan his word.

His thoughts jumped quickly to the present day, and a different recollection invaded his thoughts. The park was the same one in which Elizabeth had played as a child, but now she had grown into a beautiful woman, graceful and kind to anyone along the path. It was here he first spied her betrothed. She was laughing and talking with a tall, handsome man she called Mr. Darcy.

Certainly, he thought, *they seem happy in each other's company, and they make a striking couple.*

During that trip, he discovered the man was a neighbor of Elizabeth's, very wealthy and well respected. Most importantly, he appeared to deeply care for Elizabeth by his words, his gazes, and his slight smiles of appreciation for her beauty and charm.

Yes, long ago Bennet had made the right decision in sending his second daughter away. His wife was not just a silly, unreasonable woman. She was obsessed with Elizabeth — even a little insane. Most people, including Jane, accepted her as eccentric. It was common knowledge and often discussed that his wife would check the eye color of every girl she met and become distrustful if anyone questioned her motives. She was a difficult woman, and she insisted that she could judge the worthiness of a person by the color of their eyes. Fortunately, his wife doted on Jane, a sweet and gentle girl.

In public, he kept up a pretense that all was well with their marriage, but in private, he avoided his wife as much as possible. When he was not with Jane, he was alone in his study. He kept his exposure to Fanny Bennet to a minimum.

Mr. Bennet noted with great sadness when the Worthingtons passed away; however, he knew Elizabeth would be well looked after. Mr. Worthington had been an extremely wealthy man, so Elizabeth's dowry would be substantial, and from the little he had discovered, Mr. Darcy was also very wealthy. His Elizabeth would not be alone. Her remaining family was small, but she still had her brother and uncle, and most of all, she had Sarah. Soon, she would be having a family of her own, just as he had wanted for her.

To Mr. Bennet's surprise, Mr. Worthington's solicitor sent him a message shortly after the death of his old friend, requesting his presence in London.

He had been shocked to learn that Jonathan Worthington had left Jane the sum of 20,000 pounds! Mr. Bennet saw this gift as a way to find a suitable husband for his daughter. Worthington's only stipulation was that no one should know he had left the money to Jane. His eldest daughter was now twenty, and though she was sweet and beautiful, she had had no suitable offers of marriage. Hertfordshire offered little in the way of eligible men, so Jane had remained single.

Mr. Worthington's generosity allowed Mr. Bennet to send Jane to stay with Mr. and Mrs. Gardiner, in London. Mr. Gardiner was in trade and, therefore, not accepted into the higher echelons of London society, but an excellent marriage could still be arranged with a 20,000 pound dowry.

And now Bennet's heart raced, and he could not stop smiling. He had received a letter from his dear Jane, telling her parents she had met a Mr. Charles Bingley. He caught the excitement in her letter and knew that she was in love. He was surprised that people in high society would take an interest in his daughter. True, she was beautiful and sweet, and she was a gentleman's daughter but, other than her dowry, there was no additional money and no connections. A letter from his wife's brother, Edward Gardiner, arrived the same day as Jane's, confirming the Gardiners' good opinion of Mr. Bingley.

Yet, he felt conflicted. The happiness in his heart for Jane disappeared the instant he realized how she had met Mr. Bingley — through Mr. Darcy, Elizabeth's betrothed. His eyes misted. And now fate had intervened; his daughters had met, and they were acquaintances. Fear grabbed his heart when he read in her letter that Jane had admitted to a great friendship with Elizabeth and a connection that they had both felt from the start.

He shuddered. *How could this be? How can I let them be friends? I cannot, yet, I want this for both my girls.* He paced quickly, his legs not stopping while he marched the length of the room and back repeatedly. What was he to do now? How could he keep Elizabeth safe?

Mr. Bennet decided he needed fresh air and a fast gallop to clear his head. He rushed to the stable, saddled his own horse, and took off down the road, caring not where he went. He stopped at a neighboring estate, Netherfield, located only three miles from his own. The house had sat empty for some time, but he heard from an estate agent that a gentleman from London was making inquiries about leasing it.

Perhaps we will soon have neighbors — a wealthy family. Perhaps Jane would meet someone new. She cannot marry Mr. Bingley! I will forbid it. I cannot take the chance my wife will find Elizabeth.

The thought that Jane's Mr. Bingley might be the person inquiring about Netherfield crossed his mind. His brow creased contemplating the ramifications of that idea. He felt it would be unwise for him to live so close to Mrs. Bennet. Elizabeth might come for a visit once she was married to Mr. Darcy. He heeled the horse and took off, racing down the road.

I must find out who leased the estate and, regardless, I must stop Jane!

Chapter 10

On the night of Darcy's dinner party, Bingley was the first to arrive, leaving Caroline to come with the Hursts. As usual, Bingley bounded into the house, a big grin on his face.

"Darcy! Congratulations! Miss Worthington is a lovely lady, and you are a lucky man."

Darcy poured his friend a glass of wine. "Bingley, I consider myself the most fortunate of men. Do you know how many others tried to court her?"

"I do, indeed! Your own cousin tried the hardest. Tell me, is he angry with you?"

"No, not at all! While I believe he truly likes Miss Worthington, many of his actions were simply to make me jealous."

"And did he succeed?" Bingley asked, even though he knew the answer.

Darcy rolled his eyes. "Oh Lord, yes! I was the willing mouse to his manipulative, snoopy cat, and I admit that I did make a fool of myself, except it led me directly to the proposal. I suppose the art of being ridiculous has its value."

"A fool? Ridiculous? I am shocked! Nonetheless, not many men are able to marry for love and find that their intended also has a large dowry and excellent connections. Perhaps I should be a little foolhardy too."

"No, do not!" Darcy exclaimed, knowing how quickly Bingley could change his mind. "Have you not noticed how beautiful Elizabeth is, especially with those violet-colored eyes?" Darcy asked smugly. "Even as a child, her eyes fascinated me."

"Indeed I have, although lately, I must confess to being fascinated by Miss Bennet's blue eyes exclusively."

Both men laughed, happy with their choices.

The Worthingtons were the next to arrive, and when Elizabeth smiled at Darcy, his heart skipped several beats, racing wildly as he nearly ran to reach her.

He raised her hand to his lips, speaking so only she could hear. "You are here at last, my love."

Elizabeth gave his hand a brief squeeze before releasing it but, instead of calming his beating heart, it did the opposite, and it only quieted when Andrew and Henry Worthington greeted him.

The remainder of the guests arrived in a steady burst of activity. Included were the Hursts, Miss Bingley, Lord and Lady Matlock along with their two sons, Albert and Richard, the Gardiners, and Jane Bennet.

Darcy stood back when Georgiana rushed into the parlor, hugged Elizabeth, and then welcomed the rest of their guests. She chuckled when Bingley nearly tripped over his own feet while dashing to welcome Jane.

The colonel shared in the laughter but directed his gaze to Jane Bennet, and Darcy spied the expression his cousin used when he would spend the night in meaningless flirtation. Elizabeth had been declared unavailable with Richard's parents concurring, and so, unfortunately for Bingley, Darcy feared the colonel's target was now Jane Bennet. She was, after all, very beautiful.

For a few moments, the noise seemed almost too much for Darcy's comfort, but Mrs. Bowers chose that moment to announce that dinner was served. Many toasts were made that evening for Darcy and Elizabeth's happiness, and the party was lively.

Caroline Bingley repeatedly drew the focus to herself with remarks about London society. With a pointed remark about the superiority of ladies who lived in London, she peeked over at Elizabeth with a barely concealed smirk hidden behind her wine glass.

"Did you attend a ladies' seminary in town, Miss Worthington, and receive your lessons from the very best masters, or did you rely upon country instruction? The seminary I attended has a reputation for providing the most excellent preparation for managing a grand estate."

Darcy's eyes narrowed, and he glared at Bingley, whose face was slowly turning a crimson red.

"No, Miss Bingley," Elizabeth said, as she glanced at Caroline with an expression that remained indifferent. "The masters of London came to me in my little country estate, Rosehaven." Elizabeth then dabbed her mouth with her napkin. Lady Matlock patted her hand while she eyed Miss Bingley but remained quiet.

The remainder of the dinner was cheery with easy conversation. The women separated from the men and quickly arrived in the music room. Caroline and her sister found seats slightly apart from the other ladies, and her gaze never veered away from Elizabeth. Whatever she did, Caroline snorted and whispered to Louisa and occasionally rolled her eyes.

Elizabeth ignored her and concentrated instead on Lady Matlock, Georgiana, Mrs. Gardiner, and Jane. They were immersed in a discussion of the just-arrived China silk, and they argued, as gently as anyone would expect women to argue, as to its superiority. Every so often, Caroline would snort and laugh, catching the attention of Lady Matlock. Elizabeth, fearing a scene, approached Caroline and asked if she would like to join in the discussion. She declined and remained apart from the others until the men entered the room.

"Shall we have some music?"

Caroline jumped up and rushed to the instrument. She played a complicated piece with ease. "Music was a favorite study of mine. Miss Worthington, have you mastered Beethoven yet? His music is very complex."

Georgiana stood, her hands fidgeting with a handkerchief. "I seek Elizabeth's help often, since she studied under the most sought-after master, Mr. Rogers. I understand he only accepts students with the most talent. Did he teach at your seminary?"

Caroline's brows rose. "I imagine her sixty-thousand-pound dowry did not sway his decision to take her on as a pupil."

Everyone's brows rose in unison as they stared at Miss Bingley, shocked that she would dare make such a remark, especially in front of Darcy and the Worthingtons.

"Caroline," her brother hissed.

"Yes, Charles?" Her look was innocent, as though she had discussed nothing more important than the weather. "Now, do not be silly. Please, sit down, you are embarrassing me." Miss Bingley calmly straightened the sheet music.

Elizabeth shrugged, turned to Georgiana and Lady Matlock, and began talking about their plans for the following day, while Caroline banged on the keys, performing another difficult and, this time, not well-played sonata.

Andrew followed suit and took that opportunity to ask Darcy's advice on a few estate matters. Soon everyone's good mood was restored, and the loud music ended.

Darcy realized, however, that Elizabeth was still upset, and he moved to stand next to her, taking her hand into his. Holding it tightly, he caressed it with his thumb, giving it a squeeze before he released it.

He raised his glass and said, "Another toast to the most beautiful and kindest lady of my acquaintance, my future bride, Miss Elizabeth Anne Worthington."

After everyone toasted her, Elizabeth grinned and said, "Perhaps I should make a toast to my intended. He is, after all, the most wonderful and the most handsome man in the world. I am honored he chose me as his bride."

Before anyone could remark on Elizabeth's words, Colonel Fitzwilliam stood and declared, "Absolutely not! The very idea of toasting Darcy as the most wonderful and handsome man in the world is absurd. However, I must say that I am honored to toast the happy couple. If I could not win her, and we all know I could not, I can think of no better man than Darcy."

Everyone laughed, and soon Elizabeth and Georgiana withdrew to the pianoforte while everyone settled back into their seats. They played a duet, and when Elizabeth looked at Darcy, he sent her a smile to show he was pleased.

However, Darcy's outward expression did not match how he felt. He was still unhappy with Miss Bingley's behavior toward his betrothed, so he turned to her brother.

"Charles, your sister is still murmuring and smirking to Mrs. Hurst about Elizabeth. If you do not remove her from the room, I will."

Without a word, Bingley stood, took his sister by each elbow and escorted her out of the room. The others heard raised voices, and then a door slammed. Bingley walked calmly back into the music room, sat down, and began sipping a glass of wine.

After a few sips he looked up. "Oh, pardon me. Caroline asked to be excused. She has a terrible headache and is resting in the front parlor."

To everyone's surprise, Elizabeth laughed out loud. "Mr. Bingley, you are such a gentleman." And with that, she turned to Georgiana and they began another duet.

The evening ended on a good note, and Darcy escorted Elizabeth and the others to the front parlor while they waited for their carriages. Caroline stood up from the sofa when the others came in, signaling Louisa to join her at the window. She railed against Elizabeth for several minutes, her sister listening without comment. Caroline clutched her music tightly against her chest, and they headed out of the room while she continued to disparage Elizabeth. After a few steps, they stopped outside in the empty hallway leading toward the front door. They were paying no attention to the others, assuming they had also left the parlor.

"I have a question, Caroline," Louisa asked. "Why did you mention Miss

Worthington's dowry? It was shameless to discuss money. Lady Matlock was not pleased."

"I was not truly speaking of buying the services of a music master. I was inferring that it must take sixty thousand pounds to purchase a man of Darcy's status. Miss Worthington is not pretty and does not possess the qualities of a London girl. Money is the only reason he chose her. Or perhaps their friendship over the years was too intimate, and they must marry quickly! I will have much enjoyment suggesting that to everyone in town." She laughed until she heard a low, threatening voice from the parlor.

"Miss Bingley!" Lady Matlock exclaimed, her tone authoritative.

Caroline stepped back and peeked inside the room, shocked to find the entire party still assembled there. Lady Matlock glared at her with one of the most menacing expressions she had ever witnessed from anyone, including her own parents.

Darcy, in turn, called to her brother. "Charles!"

Once again, Bingley took his sister by each elbow, pulled her out of the hallway and outside. The others heard their voices raised in angry tones, and then the front door slammed. Bingley walked calmly back into the parlor and sat down in a chair close to Miss Bennet.

"Caroline asked to be excused. Her headache has returned, and she has decided to wait alone outside for the carriage. She is hopeful the fresh air will restore her to better health. "

The Hursts and Bingley were the first to leave, followed by Jane and the Gardiners. When the Worthingtons were ready to depart, Darcy walked them to the door. "Will I see you tomorrow, dearest?"

"Your aunt and Georgiana are taking me shopping again. Shall we stay for tea when we bring Georgiana home?"

"That would please me very much, my love. May I have a private moment with you tomorrow?" When she said yes, he tenderly kissed her hand and waited outside until the three Worthingtons entered their townhouse.

Back inside the Darcy home, the conversation was centered on Miss Bingley. Lord Matlock raised his eyebrow and frowned. "Nephew, what is wrong with that dreadful woman? And please explain why she was here tonight!"

"She is Bingley's sister, and I did not wish to offend him by excluding her. As for her remarks, she speaks out of jealousy. For as long as I have known Charles, Miss Bingley has had the mistaken idea that she will be mistress of Pemberley, even though I have never given her any encouragement."

"Perhaps you need to speak with Bingley about her. He seems a decent and likable chap. Even his sister, Mrs. Hurst, has a proper sense of decorum."

"Mrs. Hurst can be as bad as Miss Bingley although even she seemed to be as shocked as the rest of us tonight. It will be interesting to see whether Miss Bingley comes to grovel tomorrow. She might find herself left out of many social events if she does not. Miss Worthington is well liked, and Miss Bingley is not."

Lady Matlock sniffed before remarking, "It will not do for her to make derogatory remarks about my godchild in the future. She can be blacklisted very quickly."

"I do not believe she will carry her jealous rants any further. I feel certain Bingley and Mrs. Hurst will make her understand how much she stands to lose if she does."

Lord Matlock spoke. "Have you heard from Lady Catherine regarding your marriage? I imagine she is quite displeased that you are not marrying Anne."

"Uncle, you know I have never wanted to marry Anne. While I like my cousin and feel pity for her, she has never been my choice for a wife. As to your question, yes, I heard from her. Indeed, she made a point of visiting me in an effort to talk me out of marrying Miss Worthington. There was nothing negative she could say about my intended, so she focused on how my mother wanted me to marry Anne and how cruel I am to disappoint her daughter."

"Catherine will come to accept it, Darcy. Do you plan to invite her to the wedding?"

"Oh yes, Elizabeth insists on it. She does not want any discord in our family."

Lady Matlock grimaced. "With Catherine, you can always count on discord, but I am glad Elizabeth feels the way she does. Catherine will come around, sooner or later, and we may all wish she had not." At this statement everyone laughed.

ONCE INSIDE THEIR HOME, HENRY Worthington was still upset with Miss Bingley and invited Andrew into his study for a brandy. Elizabeth kissed them goodnight and retired to her chambers, where Sarah was waiting for her.

"Did you have a nice time tonight, lovey?"

"Oh, Sarah, it was lovely except for Miss Bingley. She is so jealous and she has such a vicious tongue."

"And what did that she-devil do or say to my girl? Tell Sarah all about it."

Elizabeth repeated what had happened, and told how Mr. Bingley made his sister leave. Although she tried to dismiss the subject, Sarah knew her mistress was upset.

"That shrew could never attract Mr. Darcy, even if she was the king's daughter and had a million pounds for a dowry. I am certain he would rather go to the gallows than marry her."

"Well, thank heaven he is marrying me. Oh, Sarah, Fitzwilliam is so wonderful, and I love him with all my heart. My wedding day seems so far away. I wish it were tomorrow."

"Do not rush things, lovey. It will come soon enough, and then you will have the rest of your life to be Mrs. Darcy." Sarah snidely added, "And, Miss Bingley will more than likely remain *Miss* Bingley."

Chapter 11

The following day as soon as Elizabeth came in from shopping, Darcy asked her to join him in the library, telling the others they would only be a moment. As expected, Sarah came along, but suddenly she stopped, smiled, and did not go inside with them. Instead, she pulled the door closed and stood waiting outside. At first, the couple did not notice they were alone, for they had eyes only for each other.

Darcy pulled a small box from his pocket and opened it, revealing a beautiful diamond ring within. He lifted the ring from the box, which had held it since the death of his mother. As he placed it on Elizabeth's finger, he thought how pleased Lady Anne would have been to know that he was now giving it to this beautiful woman. "This belonged to my mother, dearest. It has been passed down to Darcy brides for several generations, and now it belongs to you."

Tears ran down Elizabeth's cheeks, and for a moment, she was unable to speak. Darcy wiped away her tears with his thumbs. He held her face in his hands and bent his head to place his lips gently on hers in a tender kiss.

When she could speak, Elizabeth shared with him how she remembered seeing Lady Anne wearing it. "It is truly beautiful, Fitzwilliam, and I feel so honored to wear her ring." She smiled through her tears. "I suppose I shall have to give it up when our first son marries."

"It is yours for as long as you live," he assured her. "It will belong to no other as I will belong to no other."

Hoping that Sarah would allow him to kiss Elizabeth properly, he looked around, surprised to see that they were alone in the room and the door was closed. He wanted to kiss Elizabeth, but did he dare? Being so close to her each day since her coming out, yet always having Sarah watching them, was driving him wild with desire. Now that they were engaged, he had no worries about unwanted suitors but, blast it, Sarah was always watching!

Hardly believing his good fortune and feeling that he needed to make the most of it, Darcy quickly drew Elizabeth close and kissed her, one hand cupping her bottom, and the other her breast. Elizabeth moved closer still and pushed her body fully against his. Her unexpected actions excited him beyond measure, inciting him to lose what little control he had maintained. He lifted her until her hips came into contact with his manhood, and he rubbed himself against her. He wanted nothing more than to love her completely. To know that she felt the same was the greatest of gifts.

She moaned his name softly, her arms tightening around his neck. He knew they had to stop before Sarah returned, and he reluctantly let her go. She swayed when her feet touched the floor, and he put his hands around her waist to steady her. They were still slightly breathless when Sarah came into the room, looking at both of them with no sign that she suspected any mischief.

Sarah led the way to the sitting room where Georgiana and Lady Matlock were having tea. Georgiana knew her brother planned to give his intended their mother's ring, so her eyes immediately went to Elizabeth's hand. She jumped up and, giving a joyful cry, threw her arms around Elizabeth. They were all admiring her ring when Bowers announced Bingley's sisters.

MISS BINGLEY'S EYES INSTANTLY FELL on Elizabeth's hand. She gulped and turned pale when she saw the ring there. Clenching both hands into fists, she clamped her teeth together, and an unfortunate hiss escaped when she exhaled. Mrs. Hurst was greatly alarmed and looked at her sister, wondering if she should insist on their immediately returning home. But with a shudder, Miss Bingley appeared to recover and then smiled her most insincere smile at everyone in the room. Her hatred for Elizabeth was so intense, however, that she would gladly have cut her throat, if she could have gotten away with the deed.

Mrs. Bowers brought in the tray of tea and light refreshments, and Caroline saw Darcy signal Elizabeth to act as hostess. *That should be me*, she thought angrily.

It was difficult for Caroline Bingley to grovel, and having to do so before Elizabeth made her dislike stronger than ever. She had called, hoping Elizabeth would not be there — that she would still be out shopping. She had intended for her sister to occupy the staff while she saw Mr. Darcy alone, for she was confident that she could yet win his affections. She was certain that with enough time she could convince him to break his engagement to Elizabeth and declare himself to her instead. After all, she was more mature and gracious than Elizabeth. She had the advantage of being experienced with running a household, and she was a seasoned hostess, having served in that capacity for her brother's many social events.

Miss Bingley thought Elizabeth was nothing more than an immature, impertinent, spoiled child, and she was quite willing to point out her rival's defects to Mr. Darcy. She knew in her heart that one day he would thank her for saving him from that little chit and would declare his love and appreciation for her by asking her to marry him. But for now, here sat the little fool, wearing Mr. Darcy's ring — an heirloom for heaven's sake — and acting as though his house was already her own.

As she began to speak, Miss Bingley's voice grew shrill in her agitation, and her eyes darted from one person to the next. She began chattering, her voice sometimes trembling, but not from nervousness. She was filled with rage; she hardly knew what she was saying.

"Mr. Darcy, Miss Eliza, how nice to see you again. What a pleasure to see you, Lady Matlock, Georgiana. I am so sorry that I had such a headache last night and could not stay for the entire evening. Have you ladies been shopping today? What a beautiful day to be outside. Why, I told Louisa only this morning we should leave the house, that it was a pity to waste such a beautiful day sitting indoors when there were such pleasures awaiting us outside. And thus, we find ourselves here."

She chattered on and on until Mrs. Hurst put her hand on her sister's arm to gain her attention in an attempt to stop her. Miss Bingley took a deep breath and looked anxiously around. Although she hated groveling in front of Elizabeth, she knew if she ever wanted to be invited to another social event, groveling was necessary. It was essential for her to be in Mr. Darcy and Lady Matlock's good graces; therefore, she had to pretend to be a friend to Elizabeth.

ELIZABETH IGNORED MISS BINGLEY'S INSINCERITY and treated her with civility. Soon the ladies were chatting excitedly about the wedding arrangements, while Darcy sat quietly watching. Although his mind was more agreeably focused on Elizabeth and the memory of the blissful moments he had spent with her earlier, he did note that Miss Bingley had torn her handkerchief to shreds in her agitation, and for once, she did not focus her attention solely on him.

He found Miss Bingley utterly repulsive, and he sincerely hoped this would be the end of her obsession with him, although he was quite certain it would not be.

What drives the woman? Perhaps I should speak with Bingley again about her. She is becoming more and more hostile to Elizabeth, and I am concerned that she could be a threat to her.

Having no answers to his questions, he turned his full attention back to Elizabeth, remembering once more with great pleasure the feel of her body against his.

Before Miss Bingley and Mrs. Hurst took their leave, Caroline turned to Elizabeth. "Miss Eliza, I hope you did not think I intended any insult against you and Mr. Darcy last evening. Please believe me when I say that my remark was innocent with no malice behind it."

She then turned to Darcy. "Sir, you have known me for many years, and *you* must know that I have not a vengeful bone in my body. I would never insult anyone, especially in their own home. We have been dear and close friends too long to put our friendship aside. Those who know me know that I am a kind and caring person."

All remained uncomfortably silent, unable to formulate an appropriate response to such a declaration until Elizabeth gathered her wits and spoke. "It is forgotten, Miss Bingley. Think of it no more."

She could afford to be gracious to Miss Bingley. After all, Elizabeth had Fitzwilliam's heart, while Caroline did not and, despite any wish of hers to the contrary, never would.

Caroline turned back to Darcy. "While we are here, I would speak to you about Charles. I am afraid he is making a grave mistake in courting Miss Jane Bennet."

"How is that, Miss Bingley?"

"Surely you must know of her uncle who is in trade! She lives with them in Cheapside. Knowing you as I do, I cannot believe that you approve of Miss Bennet as a match for my brother. I wish for you to voice your opposition to this dreadful relationship. Make him see that she is not desirable as a wife."

Elizabeth's eyes flashed with anger. Knowing how much she valued her friendship with Jane, Darcy knew better than to criticize Miss Bennet in front of Elizabeth. Besides, he would not give Miss Bingley the satisfaction of agreeing with her, especially after her recent insults.

"I see nothing wrong with Miss Bennet. She is a gentleman's daughter, and I understand that her dowry is equal to yours. Your brother is his own man. I will not interfere in his life."

The expression on Miss Bingley's face told everyone that she could not believe he had refused her request for assistance.

"Mr. Darcy, I am most disappointed in you. Of all the people I know, you are the one person who should understand how important it is to marry a socially acceptable person. Miss Bennet is a sweet girl, but she is nothing more than a country nobody with an uncle in trade."

Darcy was tempted to remind Miss Bingley that her own father had earned his wealth in trade, but he did not. He only repeated that he would not interfere in her brother's life.

The sisters left, and everyone breathed a sigh of relief. Miss Bingley was always a trial to be around, especially when she was being so insincere.

Chapter 12

As the day for the wedding approached, Sarah thought about the talk that she needed to have with Elizabeth. Thus, after breaking their fast the day before the wedding, Sarah determined this was the appropriate time to prepare the bride for her wedding night. This would allow Elizabeth time to think about what they discussed in the event she had questions requiring further elaboration.

"Lovey, did your mother ever speak with you about the relationship between a man and a woman? Did she have the opportunity to share with you what you should expect to happen on your wedding night?"

"No, of course not. There was never a reason for that discussion."

"You need to listen closely then to the things I will tell you. But first, has Mr. Darcy done more than kiss you? Has he touched any part of your body?"

"You know better than that, for you have always been with us."

Sarah grinned. "That is true but, do not forget, I sometimes turn my back or stand outside the door."

"He has only kissed and held me. Of course, he touches my hands and face, but nothing else."

Sarah laughed as she said, "Oh, but once I saw him licking your palm, young lady. What do you say to that?"

"He was not licking it!" Elizabeth protested.

"Then what would you call it?"

"Hmm … well, he … just twirled his tongue around on the inside of my hand."

"Twirled his tongue?" Sarah threw her head back and laughed aloud.

Elizabeth began laughing, too. "Stop it! You were not supposed to see that. To be truthful, he was nipping at my palm with his lips."

"And the night you became engaged?"

"I do not understand you," Elizabeth said with what she hoped was an innocent look on her face.

"Oh, I think you understand perfectly, my sweet girl." Sarah laughed.

"Do you have eyes in the back of your head? Can you see through wooden doors? Very well, Mr. Darcy touched my breast and brushed his thumb over my nipple. There, are you satisfied? Am I to have no privacy?" Elizabeth pouted.

The two looked at each other, one petulant, one grinning. As Sarah held her gaze, Elizabeth's mouth started twitching and, before long, both women were laughing again and holding on to each other.

After their laughter stopped, it was time for Sarah to become serious. She took a deep breath and began telling Elizabeth what would happen in the marriage bed. At first, Elizabeth only blushed, but soon her eyes grew wide as she listened.

She remembered how she felt when Darcy kissed and held her in his arms. She had wondered what else he would do when they married, but never had she thought he would do *that* to her.

"But, what shall I do while he is doing that? Do I just lie there?"

"No, do not just lie there. Enter into the lovemaking as an equal partner to him. Truly, Mr. Darcy will love you even more if you show that you desire him as much as he desires you. Trust me, lovey, when Mr. Darcy makes love to you, you will not want to simply lie there."

"Now, Sarah," Elizabeth teased, "how do you know so much about what happens after one is married? Have you been keeping secrets from me?"

"I have never told you about my private life because you were too young and innocent. Truthfully, you still are, but soon you will be a wife and, while I will still not tell you of my private life, there are other things you need to know."

Elizabeth and Sarah spoke at length — that is, Sarah spoke but Elizabeth could hardly bring herself to say any more than "Oh? Truly?" and "Oh, my stars!" Some of what she was told made her shiver and want to be married right away, but other things made her a little afraid. She decided she would not worry about it, though. Fitzwilliam had always been wonderful to her, had always taken care of her, and she did not think that would end when they were in bed together. If the marriage act itself made her feel as good as his kisses, everything would be marvelous.

Elizabeth did confess to some anxiety concerning her duties as mistress of Pemberley. Rosehaven was as large as Darcy's estate, and her mother had been training her to become mistress of whatever estate she married into, but her mother's sudden death had brought an end to that instruction. Although Lady Matlock had been a wonderful source of information, there was still so much more Elizabeth needed to know.

"What if I make mistakes? It was one thing for Mama to discuss my duties and quite another for me to suddenly become mistress of my own house."

"Do not worry. No one expects you to be perfect. And remember, Mrs. Reynolds and Mrs. Bowers have known you all of your life, and they both love you. They will help you become comfortable with your duties."

Elizabeth considered Sarah's sage advice. "You are right. I know you are, so I will worry about this no more."

Sarah grinned slyly and said, "Just keep Mr. Darcy happy in the marriage bed, lovey, and you will have nothing to worry about at all."

"Oh, you!" Elizabeth laughed.

AFTER SARAH LEFT, ELIZABETH STOOD in front of her mirror. She discarded her clothes and examined her body. She hoped Fitzwilliam would be pleased with her. Her legs were slim, her stomach flat, and her bottom was firm and round. Her breasts were larger than was fashionable, but she thought Fitzwilliam might like them. They were high and firm, but soft too. She had heard that men liked large breasts, and if that were true, Fitzwilliam would be very happy with hers.

Sarah had told her how they would make babies, and she wondered how large Fitzwilliam was. Would his manhood fit inside of her? That place between her legs seemed quite small. Curious, she took her hand mirror and looked between her legs.

Oh my, he will have to be very small to fit in there.

But after she thought some more on it, she remembered Sarah saying that was also where babies came out. Some babies were rather large, and if a big baby could come out, then perhaps something big could go in. *My stars, I hope he is not as big as a baby.*

Although she had grown up and spent most of her time at Rosehaven, Elizabeth had been sheltered from mating farm animals. Her parents had not wanted her exposed to any behavior that was sexual in nature, and if she sometimes asked questions of her mother, the subject was subtly changed. The Worthingtons felt that she would learn all she needed to know from Sarah before her wedding.

Thus, Elizabeth was unusually naïve and innocent. When Darcy touched her intimately, all she knew was that it proved pleasurable, and she responded the way her body directed her to increase her enjoyment.

Yawning, Elizabeth decided it was all too much for her to try and understand, so she would put it out of her mind. There was no way of knowing anything for certain until her wedding night, so there was no good to come of her worrying. She loved Darcy and trusted his love for her. It was enough.

SARAH HAD PREPARED ELIZABETH AS well as she could for her wedding night, but she was concerned about Darcy. She had listened to the other servants, and what she overheard led her to believe that Darcy was inexperienced with women. There was not even a hint of gossip to indicate that he had ever been intimate with a woman. Although she was aware that Darcy and Elizabeth had experimented when they thought she was not looking, Sarah made the decision to go to Darcy and speak with him. He would, no doubt, respond with anger at first, but it could not be helped. Their wedding night must not be a failure!

That afternoon after she spoke with Elizabeth, Sarah walked to the Darcy's townhouse. Darcy was in his study when Sarah was announced. As the door closed behind her, he jumped up.

"Sarah, what is wrong? Is Elizabeth unwell?" he asked anxiously.

"All is well, Mr. Darcy. May I sit?"

"Certainly! Would you care for tea?"

"No, thank you, but if I may, a glass of brandy?"

He was surprised, but poured her a glass and handed it to her. She took several sips, and then said, "I have come on a rather personal and intimate matter, sir."

Darcy was even more surprised at her words. He lifted an eyebrow and said, "Oh? *How* intimate?"

"Sir, I am sure you are not surprised that I have spoken with Elizabeth on what to expect on her wedding night."

His face was beginning to turn red, but he nodded his head.

"Mr. Darcy, I know of no other way to ask this, so...I need to know if you are experienced in how to please a woman in bed."

He jumped up, his face a brilliant red, and exclaimed, "This is most improper! You and I...we cannot speak of this! It is simply not done." He walked to the window with his hands behind his back, nervously twirling the ring on his little finger.

"For the moment, let us forget what is proper and what is not. I am only

91

interested in you and Elizabeth — in your having a successful wedding night. I have seen the passion you two have for each other, and that is a very good thing as it bodes well for your future happiness. But, surely you must know that my young mistress is innocent in the art of lovemaking. That is why I have come to you. Out of inexperience, you could make a blunder that could cause problems between you for the rest of your married life. So I ask you again, are you experienced? Have you ever been intimate with a woman?"

Taking a deep breath, still looking out the window, Darcy replied in a low voice. "If this were anyone but you, Sarah, I would have you thrown out of my house. I do not like speaking of my intimate life, for I consider that highly personal. But since it is you, and I know you have only Elizabeth's best interest at heart, I will answer. No, I am not experienced, and no, I have never been intimate with a woman."

"Thank you for your honesty, Mr. Darcy," Sarah said. "Now, I suspect you are wondering what I, a woman who was abused by her father, could tell you about having a successful wedding night." For a moment, Sarah's eyes took on a faraway look and a small smile graced her lips, but in an instant, she shook herself and continued.

"You see, I once had a grand romance that taught me the beauty of true love, and the difference between being forced into submission, and willingly giving myself to a man I loved and respected. So, I do have words of value to impart to you.

"I have much to tell you regarding how to make a woman happy and how to keep her satisfied in the marriage bed, but I will promise not to be too explicit. You need not face me, if you so desire, but listen carefully."

DARCY LET OUT A SIGH after Sarah left. Never had he been so embarrassed, but Sarah had kept her promise not to be explicit. She was so matter-of-fact with things that were not actually intimate, that he soon grew more comfortable and sat down again. Now that he was alone, he pondered the things she had told him and realized that she may have done him a great favor.

She had primarily spoken of the little ways he could assure Elizabeth that she was loved, and the things he could do that would put her at ease. So many things she had told him were things he had never heard from anyone, not even the men of his acquaintance. He wondered if the lack of this knowledge was why so many men and women looked outside their marriage for love.

Darcy then looked at the book she left with him. She did not speak of it, but had simply laid it on his desk as she left the room. So many positions! It would take a lifetime to try them all. There was no title anywhere on the book and nothing to indicate where it came from or who had published it. She told him it was his decision whether to share the book with Elizabeth after they became comfortable with each other.

He took the book with him when he went to his chambers that evening and stayed up most of the night reading it, amazed at what was possible for two lovers. He was eager for their wedding night, for Elizabeth had already shown that she felt passion for him.

Between the announcement of their engagement and their wedding, many dinner parties and several balls were given for the happy couple. Darcy, with his new animated spirit, was the talk of the *ton*. Never had their friends seen him so happy or talkative. His manner was described by more than one as giddy, but his happiness was so great that he endured all teasing with surprisingly good humor.

Once, when Bingley joked about how much he smiled, Darcy laughed as he replied, "Jest all you like Bingley, for you cannot find a happier man than I in the entire world. Elizabeth Worthington loves me and will soon be my wife. That is worth all the teasing I am receiving."

Caroline Bingley had begun to suffer from the remarks she had made when a number of dinner parties given in honor of Darcy and Elizabeth excluded her. Lady Matlock had declared that Miss Bingley would not receive an invitation to the engagement ball she planned for the couple, but Elizabeth had asked her to reconsider for Mr. Bingley's sake. It was not that she cared whether Miss Bingley attended the ball, but she did not want Mr. Bingley's feelings hurt. Lady Matlock finally yielded to her wishes, and Miss Bingley's invitation was delivered.

Everyone who received an invitation had accepted and, for Elizabeth and Darcy, the night of the ball was glorious. Darcy was clearly happy as he proudly stood in the receiving line with his beautiful betrothed at his side. Many people discovered, for the first time, that Fitzwilliam Darcy had dimples. When they led off the first dance, there was almost a collective sigh from the other participants as they witnessed a couple utterly engrossed in each other.

Before the dance, however, Darcy had come close to having a row with his aunt. He did not want Elizabeth dancing with anyone but him while Lady Matlock insisted he could not fill her dance card with only his name.

"Elizabeth must be allowed to dance with Andrew and her uncle. And you know your uncle wants to dance with her as, I am sure, Mr. Bingley and Richard will also. Now, stop your pouting; it looks undignified on a grown man."

Finally, Darcy relented, but when he was not dancing with Elizabeth, he stood in a corner, a scowl on his face. Quite a number of people laughed behind their hands and remarked on how a scowling Darcy was the one they all knew so well.

Miss Bingley was the only person not enjoying the engagement ball, as she watched the couple with hate-filled eyes. Unfortunately, she voiced her harsh criticism of Elizabeth to Miss Henrietta Stokley and several other young ladies.

The ladies sniggered when Miss Stokley remarked, "Apparently, you are unaware that you were not originally invited to this ball. Lady Matlock told my mother, who is a close friend, that you were invited only at Miss Worthington's insistence."

Miss Bingley stood frozen, her mouth slightly agape as she received this news. "But…but…Mr. Darcy never would have allowed me to be excluded. We are very dear friends of long standing."

She was only vaguely aware of the giggles of the other ladies as Miss Stokley laughed. "Think that if it gives you pleasure, Miss Bingley."

When she was able to gain control of herself again, Miss Bingley realized that everyone had left her, and she was standing alone. She looked around the room and saw that Miss Stokley was standing next to Lady Matlock, whispering into her ear. Lady Matlock looked most displeased as she turned her gaze toward Miss Bingley.

Mr. Bingley had noticed the expression on his sister's face and rushed to her side. "Caroline, what is wrong? Are you unwell?"

Miss Bingley could not bear to tell her brother of her humiliation, even though she knew he would hear of it before the night was over.

"Yes, Charles, I have a pounding headache, and I must leave now. Perhaps Louisa and Hurst would see me home."

"Of course, I will speak to Louisa immediately and see to your departure."

When he approached Mrs. Hurst and her husband, they had already heard the gossip, and to Bingley's surprise, Louisa Hurst refused to leave the ball.

"We will send her home in our carriage, if you will see us home after the ball. You should know that Caroline spoke harshly of Miss Worthington this evening, and Miss Stokley would not let the remark stand. Perhaps you have noticed that no one has asked her to dance. If she has a headache, it is from being humiliated, and it is her fault. I will no longer be punished for her spiteful words. She has persisted in her delusions despite all evidence to the contrary, and she alone will suffer the consequences of her actions."

Mr. Bingley's face had become grim as he listened to his sister. "You are right, of course. It is my responsibility to take care of Caroline. We will speak further on this tomorrow morning and decide what must be done."

Bingley turned and walked to Miss Bennet. "I must leave for a short while, but I will soon return. My sister has a headache that necessitates her removal from the ball, and I must escort her home."

Miss Bennet smiled serenely and assured him she would be waiting for his return.

THE TWO LOVERS WERE UNAWARE of the tension provoked by Miss Bingley, and they continued to enjoy their engagement ball. As it was drawing to its conclusion, they slipped out to the terrace to enjoy a stolen kiss.

Darcy's voice was low and husky as he spoke. "I am all anticipation for our wedding night. It is driving me insane to have you so near and yet be unable to touch you as I desire."

She leaned into him and whispered, "I know, Fitzwilliam. I hate to part from you, but we should go back inside, or Sarah will come looking for us."

Darcy groaned and kissed her one last time.

THEIR WEDDING DAY FINALLY ARRIVED, and as Sarah helped Elizabeth dress, there was much giggling and nervousness. When her hair was finished, Sarah stood behind her as Elizabeth looked at her reflection in the mirror. With tears in her eyes, Sarah told her how beautiful she looked. *If only the Worthingtons were still alive to witness their daughter's happiness. They would be so proud of her.*

Her gown was white satin with tiny seed pearls scattered throughout the bodice. Sarah had woven fragrant orange blossoms and seed pearls into her dark curls, and her only jewelry was a pair of pearl earrings that had been a gift from her father. Instead of a wedding bonnet, she decided on a veil of the finest lace. It was secured by pearl pins and fell to her shoulders. Georgiana was her attendant, while Darcy chose Charles as his witness.

As Elizabeth walked up the aisle on the arm of her brother, she beheld Darcy waiting for her at the altar. He was standing very straight, with the usual scowl on his face, but when he saw her coming toward him, his eyes lit with joy, and his scowl was replaced with the most beautiful smile Elizabeth had ever seen.

The ceremony passed in a blur until Darcy slid the ring on her finger, and the bishop pronounced them man and wife.

Man and wife, she thought happily, *Mr. and Mrs. Fitzwilliam Darcy.*

A wedding breakfast and ball were held at Lord and Lady Matlock's mansion, and the newlyweds led off the first dance.

"How long do we have to stay?" Darcy whispered to her.

"Long enough to be polite," she whispered back.

"I do not know why we are being asked to stay with all of these people," he grumbled. "All I want is to be alone with my new wife."

As far as Darcy was concerned, the ball lasted too long and there were far too many speeches. First, Andrew made a toast to the couple and welcomed Darcy as his new brother. That was followed by Henry Worthington's toast and, of course, Bingley, the colonel, and Lord Matlock had to make their own toasts and say a few additional words.

The couple finally made their escape, unabashedly pretending to be leaving for Pemberley with a long trip ahead of them. In truth, they were staying in London that night and leaving for Pemberley the following day. Georgiana would stay with the Matlocks for two weeks, and the colonel would then escort her to Pemberley.

They settled into their carriage, and Darcy took her hands in his and smiled. Before he could speak, Elizabeth giggled and launched herself at him, licking both of his dimples.

Surprised, he could only stare at her with wide opened eyes before saying, "I beg your pardon?"

She giggled again, suddenly shy. "I am sorry, Fitzwilliam, but I have wanted to lick your dimples since I was a little girl. I promised myself I would do so if ever given the opportunity. They fascinate me, they always have. You look so delicious when you smile." Her smile had been replaced with a look of genuine concern as she realized the impropriety of her actions. "Are you angry with me?"

Darcy, having had time to recover, pulled her over to sit by his side. Snuggling her, he laughed. "How could I be angry with you, my love? I was only surprised, that is all. Feel free to lick my dimples anytime you wish."

They enjoyed deep kisses, long denied them, lasting until the carriage pulled up in front of their London townhouse.

As soon as they stepped inside, Darcy reminded Mr. and Mrs. Bowers not to tell anyone they were in residence. "We will ring if we require anything of the staff."

Darcy kissed Elizabeth's hand as they stood in front of the door to her bedchamber. "When should I come to you, my love?"

She looked down at the floor, suddenly shy. "I should be ready in a half-hour."

He left and went to his chamber where Williamson had hot water waiting for him. His nightshirt and robe were lying on his bed. "Will there be anything else, sir?" his valet asked.

"No, that will be all. Good night."

In Elizabeth's bedchamber, Sarah helped her mistress undress and then slipped a pale blue gown of translucent silk over her head. Sarah quickly took the pins from Elizabeth's hair and brushed it, all the while whispering and giggling as she reminded Elizabeth of the things she had told her about the marriage bed.

At the agreed upon time, Darcy knocked on the door leading to Elizabeth's bedchamber. He shivered in anticipation when he heard her soft voice calling out for him to enter. He opened the door and stood feasting his eyes on her as she stood waiting in the middle of the room. Her dark, curly hair flowed down her back and the silk gown that clung to her curves left little to the imagination, firing his blood. He was having trouble swallowing, so he cleared his throat instead.

As though in a daze, he drew her close. Fighting to control his breathing, he whispered, "You are so beautiful! I can hardly believe you are now my wife. What have I done in my life to deserve you?"

She stood on her toes and kissed him softly on his neck. "This seems a dream to me as well, Fitzwilliam. I have waited so long to be your wife."

To his surprise, she pulled away and ran to her trunk, lifting out a wrapped package. Handing it to him, she said, "My darling Fitzwilliam, this is your wedding gift from me."

He tore off the paper and found a beautiful, leather-bound book. Written in gold were the words, *Love Poems to My Husband*. When he opened it, he saw the inscription penned by her hand: *To my husband, Fitzwilliam Darcy, on our wedding day, June 4, 1809.*

"It contains poems I wrote to you over the years, and I have included poems others have written that I thought pertained to us or that expressed my feelings for you. Read the first poem, Fitzwilliam, and then put the book away until later. This first poem was written when I was nine years old, the night after I made my declaration of intent to someday marry you."

Tears filled his eyes even though he laughed as he read.

I love Fitzwilliam Darcy.
He is as sweet as he can be.
And when I am a lady,
I know he will marry me.

He looked up and saw her grinning at him, and his heart felt as though it would burst from happiness. Laying the book aside and drawing her close, he whispered, "Oh, Elizabeth, I love you so much."

She stood on tiptoes and raised her lips to his, and he forgot his vow to go slowly as he hungrily kissed her. Her own hunger matched his, and his arousal pushed against her stomach. Darcy quickly picked her up in his arms and carried her to the side of the bed. He sat down, standing her in front of him and, with trembling hands, slipped her gown off her shoulders letting it fall to the floor, a shimmering puddle of blue silk at her feet.

"Do not be frightened, dearest. Did not Sarah tell you what to expect tonight?"

Elizabeth ran her hands through his hair. "I am not afraid of you, for I know you would never hurt me. And, yes, Sarah told me what I should expect."

"What did she say?"

Teasing him, she answered, "I cannot tell you everything, dearest. It would embarrass me. But I can tell you that she told me to relax and let my husband teach me what will please him."

"Sarah is a very wise woman, but tonight we will learn together. This is as new to me as it is to you. I have never been with a woman until now, my love."

"It would break my heart had you known another woman."

"You are the only one I have ever wanted."

His eager hands caressed her while his hungry eyes traveled over her, drinking in her beauty. She felt so soft under his hands, and her scent drove him mad with desire.

"Does my body please you, Husband?"

"Oh yes, my beloved, it pleases me very much," he whispered, as he cupped her breasts, and his fingers teased her nipples. "You are perfect in every way."

"I want to see your body, Fitzwilliam."

Darcy stood and removed his robe and nightshirt. Elizabeth's eyes grew wide when she saw him standing before her in all his naked glory. He was quite large, and again she wondered how he would fit inside of her. She marveled at the firmness of the muscles under her fingers. Then she walked around to face him and caressed his chest, running her fingers through the soft hair that grew there.

"You are magnificent with your broad shoulders and narrow hips." She grasped his arms. "They are so strong! You are beautiful, my husband, and you are all mine."

"Yes, we belong only to each other." Darcy was breathless with desire as he sat back on the bed and again placed her between his legs. He cupped her breasts and allowed his fingers to tease her nipples. Bending his head, he brought his mouth to her breast, tasting and nipping her gently with his lips. She tangled her fingers in his hair and moaned, arching herself toward him as he sent waves of desire coursing throughout her body.

He lifted her and carried her to his bed chamber. He had dreamed of taking her as his wife in his bed. Laying her down gently, he quickly slipped in next to her, thrilled by the sensation of her nude body pressing against his.

Darcy felt his control slipping, but he was determined to give her pleasure before taking his own. He had trouble keeping his resolve, however, as she ran her hands and nails up and down his back and slid her body against his.

"My beloved, I fear I will not be able to satisfy you if you continue. Give me time to give you pleasure."

Sarah had not told her this might happen, but she trusted her husband enough to stop moving. He kissed her face and lips, teasing her with his tongue, and then moved to her neck and earlobes. Her skin was softer than he had imagined, and her scent continued to arouse him. Darcy moved back to her lips, and when his tongue entered her mouth, she moaned softly. Her hands continued moving over him, and he groaned with pleasure at her touch.

As his mouth and tongue moved slowly over her body, she cried out his name. He continued exploring until he reached the sensitive area between her legs. She gasped in surprise, and for a moment, her body became stiff.

"Relax, my love," he whispered. "We are married now and whatever we do in our bed is proper. Let me, dearest. I promise you will like it."

Elizabeth tried to relax, and almost immediately, she decided that she liked very much what her husband was doing. "Fitzwilliam," she cried out again, as a sensation she had never felt before flowed over her. She pulled him closer and kissed him as he rolled on top of her.

Trying to be gentle, he pushed slowly into her. She was very tight, but when she felt him entering her, she responded by wrapping her legs around his waist and lifting her hips. Her movements almost sent him over the edge.

Calling her name, he lunged and broke her maidenhead. She let out a whimper, and he stopped, fearing that he had been too rough with her.

"I am sorry, my love. Shall I stop?" He prayed she would say no. He was not sure he could bear it.

To his relief she gasped, "Do not stop. Please, do not stop."

Hearing her cries of pleasure, he whispered how much he loved her, how he adored her. Their bodies came together in a frenzy that surprised them both. It took all of his control to wait until she reached her peak once more before he took his release and spilled his seed deep inside of her.

Exhausted, he did not move until he realized that her breathing was as labored as his, and he rolled onto his side. Pulling her close, Darcy placed small kisses over her face. "Are you pleased with your new husband?" he asked.

She answered by tangling her fingers through his curls and drawing his mouth to hers for a tender kiss.

"I could not be more pleased. I was assured I would enjoy the marriage bed, but I did not realize how wonderful it would be until now." They lay in each other's arms and looked at one another. "You are looking very smug, dearest."

He laughed and nuzzled her neck. "I am feeling very smug, my beloved. Every man dreams of marrying a lady who turns into a passionate woman each night, but few men are so fortunate. Thank heaven I am one of the fortunate."

She smirked. "Perhaps some men do not know how to turn their lady into a passionate woman, as do you."

Darcy laughed out loud, but his laughter quickly turned into a moan as he felt her fingers stroking him.

"Do you mind me touching you here, Fitzwilliam? I wish to give you the same pleasure you gave to me."

Darcy took her hand and showed her how he liked to be stroked, surprised at how quickly she learned. Elizabeth was delighted when she felt him enlarging, and the growling sounds he made deep in his chest excited her. His hips began to move, and he attempted to remove her hand, but she slapped at him and whispered, "Do you not like what I am doing?"

"I like it very much, my love," he groaned, "but if you do not stop, this bed will soon be a mess."

Elizabeth declared that she did not care, as long as she pleased him. He reached into the drawer of his bedside table, grabbing a handkerchief to catch his seed while his body trembled with release.

Not surprisingly, they made love several times throughout the night. They could not seem to get enough of each other. Their love was consuming; their passion unquenchable.

Later, she teased him about having a handkerchief at hand. When he replied that he always kept one nearby in case he caught a cold, she crawled over him before he could stop her and opened the drawer.

Peals of laughter shook her when she saw a drawer full of plain, white handkerchiefs. "My stars, Fitzwilliam, what a lot of colds you must have!"

He scowled at her, pretending to be displeased at her jest, but she kissed his lips and told him how much she loved him. He laughed and said he would remove the handkerchiefs.

"Do not move them, Husband, for we will have future need of them, and you know we do not want a messy bed. From now on, I will be the one to pleasure you, and I plan to do it often."

He gave a happy sigh of contentment and snuggled closer to her. Before drifting off to sleep, he murmured, "I must remember to give Sarah extra when I next pay her."

Chapter 13

Darcy and Elizabeth left London the following day for Pemberley. Their departure was later than originally planned, but that was not really surprising, considering the fact that they were newlyweds and enjoying every privilege that was now theirs to savor.

The trip was long, but Darcy made use of the time by showing Elizabeth the book Sarah had given him. They took great pleasure in discussing the various positions they could try, while laughing at the ones they saw little hope of achieving — at least in comfort.

When the familiar house finally came into sight, they smiled at each other and sighed contentedly. They were glad to be home.

"I remember when I used to visit Pemberley, Sarah always made them stop the carriage here, so we could see the house from this view. The sight never failed to move me." Elizabeth turned from the carriage window to catch her husband's expression.

"When I returned from London, this is where I stopped to view it. No matter the turmoil in my life, this house soothed my soul. Nothing bad could touch me when I was at Pemberley. It was my haven."

Mrs. Reynolds and the other servants were all waiting on the front steps to greet them as they arrived. The housekeeper stepped forward with a smile, and took Elizabeth by both hands. "Mrs. Darcy, we are so happy to see you again and to welcome you as the new Mistress of Pemberley."

"Thank you, Mrs. Reynolds. I feel as though I am greeting old friends when I look at everyone. There are many faces I remember from my past visits here."

They walked into the great hall as Mrs. Reynolds remarked, "Your trunks should be in your chambers by now. Mr. Darcy, would you and the mistress like to freshen up and perhaps rest a bit before dinner?"

"That sounds wonderful," Darcy said. He looked at Elizabeth, and she nodded her agreement.

"I will have refreshments sent up immediately." Mrs. Reynolds hurried away to set all of the arrangements in motion.

The door to her bedchamber was open, and they stepped inside to find Sarah unpacking Elizabeth's trunks. She looked at them and grinned.

"Mr. Darcy, Williamson is preparing your bath, and I have your wife's bath almost ready. If you like, I will let you know when tea arrives. I am going to the kitchen now and ask Mrs. Reynolds to delay bringing it until your baths are completed."

"Thank you, Sarah," said Elizabeth.

Sarah turned and left the room, and Darcy leaned down to kiss his wife. "Sarah cannot scold us now for kissing whenever we want. Mmm, marriage definitely holds an advantage over an engagement."

Elizabeth smiled as she put her arms around his neck and returned his kiss. "Will you nap with me after tea, my love?"

"Try and stop me, madam, although, I am not sure how much sleep you will enjoy. I may be tempted to engage you in more pleasant activities."

She smirked and asked, "Will those activities be as beneficial to my health as a nap?"

"Even more so," Darcy whispered, before leaving for his chambers.

After tea, Darcy swept Elizabeth into his arms and carried her to their bed. He quickly undressed them, but instead of joining her, he paused and looked down, greedy to see what now belonged only to him.

"I love the way your hair fans out over your pillow and the way you look at me when I make love to you. I even love the way your eyes flash when you are angry. I have always adored your very fine eyes, my love."

She held out her hands. "Join me, Fitzwilliam. I feel lonely without you lying by my side."

He lay down and pulled her into his arms, kissing her until they both gasped for breath. His mouth and tongue teased her neck, moving downward. She moaned softly, and ran her fingernails up and down his back. Shivering from the sensation, he gently pushed her onto her back.

Elizabeth raised her hips. She wanted him inside her, but he chose to move between her legs and open her knees wider. She let out a loud squeak of pleasure and yelled loudly, "Oh my stars," and grabbed him by his hair.

Darcy dissolved into laughter at her reaction, and he stopped what he was doing in order to control himself.

"What? What?" she cried. "What are you doing? Why have you stopped, Fitzwilliam?"

He could not control his laughter any longer and rolled on his side. She pounded him on his back with her fists, demanding to know why he was laughing at her. It was obvious to Darcy that she was angry with him, for she moved to leave the bed.

Still laughing, Darcy tried to grab her, but she slapped his hands away and stood by the bed looking down at him. Crossing her arms over her chest, she huffed her displeasure.

His laughter suddenly gone, he jumped up and enclosed her in his arms. "Please dearest, forgive me; I was not laughing at you."

"Do not take me for a fool, Fitzwilliam! Of course, you were laughing at me. Never did I think my husband would laugh while making love."

Her beautiful, violet eyes flashed in anger, and her lips formed a straight line. He had to make her understand why he laughed. He did not want their intimate life to be over just as it was beginning.

"Please, dearest, let me explain. I am sorry I laughed, but I could not help myself, and I was not making fun of you. Here, let us sit on the side of the bed, and I will explain everything." He patted the bed indicating she should sit.

"You sit on the bed, I will sit here," she said in a hurt voice and moved to a chair away from him. Darcy sat on the bed and sighed, running his hands through his hair. Looking down at the floor, he explained that her reaction of squeaking and then yelling, "Oh my stars," simply struck him as funny, and once he started laughing he could not stop.

"I was not making fun of you, my love. In truth, I am pleased you enjoyed what I was doing enough to have such a reaction. I desire to give you pleasure in all that I do."

He looked up at her, trying to gauge whether she was still angry, only to see her hands over her face and her shoulders shaking, as though she was sobbing.

Oh Lord, she will never let me in her bed again.

He knelt down on the floor in front of her and laid his head on her lap. "Please forgive me, my love."

Suddenly, she gave him a light shove, and he landed on his back. Before he knew what was happening, she had straddled him and was pounding him on his chest with her small fists. He was surprised to see her laughing and to hear her almost yelling, "You insufferable man!" He laughed with her, grabbed her hands, and rolled her over on her back, kissing her face and neck. When she kissed him back, he knew that she was as excited as he was.

He picked her up and put her back on the bed on her stomach, asking her to get on her knees with her bottom in the air. She looked at him in confusion, but when he smiled, she did as he requested. She could not resist teasing him by asking, "Do you want me, my love?"

"Oh, yes," he panted, his breath husky, "you have no idea how much I want you."

It was not long before she cried out his name and reached her peak. His own release seemed to last forever.

He slumped against her for a moment and then rolled her over on her back. At last, they were able to control their breathing, and Elizabeth snuggled her face against his neck. He yawned and, before long, his even breathing could be heard. He was sound asleep. Darcy would have been pleased had he known that Elizabeth then rolled over on her side and spooned her body against his, before gently taking his hand and placing it on her breast, soon falling asleep herself.

Chapter 14

The Darcys spent two glorious weeks by themselves without having to schedule their time or see anyone. They stayed up most of the night making love and talking and slept late each morning. Breakfast was brought to their chambers, where they fed each other.

They had picnics by a stream in a spot where Elizabeth and Georgiana had played as children.

"Do you remember the time, dearest, when I wanted to cross this stream, and you insisted on carrying me? You were afraid I would slip and fall in."

Darcy threw back his head and laughed. "And I slipped on a rock and we both went into the water. You were so angry with me! I shall never forget you marching back to the house, your little hands in tight fists, and your arms swinging back and forth, huffing and puffing the entire way."

"Oh yes, I was very angry. I had not wanted you to carry me. I thought I was big enough to walk across by myself."

His eyes softened as he remembered how she had not betrayed him when they reached the house. "You told my mother that it was your fault. That you fell and I jumped in to save you. You never wanted anyone to be in trouble, even when you were punished through no fault of your own."

"I was not punished so very often, my love. Sarah never told on me, and she often took the blame for things I did. I think Mama knew the truth, which is why she did not punish her. Besides, Mama was much too tenderhearted to punish."

IT WAS A BEAUTIFUL DAY, and they had walked to the stream for a picnic. After they had eaten, Elizabeth looked around, as though searching for something.

"Does anyone ever come here? Will we be disturbed?"

"It is unlikely! This place is well hidden."

She smiled shyly, rose to her feet, began singing a tune they had recently heard at the theater, and then started dancing. After she had finished, Elizabeth knelt before him, took his face between her hands, and kissed him. He reached for her, but she whispered, "No, not yet. Let me love you first."

She began kissing him the way he often kissed her, beginning at his temples. Slowly, her moist lips slid over his face, nibbling and kissing his neck and ears, whispering words of love as she lingered there.

He closed his eyes, and her mouth continued to move over him while he moaned her name. Again, Darcy reached out for her, but Elizabeth gently pushed his hands away. Her hands rose to her hair, and she pulled the pins out, so that her curls tumbled down around her shoulders and back.

"You look like an enchanted wood nymph."

Before she could stop him, he swiftly lifted her atop him, pulling her down to his chest. With their arms wrapped around each other, they lay together quietly, whispering words of love and caressing one another.

LATER, THEY STROLLED BACK TO the house, their arms around each other's waist, with Elizabeth's head on his shoulder. Darcy marveled at this loving and exciting woman who was his wife, and he was glad he had never been with another woman. Now that she was his, he knew he could not live without her. For a moment, he felt fear dart through him, as though they were tempting fate with such happiness, but when she looked up at him and smiled, he forgot his fear and thought only of their love.

Some days they rode around the estate, and Darcy took her to the tenants' homes so she would know them as he did. Elizabeth's horse, El'Zora, had been brought to Pemberley, and they often raced. She had never liked riding side saddle, so when she was younger, Elizabeth talked her parents into having riding clothes and boots made to fit her, so she could ride astride with a regular saddle. Even when she rode with others outside her family, she never used the side saddle.

Darcy knew she loved riding and racing against him, and he loved watching her hair streaming in the wind. Elizabeth never won a race against him, although she came close several times.

In the evening, they read to one another or lay in each other's arms in front of the fire. No one disturbed them. They were on their honeymoon, and meals and baths appeared as if by magic. They were in a world of their own and wished this time never had to end.

BUT EVERYTHING HAS AN ENDING. Elizabeth was wandering through the gardens one morning, waiting for the arrival of Georgiana and Richard, when she heard familiar voices. Peeking around a hedge, she saw, to her great surprise, Jane Bennet and the Gardiners. They were admiring the roses.

"Ladies! Mr. Gardiner! What a pleasant surprise. I did not know you were visiting this area."

Jane Bennet rushed to embrace Elizabeth, happy to see her friend again. "Yes, we have been planning this journey for many months. We hesitated about touring Pemberley as we knew you and Mr. Darcy were on your honeymoon, but we did so want to see the house and grounds,"

Elizabeth laughed. "I am afraid the honeymoon is over. We expect Miss Darcy and Colonel Fitzwilliam sometime today. But why did you not tell us of your traveling plans before the wedding?"

Mrs. Gardiner explained. "There was so much happening, and you were so busy planning, that there never seemed to be a right time."

Elizabeth looked at Miss Bennet. "And Mr. Bingley — is he well?"

Jane blushed and looked at the ground. "Quite well, thank you. We are engaged now. The day after your wedding, Mr. Bingley rode to Longbourn to petition Papa for his consent."

"And Charles let you make this trip so soon after your engagement?" Elizabeth teased.

"Indeed," Mrs. Gardiner laughed. "He looked as though he was losing his best friend the day we left, but we had planned this months ago, and he did not wish to deprive Jane of her promised diversion."

At Elizabeth's insistence, they went back into the house for tea. "I am sorry that Mr. Darcy is not here to greet you personally. He is helping one of his tenants, but perhaps he will return before you leave."

At that moment, they heard loud footsteps and Darcy's voice. "Elizabeth, are Georgiana and Richard here?" He stopped in the doorway, conscious of his disheveled appearance. Elizabeth saw at once that he was embarrassed at being caught in dirty clothes, so she stood and went to him.

"Look, my love, Miss Bennet and the Gardiners are touring Derbyshire. I met them in the rose garden and insisted they come inside and join us for tea."

Darcy bowed. "Welcome to Pemberley. Please forgive my appearance. I have been with a tenant all morning. Please excuse me."

After he left, Elizabeth asked her friends to stay for dinner; however, they had other plans for the afternoon and evening. After tea had been served and they walked out to the Gardiner's carriage, a servant, at Elizabeth's request, met them with a large bouquet of roses. He bowed and held them out to Miss Bennet.

"They are beautiful," Jane exclaimed as she held them to her face. "And look at all the varieties. Thank you so much, Mrs. Darcy."

Elizabeth stood at the door waving until they were out of sight. Then she went back inside and up to her husband's chamber. Williamson answered her knock and informed her that he was shaving the master. She pushed past him. "Carry on, Williamson. I will not be in your way."

Darcy looked at her and laughed to himself. *Williamson will have to adjust to Elizabeth's ways, as she will not adjust to his.*

The valet seemed amused at her lively spirit. He quickly finished shaving Darcy and left the room, whereupon Darcy pulled his wife onto his lap and kissed her.

She put her face in his neck and breathed deeply, "You smell so good, my love, so spicy and manly. Mmm, and you feel good too."

Darcy laughed and hugged her, giving her one last kiss before they went downstairs for a bite to eat. They had just begun when voices alerted them that Georgiana and the colonel had arrived.

Georgiana ran to her brother and hugged him, before breaking away to hug Elizabeth. "Oh, it is good to be home," she cried. "Of course, I enjoyed my time with my aunt and uncle too, but home is the best place of all."

After all had exchanged greetings, they sat down to finish eating. Richard turned to Darcy and started talking about the news he had learned of George Wickham.

"I hear that someone bought him a commission in the Yorkshire militia. Too bad he is not under my command," the colonel smirked.

"Old Sticky Wicky, I never liked him," Georgiana exclaimed. "Remember how you made him cry, Lizzy, and Brother told him to leave you alone?" She grinned at her sister.

"I remember that well," Darcy laughed. "That was the day a certain young lady told me not to marry until she grew up." He and Elizabeth smiled at each other.

"I see she began training you at an early age, Cousin. No wonder I did not stand a chance with her. She had already decided on you," Richard snorted.

"Yes, I had only to wait until she grew up."

"Do not look so bloody smug, Cousin."

"Richard, mind your language around Elizabeth and Georgiana," Darcy answered sternly.

"Sorry, sweetheart," Richard said as he looked at Georgiana. He turned to Elizabeth. "Sorry, dearest Elizabeth, I cannot help but be carried away sometimes, especially when I behold your beauty." He moved his hand as though to put it on top of Elizabeth's, but with a look of displeasure, she quickly moved her hand to her lap.

A frown appeared on Darcy's face. He hoped Richard's visit would not be too taxing.

Chapter 15

Elizabeth sent a message to the Lambton Inn, inviting the Gardiners and Jane to dinner at Pemberley in two days' time, but they sent their regrets, saying their days and evenings were filled with planned visits to family and friends. They hoped to see the Darcys either when they next came to London or when Jane and Bingley married.

Darcy soon received the expected letter from Bingley, with its usual blots and smears, informing him of his engagement to Jane Bennet. He told him that a mutual friend, Lord Heatherby, would be his witness. He included a short line about looking for an estate in Hertfordshire, and then went on to say:

Jane's father is all that is pleasant, but Mrs. Bennet is very odd. I am not certain that Jane and I should live near her. For that reason, I will lease an estate, rather than buy one at this time. I am curious as to what you would make of Jane's mother, and you must visit as soon as I am settled.

After reading Bingley's letter aloud to Elizabeth, he voiced his opinion as to the wisdom of Bingley's involving himself with the Bennet family.

"She must be very strange, indeed, for Bingley to be cautious of her. He is such an impulsive man and always tends to see things in a rose-colored hue."

"The choice of a wife is up to Mr. Bingley, is it not?" Elizabeth asked.

"Yes, that is true, but a peculiar mother-in-law could hurt Bingley's position with the *ton*," Darcy replied.

Elizabeth rolled her eyes but said no more. Although she had many friends in London society, she thought most of them were snobs and many were of questionable character and were to be avoided. She enjoyed the company of others not of that social sphere, in particular Jane Bennet. The Worthingtons had taught their children to place a higher value on good character: qualities such as honesty, loyalty, and the way a man treated others, rather than wealth and rank in society. Elizabeth felt very strongly that Jane Bennet should not be judged by her mother.

SHORTLY AFTER GEORGIANA'S RETURN, ELIZABETH decided they would take up visiting the tenants, a practice that had died with Lady Anne. The servants and tenants all loved and respected her. She showed a remarkable maturity for one so young, and her closeness to Georgiana deepened.

Darcy ordered two male servants to go with them, as he did not want them traveling by themselves on the extensive estate. Several of the women had recently given birth, and the Darcy ladies brought them clothing they had sewn and food provided by the Pemberley kitchen staff.

After a few moments' pause in their conversation, Georgiana took advantage of being alone with her sister to bring up a subject that had preyed on her mind.

"Lizzy, has my brother said anything to you about Richard?"

Although she knew to what Georgiana referred, she nonetheless asked, "Regarding what, dearest?"

"Oh, about all the attention Richard pays to you. I never realized what a flirt he was until now. Brother is irritated, even though he tries not to show it, and it makes him jealous to see the way Richard tries to dominate your time and claim your undivided attention. He uses every excuse to try and touch you."

Elizabeth looked down at her hands, folded in her lap. "We have discussed our cousin's behavior several times, and your brother is trying to stay calm when Richard is in company with us. He began acting this way before I came out, and I do not understand why he persists in trying to make Fitzwilliam jealous. I have never particularly cared for Richard and, if he continues this type of behavior, I shall have to avoid him."

"Perhaps I should talk to him," Georgiana offered, her voice very determined.

"No, dearest, let your brother handle it. As my husband, it is his place to do so."

"Why do you not care for Richard?"

"It goes back to our childhood. You were never a victim of his harsh teasing, but I was, and I grew to dislike him for it. I do not know if he meant to be cruel, but he was. Several times I had to stop Sarah from hurting him in retaliation for his mistreatment of me, else she surely would have cut him as she did Wickham.

112

"Your brother, on the other hand, was always kind, always considerate, even to one much younger than himself. We teased one another, but we also knew when to stop. He never caused me to be uncomfortable the way Richard did."

Georgiana hesitated before speaking again. "I have wanted to ask you something for a long time. I overheard the servants talking about Richard having a mistress. Do you know whether it is true?"

Elizabeth was uncertain if she should be truthful or if she should say she did not know, however, she remembered her own curiosity had prompted her to ask Sarah the same question, and she did not like lying to Georgiana.

"Dearest, according to Sarah and from the talk I have heard from my friends, it is unfortunately true. I understand that they care a great deal for each other, and their relationship is of long duration. That is yet another reason I do not understand why he pays so much attention to me."

Georgiana sat quietly as she digested this information. "I suppose it is none of my business. It does not affect me. Richard has always been kind and loving to me, so I will not judge him for his indiscretion."

Elizabeth reached over, patted her sister's hand, and smiled at her. That was the last time the two discussed Richard's mistress.

AT PEMBERLEY, SARAH MADE PLANS to confront the colonel about his flirting with her mistress. Sarah went to great lengths to blend into the background when others were present, and she was often overlooked when people should have been aware of her presence. She saw and heard everything.

Sarah knew that the cousins were close and usually very loyal to each other, but the colonel also had that streak of the devil in him. He had spent a lifetime trying to make Darcy jealous of one thing or another. He was much too attentive to Elizabeth, stopping just within the limits of propriety, and he was making Darcy's life miserable. Anything that affected Darcy eventually affected Elizabeth.

Elizabeth was unfailingly polite to the colonel, and she never gave Darcy reason to doubt her total devotion to him, but they were beginning to feel the strain of Richard's imposition, especially in the evenings when they were always together. The colonel would not stop flirting with Elizabeth, despite her efforts to repel him, and he carried it too far for everyone's comfort.

Today, with Darcy attending to a problem with one of his tenants and Elizabeth and Georgiana making their rounds, Sarah planned to stop this nonsense with the colonel once and for all. What she had no way of knowing was that Darcy had returned to Pemberley early. As he sat in his library with the door half closed, he overheard the confrontation.

"COLONEL, PLEASE, I WOULD HAVE a word with you."

The colonel stopped, wondering why Sarah, a servant, would need to speak with him.

"And you are?" he asked, knowing full well who she was, for he had known her most of his life.

"I am Sarah, as you know, and I have attended Mrs. Darcy since she was born. I must tell you, Colonel, that I have watched you closely for the past week, and I am most displeased with your forward conduct toward my mistress."

Colonel Fitzwilliam was speechless that a servant, even if it was Sarah, would speak to him in this manner. Greatly annoyed, he tried to brush her aside. "And I must tell you that I will have a word with Mr. Darcy about your presumptuous conduct."

"You are going out of your way to annoy Mr. Darcy by flirting with my mistress. This causes great discomfort to her, and Mr. Darcy is not pleased."

"You forget your place. You are a mere servant in this household, and I am Mr. Darcy's cousin and the son of an earl." The colonel's face was red, and his voice was cold. "I will see that Mr. Darcy has you dismissed immediately. Now, move out of my way."

A small smile briefly crossed Sarah's lips, but she stood her ground as she warned the colonel, again, to stop his flirting, or else.

"Or else what?" he sneered. "There is nothing you can do to hurt me, but there is much harm I can do to you." The colonel had heard of what Sarah did to Wickham, but he was not worried for himself. Wickham was a coward while he trained men to fight in battle.

Without warning, Sarah had a knife pushed against the colonel's throat. He was stunned and froze, hardly breathing.

"Do not move or you will be dead before you hit the floor. Now, promise me you will desist in your unwanted attentions toward Mrs. Darcy."

At that point, the colonel would have promised Sarah anything, but he only whispered in agreement.

"Excellent, I am glad that we understand each other. Now, if you will excuse me, I have work to complete."

Sarah walked upstairs, leaving the colonel with his mouth hanging open.

Darcy burst into laughter, letting Richard know he had heard every word.

Walking into the library, the colonel growled, "Quiet, Darcy! Never have I heard such insolence from a servant. Why do you put up with her? I insist that you dismiss her immediately."

Still laughing, Darcy informed his cousin that he would not turn Sarah out, for if he did, Elizabeth would divorce him. "Sarah is like a lioness protecting her cub, and now that I am Elizabeth's husband, she affords me the same protection."

"I cannot believe you would stand for such insolent behavior."

"Richard, you need to understand something. Elizabeth's father had Sarah given special training so that she could always protect Elizabeth and Andrew. She does not worry about Andrew now that he is a man, but Elizabeth is another matter altogether. She will not allow anyone to upset her mistress for any reason. As for me, she has always liked me because I make Elizabeth happy. For my continued health, I shall always strive to keep my wife happy and content." He smirked.

"Someone will kill her someday unless you rein her in. Another man would not care that Sarah is a woman, Darcy. He would kill her or have her killed."

"Nonsense! She is my superior with a pistol or a foil, and you know better than anyone what she can do with a knife. By the way, do you realize that you have a trickle of blood running down your neck?"

Richard slapped at his neck. "Blast her! Do you know what scared me the most about her? She never raised her voice, and her eyes were stone cold. Someone in her past hurt her deeply and that makes her especially dangerous."

"Perhaps you are right, but she is here to stay. I accept that she is more than just a servant to Elizabeth, and I would never try to change that. She is also fiercely protective toward Georgiana. You would be wise to take her words to heart."

The men stopped talking when they heard voices in the hallway. Elizabeth and Georgiana swept into the library, chattering happily, but stopped when they saw the look on the gentlemen's faces.

"Is something wrong?" Elizabeth asked, at the same time that Georgiana rushed to Richard and exclaimed over the blood on his neck.

"It is nothing, sweetheart," Richard assured Georgiana, not looking at Elizabeth. She glanced at Darcy, her eyebrow raised in question. He smiled slightly and looked toward the ceiling.

She understood and smiled. Elizabeth had known that Sarah would eventually reach an understanding with Richard.

Excusing herself, she went to her chambers, where she found Sarah repairing one of her gowns. There was nothing unusual about Sarah's manner, but she had a satisfied smile on her face as she greeted her mistress. Elizabeth sat and began telling Sarah about the new babies they saw that day. After she exhausted the subject, Elizabeth asked nonchalantly, "Did anything happen while Georgiana and I were gone?"

"No, lovey. Now come and try on this gown."

She knew she would get no explanation from Sarah until she was ready to talk, but Elizabeth intended to speak with her husband later. She was certain he knew exactly what had happened.

Chapter 16

The following week passed pleasantly enough, and to Darcy's amusement and relief, Richard stopped flirting, and Sarah blended back into the background.

After the colonel left, the rest of the summer was spent with Darcy working on estate matters, Georgiana practicing on her pianoforte, and Elizabeth becoming more familiar with managing Pemberley. The couple talked of giving a dinner party for their neighbors, but they were too content with each other's company to bother.

Georgiana enjoyed riding and was an excellent horsewoman. The three Darcys rode several mornings a week. They all loved fast horses and were very competitive when they raced against one another. Although uncomfortable at first, Georgiana soon adopted Elizabeth's less conventional method of riding and had a saddle made to allow her to sit astride her horse.

The Darcys continued to enjoy picnics whenever time and the weather would allow, and Georgiana was always welcomed to join them. The small stream but a mile from the house was their favorite spot to spread a blanket and enjoy the delicious treats that were prepared and packed for them. Trees shaded the area, giving them relief from the summer heat. Georgiana, conscious of the fact that her brother and his wife were newly married, left them to enjoy their picnics alone more often than not.

Charles Bingley sent another letter to Darcy the first of October, inviting them to visit him and his family at the estate he had leased in Hertfordshire, called Netherfield.

You must come and help me, Darcy, for I know nothing about running an estate. My sisters and Hurst travel with me in ten days' time, and I am inviting you and your family to join us for a visit. Netherfield is located only three miles from Longbourn, the Bennet's ancestral estate.

While Netherfield is nothing to Pemberley, it presently suits my needs, and I would like your opinion of the place. I believe that the running of Netherfield will be an invaluable experience once I buy a larger estate.

Darcy read Bingley's letter to Elizabeth and Georgiana that evening after dinner.

"So what do you ladies think? Shall we go? This is a good time for me to be away, and when our visit is over, we can either spend Christmas in London or come back to Pemberley."

"Oh," Georgiana cried, "I would like to see Mr. Bingley's estate and then come back here for Christmas. This will be our first Christmas as a family, and I do so want to spend it at Pemberley." The smile that covered Darcy's face was confirmation that she had pleased him immensely with her suggestion.

Elizabeth sat silent, looking thoughtful. Darcy asked, "Elizabeth, my love, what are your thoughts on this matter?"

"I would love to visit Mr. Bingley, but I cannot help but be concerned with what he said about Mrs. Bennet. However, I am anxious to see Miss Bennet again. I hope her mother will not be a problem for them, as I believe Miss Bennet and Mr. Bingley are perfect for one another."

"What do you say to leaving on the twenty-fourth of this month? Although I do not look forward to seeing the Superior Sisters, I would very much like to see Bingley and look at his estate."

SARAH WAS NEARBY AS THEY discussed visiting Bingley in Hertfordshire. She tried to think of ways to prevent them from going, but she could think of nothing that would not raise questions she could not answer.

She had promised Mr. Worthington that Elizabeth would never discover the truth about her birth, and she would do whatever it took to keep her promise. So, Sarah stayed quiet, but she was determined that she would never leave Elizabeth alone if they should go to Bingley's estate. She knew there would be times when Darcy's presence would prevent her from being with her mistress and, at those times, she would have to trust him to keep Elizabeth safe.

THE TRIO ARRIVED AT NETHERFIELD on the twenty-seventh of October, tired but happy. Bingley was waiting outside and greeted them with his usual enthusiasm when they arrived.

The Darcys were shown to their rooms so that they might rest and refresh themselves before dinner. Sarah and Williamson left to arrange baths for their mistress and master, and Darcy took that opportunity to take Elizabeth in his arms for a kiss.

"Are you tired, dearest? Shall we have a quick nap this afternoon?"

She laughed and kissed him. "Why do I feel that a nap is not what you have in mind, Husband?"

"Just a quick one, please?" he said with a pleading look that she found difficult to refuse.

"We shall see."

Just then, Sarah knocked and came back into the room. Elizabeth looked at Darcy with her eyes full of mischief, while he mouthed the word, "Please."

She was quiet for a moment but then said, "Sarah, you and Williamson must be tired. May I suggest you both have your tea first, while the bath water is prepared, and Mr. Darcy and I will ring for you later?"

"Yes, mistress." Sarah smiled as she stepped next door to inform Williamson of the change of plans.

"Quick nap?" Williamson asked when he saw Sarah enter the room.

"Mmm," Sarah responded as they walked downstairs together.

As soon as he heard their footsteps down the hall, Darcy quickly stripped Elizabeth of her clothes. Removing his own, he picked her up high enough that she could curl her legs around his waist.

"Elizabeth," he growled, "I ache for you. I want you now." His release came quickly and then he kissed her, his body still trembling.

"That certainly was a quick nap, Fitzwilliam," she smirked.

"I am sorry, my love." Still holding himself inside of her, he walked to the bed and kissed her again. "Wait here," he said, as he laid her on the bed.

"Where do you think I would go, Fitzwilliam?" she asked, laughing. When he returned with a wet cloth in his hands, he gently cleaned between her legs.

Lying down beside her, he said softly, "Now, it is time for your nap, dearest." Elizabeth whimpered as he began a slow journey over her body with his mouth and hands. She felt him becoming excited again and reached down to stroke him, but he moved her hand away. "No, dearest, let me pleasure you first." Darcy continued until her body shuddered and, crying out his name, she reached her fulfillment.

Her muscles were still contracting when he nudged her thighs apart with his leg and pushed his way inside. She matched his rhythm, clinging to him as their bodies moved in perfect harmony, their cries of pleasure becoming louder and louder. She was ready to peak again, so he brought them to a noisy and explosive release.

She lay limp in his arms, sweat dripping in rivulets off their bodies. Finally, he found the strength to roll on his side. She snuggled close and kissed his chest, while he ran his fingers through her hair. Burying his face in her neck and caressing her with his hand, he whispered, "I love you, Elizabeth. You are my life."

They dozed for a while, but Elizabeth soon sat up and told Darcy she was going to ring for Sarah. He stretched and yawned but agreed they should bathe and dress so they would not be late for dinner. She put her hand up to caress his cheek, and he turned his head so that he could kiss her palm. They looked into each other's eyes, and as he had done many times before, Darcy gave thanks that Elizabeth loved him.

EARLIER, CAROLINE BINGLEY HAD BEEN standing in the hallway, listening. She was passing by on her way downstairs when she heard their cries, and she stopped, putting her ear against their door. She was astonished at the noises.

Just as I thought, she said to herself. *She is no better than a woman of the streets, regardless of how much money she has.*

Caroline knew that she never would have made such disgusting noises had she married Darcy. No, she always would have conducted herself as a lady.

Chapter 17

A t dinner that evening, Bingley expounded on the neighbors who had made social calls at Netherfield, obviously pleased at his welcome to the neighborhood.

"We are all invited to a ball and supper at the home of Sir William Lucas tomorrow evening. He informs me that it will be a fairly large party, so the Darcys will be able to meet most of my new neighbors."

Before he could stop himself, Darcy groaned aloud. Bingley laughed and asked Elizabeth, "Have you not civilized him yet, Mrs. Darcy? I had so hoped to see improvement with your influence on him."

She looked at her husband affectionately. "No, I am afraid he is still a stubborn creature, Mr. Bingley. He still prefers the confined society of his own home."

Darcy smiled at the truth of her statement. "You know how I am around strangers. I will not like them, and they will not like me. I can never think of anything to say that they are desirous of hearing, and I cannot abide mindless chatter."

"All you have to do now, after taking such an agreeable partner, is smile and let your lovely wife do the talking." Thinking to tease his friend, he added, "Perhaps she could explain that you are deaf, and born without a tongue, thereby decreasing the expectation that you can actually, if prevailed upon, carry on an intelligent conversation."

Elizabeth had just taken a sip of her wine when Bingley made the statement about Darcy's lack of a tongue, and she choked and quickly brought her napkin to her mouth in order not to spew wine over everyone. Realizing what had caused his wife's discomfort Darcy smiled and patted her on the back.

"Mrs. Darcy," Bingley cried, "are you unwell? Is there anything I can bring you for your relief?"

"Thank you, Mr. Bingley; I am well now. I am sure I do not know what caused me to choke, but I am well, truly."

Darcy snorted before he could stop himself and, biting the inside of his mouth, pretended he had to clear his throat.

Caroline Bingley gave a false smile, betraying her insincerity, and looked at her sister, rolling her eyes. She still could not abide Elizabeth Darcy, but she knew it was in her best interest to pretend that she did. So far, she had given Charles no reason to scold her, but keeping silent had been difficult when presented with so many opportunities to expose further the rude manners of the new Mrs. Darcy.

The evening went by slowly, but finally everyone retired. Inside her chambers at last, Elizabeth dismissed Sarah and then knocked on the door leading to Darcy's room. She silently thanked Bingley for giving them adjoining rooms, fully aware that Caroline would have placed them on separate floors had it been possible for her to do so. As he opened the door to her himself, she was surprised to learn he had also dismissed Williamson.

With a gleam in his eye, he smirked, "I believe that I am able to undress both of us. Do you not agree?"

She laughed wholeheartedly.

ELIZABETH WAS EXCITED AS SHE was dressed for the ball the next evening. She looked forward to seeing Jane Bennet again, and she wanted to satisfy her curiosity about Mrs. Bennet.

Sarah was not happy, for she did not want Elizabeth in contact with either Mr. or Mrs. Bennet, but she knew there was nothing she could do to prevent it. Elizabeth's present situation demanded that she attend the dinner, but knowing there would be a large crowd assembled, Sarah thought Elizabeth would be safe with Darcy by her side.

Georgiana entered while Sarah was pinning Elizabeth's hair. There was a pout on her mouth. "Lizzy, will you not talk to my brother again? I do so want to go tonight."

"I am afraid, dearest, that you will have to stay home with Sarah. I will try to persuade Fitzwilliam to give his permission for you to attend the next engagement after we have met some of the prominent families here. Perhaps Sarah will be allowed to go as your companion to keep you company in case there is dancing."

Their party arrived late to the Lucases' ball. Caroline had kept them waiting as usual as she changed gown after gown, finally deciding on a horrible shade of orange with yards of lace. Her hair was decorated with matching feathers.

Elizabeth looked around the room eagerly and was happy to see Jane Bennet standing next to a fairly pretty, older woman. At that moment, Miss Bennet looked up, and seeing Elizabeth, she smiled and rushed toward her.

"Mrs. Darcy, how good it is to see you again. I was delighted when Mr. Bingley told me you would attend tonight."

"Yes, we arrived yesterday. Mr. Darcy, come greet Miss Bennet."

Darcy bowed. "It is good to see you again, Miss Bennet. Congratulations on your engagement to Bingley. You have made him a happy man."

"Thank you, Mr. Darcy. It is a pleasure seeing you again as well, sir."

Elizabeth turned to Bingley and his family, but discovered only Charles was present with a silly grin on his face. He and Jane Bennet stood staring at each other — their love for each other obvious to all.

ELIZABETH AND HER HUSBAND DID not notice the gentleman standing alone in a corner, sipping a glass of port. Mr. Bennet watched them closely, his heart pounding. He did not care for social gatherings, but rumors had circulated that a Mr. and Mrs. Darcy from Derbyshire were joining the new owner of Netherfield, and Mr. Bennet wanted very much to see them. He noticed that Mr. Darcy looked a little stiff and uncomfortable, but Mrs. Darcy seemed at home in a room full of strangers. She was, indeed, everything lovely.

After Jane and the Gardiners had returned from their northern trip, they had told the Bennets about touring the Darcys' estate, of the kindness Mrs. Darcy had shown them, and that she liked them very much.

The music began, and Mr. Darcy led his wife to the dance floor. Watching them, Mr. Bennet saw a couple very much in love and, once again, knew that he had done the right thing all those years ago. As he stood musing, he realized that the first dance was over, and that Jane was leading Mr. Bingley and the Darcys over to his wife to make the proper introductions. He noticed that Mrs. Bennet narrowed her eyes when she looked into Elizabeth's face.

Moving swiftly to his wife's side, Mr. Bennet gripped her elbow tightly, hoping to distract her attention from Elizabeth.

"Mama, Papa, may I introduce Mr. and Mrs. Fitzwilliam Darcy of Derbyshire. I met them in London. Mr. Darcy, Mrs. Darcy, may I present my parents, Mr. and Mrs. Thomas Bennet."

Darcy bowed while Elizabeth curtsied. "It is a pleasure to meet you both," Elizabeth exclaimed. "We are very fond of your daughter and the Gardiners."

Mr. Bennet was dismayed to see that Mrs. Bennet had focused her complete attention on Elizabeth. "Where are you from, Mrs. Darcy?"

"We live at Pemberley in Derbyshire, ma'am. I grew up in Staffordshire."

"Ah yes, Mrs. Darcy. I hope to know you better, as Jane and the Gardiners speak highly of you. You must dine with us one evening."

Elizabeth smiled. "We would be happy to do so. Thank you, Mrs. Bennet," she replied.

Jane's mother continued looking at Elizabeth, and Mr. Bennet saw that her gaze was not friendly but appraising.

Sir William Lucas approached and, seizing the opportunity, Mr. Bennet drew the Darcys aside and began conversing with them. "So, Mr. Darcy, your estate is in Derbyshire."

"That is true, sir."

"And Mrs. Darcy, you are from Staffordshire."

"Yes, sir, I grew up there, but I was a frequent visitor of the Darcys at Pemberley. My parents and Mr. Darcy's parents were close friends."

"Ah, yes," Mr. Bennet smiled. "I can see that you are a few years older than your wife, sir. Still, you two must have been often in one another's company."

"Quite often, sir. I am eight years older than my wife; however, she proposed to me when she was only nine and I seventeen, so I had to wait for her to grow up." Darcy turned to his wife and smiled lovingly at her.

Elizabeth was clearly surprised and delighted to see her husband speaking and joking with a total stranger. They talked until the music started once again, and Elizabeth nudged Darcy.

"Excuse us, sir. My wife dearly loves to dance."

Mr. Bennet nodded, Darcy took his wife by her hand, and they walked to the dance floor. As he stood watching them, Mr. Bennet felt mixed emotions. On the one hand, he would have dearly loved rearing Elizabeth as his daughter. She would have been a delight to his dreary, sad life and a wonderful sister to his dear Jane.

On the other hand, she would have been an entirely different woman had she grown up in a house where she was hated by her mother — had her mother even allowed her to live. Chances were that she never would have known Darcy or her present happiness. No, it was better that he had sent her away. She was alive and happy, and that was all that mattered.

On their way home that evening, Mrs. Bennet was unusually quiet, but Mr. Bennet asked no questions. He did not want to know what she was thinking, having observed her reaction to Mrs. Darcy earlier that evening.

Jane, however, asked, "What is the matter, Mama? Are you unwell?"

"No, child, I am well." Turning to her husband she asked, "Mr. Bennet, did you notice the color of Mrs. Darcy's eyes?"

"No, my dear, I was not paying attention to her eyes."

"They are violet-colored, and you know what that means."

"Yes, dear." Mr. Bennet attempted to temper the panic that burst upon his heart.

"What, Mama? I think Mrs. Darcy's eyes are beautiful. They are such an unusual color."

"Hush, Jane. Demons have violet-colored eyes, so be very careful of her."

Jane Bennet forced herself to laugh at her mother. "Oh, Mama, Mrs. Darcy is the nicest woman I know. I have told you how kind she was to me and my aunt and uncle. They are very impressed with her."

"Well, just remember what I said, and be careful. Demons are good at fooling people." Mrs. Bennet cut her eyes around and looked slyly at her husband. "By-the-by, Mr. Bennet, did you notice how much Mrs. Darcy favors your mother?"

Mr. Bennet glanced at Jane and rolled his eyes while Jane giggled. "Nonsense, my dear, she looks nothing like Mother."

Mrs. Bennet had always wondered if her demon daughter had in truth died. She seemed perfectly healthy when she was born. Perhaps Mr. Bennet had managed to smuggle her out of the way.

Chapter 18

Caroline Bingley broke her silence the moment they entered Bingley's carriage. At the party, she had conducted herself with her usual superior airs but, fortunately, she had not openly expressed her opinions. To the irritation of Bingley and the Darcys, she did so now.

"Charles, what were you thinking, dragging us to such an uncivilized place? The ladies were wearing gowns that are three years behind the fashion! The men are all backward oafs, the music was unbearable, and the country dancing was laughable, to say nothing of Sir William Lucas being a total bore! The very idea that he would think we need his help in navigating London society! Insufferable man!"

"I quite enjoyed myself, Caroline. Our neighbors are friendly, and the ladies are uncommonly beautiful."

"All ladies are beautiful to you, Charles. Granted, your Miss Bennet is a sweet, lovely girl, but did you talk to her mother? You would do well to reconsider your engagement to Jane Bennet. Her mother is very strange, to say nothing of being loud and common. Did you hear her carrying on about your 5,000 a year? You surely must have; everyone else did," Caroline sneered.

Without a pause, she continued. "And her father! Such a disagreeable man — the way he stood against the wall, looking all dark and somber with a smirk on his face."

"Are you sure, Caroline, that you are not talking about Darcy?"

Elizabeth laughed, but spoke up in her husband's defense. "Mr. Bingley, my husband was quite civil this evening. Did you not notice how many times he danced?"

Bingley looked at his friend and laughed. "That is only because he is too jealous to allow you the opportunity of dancing with other men."

"You are correct, Bingley," Darcy remarked as he squeezed his wife's hand.

"And Fitzwilliam not only talked to Mr. Bennet, he joked with him," Elizabeth said.

"Upon my word, Darcy, I can scarce believe that you talked and joked with a stranger."

"My wife has apparently succeeded in partially civilizing me," Darcy grinned.

Everyone laughed with the exception of Miss Bingley. Mr. Darcy almost irritated her since he married that silly chit, and she vowed to put a stop to those kinds of remarks just as soon as he divorced Elizabeth and married her.

Alone in their chambers, Elizabeth and Darcy discussed their impressions of the evening. "I enjoyed myself tonight, and like Mr. Bingley, I thought the people were friendly. Some members of the *ton* have conducted themselves much worse than those we saw this evening."

"You are correct, Elizabeth, although I would not want to socialize with them outside of Hertfordshire. They are our social inferiors."

Elizabeth rolled her eyes and leaned over her husband so she could kiss him, at which time he pulled her onto his lap and nuzzled her neck. "My dear husband, you are such an arrogant snob, but you are my arrogant snob, and I love you very much."

After a few kisses, Darcy was trying to disrobe her when Elizabeth sat up straight. "Miss Bingley disturbs me, my love. There is no warmth to her; her eyes are cold as ice. Sometimes I am afraid of her, for I can see that she hates me."

"I, too, have seen the hatred in her eyes when she looks at you, Elizabeth. Hopefully, she would not attempt to harm you, but it would be well if you were not alone with her."

"I find it hard to believe that she is Mr. Bingley's sister. She looks nothing like him or Mrs. Hurst nor is her personality anything akin to theirs."

"She and Mrs. Hurst are very much alike."

"No, they are not. Oh, Mrs. Hurst is a snob and a gossip, but she is not cruel like Miss Bingley. She can be quite pleasant when her sister is not around. Mrs. Hurst may not like me, but she does not hate me as does her sister."

"Come, dearest, are you not tired of talking about the Superior Sisters? I much prefer spending my time making love with you."

She laughed aloud. "Fitzwilliam, do you think of nothing but making love?"

Darcy leered at her, "No. Why should I think of other things when I have a beautiful wife to attract and entice me?" He drew her closer to him, fondling the curls at the back of her neck. "Do you have any idea how aroused I become when I see these curls bouncing on your neck? They have excited me since you turned fifteen."

His voice dropped lower as he spoke, until it became a whisper. He caressed her face and then moved to her hair where he pulled out the pins, tangling his fingers in her curls, bringing her lips closer to his. "Your scent drives me wild, my beloved. Oh, I could not live without you. When you were a child, your liveliness was amusing and made me laugh, but now it makes me want to love you again and again until we are both exhausted and spent."

His mouth seized hers and they clung to each other, kissing greedily until they both gasped for air. His voice trembling, Darcy whispered, "Elizabeth, I will always love you! You are everything to me! You are in my soul. I cannot tell where I stop and you begin. We merge into each other, and my spirit soars higher and higher until I feel that I have reached the heavens."

His voice was like fog swirling around and encircling her, permeating her very being. Holding Elizabeth tight against him, Darcy stood and carried her to the side of their bed where they slowly undressed, their eyes looking deeply into the other. When their clothing had been discarded, they moved to lie on the bed. Soon, their cries rang out in pleasure, and shortly thereafter, only Darcy's soft snores could be heard.

Chapter 19

The moment the Bennets arrived home from Lucas Lodge, Mr. Bennet headed for his library with his wife close behind. She closed the door and confronted her husband.

"Mr. Bennet," she said, her suspicious eyes boring into him, "are you certain that murderous demon child is dead? Perhaps she survived." She looked at her husband as if seeing back in time. Approaching him purposefully, her speech was slow and direct. "Perhaps you saved her from the fate she deserved by giving her away, only pretending that she died so you would not be found out."

"Fanny, have you lost your senses? I buried two bodies, as you well know."

"I know nothing of the kind! You sealed the coffin during the night, and I did not see them before they were buried. Mrs. Darcy has violet-colored eyes, and she looks like your mother. She even has the same name as the babe you said died, so perhaps she is that murdering child come back to kill me."

"Madam, I will listen to no more of this nonsense."

Mrs. Bennet left, but she was still determined to find out the truth.

ELIZABETH WOKE TO A BEAUTIFUL, sunny day and discovered her husband dressed. He leaned down and kissed her. "Good morning, dearest. Would you care to join me for a ride this morning?"

Yawning and stretching, Elizabeth shook her head. "I am invited for lunch with Miss Bennet's aunt today. With your approval, I would like to take Georgiana with me."

"Will Bingley's sisters also attend?"

"I do not know. Hertfordshire society is not to their liking, but they may surprise me."

Darcy gave Elizabeth his approval to bring Georgiana, and cautioned her to take Sarah with them. He did not want her and his sister traveling alone, even though it was a short distance. Giving his wife another kiss, he left.

Not surprisingly, Bingley's sisters made their regrets, claiming to have headaches. This news delighted both Darcy ladies as it relieved them of the obligation of spending time with them, and they set off with Sarah in their carriage.

Elizabeth and Georgiana arrived at the Philipses' house where they were to have lunch, only to find a large gathering of the Yorkshire militia. They looked at each other. "I understood that we would be the only guests today, but this is a large group."

Elizabeth shrugged. "Apparently, Mrs. Philips changed her mind." They continued into the room until, suddenly, Georgiana nudged her sister. "Look, Lizzy, there is Wickham. What is he doing here, and why is he in uniform?"

"I have no idea, but I will wager he is still up to his old tricks. Someone should warn the good people of Hertfordshire to lock up their daughters and not issue him credit."

Sarah stepped behind Elizabeth and Georgiana as they walked toward George Wickham. As they drew closer, they heard him telling a young lady his sad tale of being wronged by Darcy. Elizabeth and Georgiana looked at each other and grinned.

George Wickham's body went stiff when he heard Elizabeth say, "Mr. Wickham, are you by any chance telling this charming young lady your usual lies about my husband? Really, your stories are becoming very tiresome. Perhaps you would like to tell her the truth instead. Or shall I?"

Elizabeth kept a smile on her lips, and her voice was low enough that only the ones in their small group heard what she said. Mr. Wickham's face went pale, and he was momentarily speechless. He looked at the young lady to whom he had been speaking, but she stuck her nose in the air and left in a huff. It was not long before they saw her talking with others and pointing to Mr. Wickham.

Her smile now gone, Elizabeth hissed, "I think it is time you left this gathering, and I would advise you to keep away from the good people of Hertfordshire. Do not let me hear of you spreading anymore of your lies about any member of the Darcy family."

"Someday I will take my revenge, Mrs. Darcy," he growled.

Elizabeth rolled her eyes. "Empty threats! I must inform you that my maid, Sarah, is with me today. Shall I remind you what she did to you the last time you threatened me?"

Sarah stepped forward and grinned. "Good day, dear Wicky! I see you did not learn your lesson the first time. Shall we step outside?"

His face turned positively white, and he turned around and rushed out of the house without speaking to anyone else. By the time the afternoon was over, word had circulated about Mr. Wickham's encounter with Mrs. Darcy, and the general consensus was that his word could not be trusted.

THE THREE LADIES LAUGHED ALL the way back to Netherfield, where Georgiana gleefully informed her brother about the incident. Told that Elizabeth was lying down, Darcy soon left Georgiana to join his wife in her chamber. Elizabeth was lying on her bed when Darcy came in. "A nap, my dear?" he teased.

She smiled briefly and then remarked that she felt a little tired. "I suppose Georgiana told you about Wickham."

Darcy lay down next to his wife and pulled her close. "Yes, she said you were discreet in allowing only one young lady to hear you. I understand, however, that word about him had spread before you left."

"I also let him know that Sarah was with us. He turned quite pale when he saw her and left in a hurry."

Darcy laughed out loud. "Wickham came close to losing his manhood that day. If Sarah had cut just a little to the left, Wickham's voice would be considerably higher. I doubt we will have any more trouble with him. But let us not talk about Wickham, my love, when we could be enjoying ourselves." He cupped her breast and then kissed it through her clothing. "Shall we make a son this afternoon?" he whispered against her neck.

She turned her face toward him and smirked. "Would not a daughter suffice, Fitzwilliam? You know nothing about rearing a boy child; all of your experience has been with Georgiana."

He stared at her in mock horror. "Absolutely not, Mrs. Darcy; we must have a boy. I insist on it! There are not enough males in this family, and we need another one to help balance things. I do not stand a chance against you and Georgiana, to say nothing of Sarah."

Elizabeth laughed and kissed Darcy's chin. "Thank you, my love, for understanding about Sarah. She attends me, yes, but she is not just a servant. She is my friend, my confidant, my mother, and my sister all rolled into one."

"Most important, she is your protector, and she protects all those you love." He hesitated for a moment. "By the way, Elizabeth, you should know that Miss Bingley cornered me while you were gone."

Elizabeth's expression turned to concern. "What did she do?"

"I was in the library when the door was flung open so forcefully that it hit the wall. Before I could react, she was in the room, had the door locked, and was on my lap yelling gleefully, 'Alone at last, Mr. Darcy!'

"I stood quickly, which caused her to land on the floor. Of course, I headed immediately for the door, but she grabbed my leg and hung on tight. I had a devil of a time shaking her off."

Darcy scowled at Elizabeth when a giggle escaped her lips.

"She begged me to tell her why I married you instead of her. I tried to be a gentleman, but Miss Bingley honestly believes she is superior to you." Darcy shook his head. "It is amazing how she closes her mind to everything but what she wants to see and hear. I finally informed her that I would not have married her, even had I never met you. When she continued to insist on knowing why, I said that I simply did not like her — that I knew she loved the idea of being mistress of Pemberley more than she cared for me."

"Oh dear, that could not have made her happy."

"Indeed, it did not! You should have seen me darting around the room, trying to avoid her. I tell you, Elizabeth, that woman is quick! I have never seen anyone move so fast. When I was finally able to unlock the door, she picked up a vase and threw it at me. I ducked in time, but her actions have forced me to speak with Bingley about her behavior."

They looked at each other, and then Elizabeth dissolved into laughter. "Oh dear! I can picture you running from her, and then ducking that vase! Do you wish me to scratch her eyes out for you?"

Darcy began to see the humor and he laughed with her. "No, leave that job to Sarah. It is more her forte."

Their laughter soon died, and they lay still, thinking of their day. Darcy shuddered, as he thought of being married to Miss Bingley. There was only one way to wipe out that unwanted image, and he turned to his wife.

"No more talk of Miss Bingley, let us speak of sons," he growled, as he began an assault on Elizabeth's neck. She squealed with laughter and pretended to fight him, but when he removed her gown and began to make love to her, her laughter soon turned to sighs and cries of pleasure.

WHAT NO ONE KNEW WAS that Miss Bingley had begun sipping brandy as soon as she awoke that fateful day. She was determined to catch Mr. Darcy alone after Elizabeth and Georgiana left, but she needed a bit of liquid courage to do so. In her heart, she knew that her charms would capture him, but her mind had doubts. She fortified herself with brandy — not enough to be drunk, but enough to wipe those doubts from her mind.

After returning to her chambers, Miss Bingley finished drinking what was left in the bottle of brandy. Then, fully dressed, she fell face down on top of her bed, still determined to somehow win Mr. Darcy.

Chapter 20

While at the Philipses' home, Jane Bennet had invited Elizabeth and Georgiana, as well as Bingley's sisters, to Longbourn for tea the following day. The sisters sent their regrets, saying they had another engagement, so at ten o'clock the following morning, the two Darcy ladies and Sarah stepped into their carriage and left for Longbourn.

Jane was anxiously waiting for them, wondering if she had been wise to invite Elizabeth to her home. Some days her mother's behavior was normal, and she hoped this would be one of those days.

"Mrs. Darcy, Miss Darcy, welcome to my home. Do you remember meeting my mother at Lucas Lodge?"

"Yes, thank you, Miss Bennet."

"Please call me Jane."

"Very well, and you must call us Elizabeth and Georgiana."

Turning to Mrs. Bennet, Elizabeth smiled, "It is good to see you again, ma'am, and a pleasure to be in your home."

To everyone's surprise, Mrs. Bennet only stared at Elizabeth before asking, "What is your full name, Mrs. Darcy?"

It was not the question that startled Elizabeth, but the way Mrs. Bennet stared at her and the harshness of her voice.

"Why...my full name is Elizabeth Anne Darcy. My family name was Worthington."

Mrs. Bennet was taken aback by her reply, and a cunning smile spread across her face. "And where did you say you lived before you married Mr. Darcy?"

"Our estate is in Staffordshire. My brother and I were born and raised there."

"And your parents still reside there? Is your brother older or younger than you? How old are you and your brother?"

Elizabeth felt as though Mrs. Bennet was interrogating her, rather than making polite conversation. "No, Mrs. Bennet, unfortunately our parents were killed in an accident when my brother and I were seventeen. Andrew and I are twins."

Mrs. Bennet's face showed a flash of alarm, before she composed herself. With a sly look she said, "I had twin babies when Jane was two years old, but they both died. The girl was named Elizabeth Anne, as are you. Her eyes were also violet-colored. Are you aware of that, Mrs. Darcy?"

"No, ma'am, I would have no way of knowing that. Until now, I have never been in Hertfordshire."

Mrs. Bennet continued speaking. "Yes, they died. My daughter wrapped the cord around my poor son's neck while they were still in my womb. She was a demon child!" Mrs. Bennet paused but did not take her eyes off Elizabeth. "And what is your birth date, Mrs. Darcy?"

Elizabeth wanted to tell her it was none of her business but, because of Jane, she answered politely. "Andrew and I were born on the eleventh day of May, in the year 1790."

Mrs. Bennet gave an audible gasp, and put her hand to her mouth. "That was but two days after my twins were born. Tell me, madam, did your late father know my husband?"

Jane's face had turned red, and Elizabeth could see that she was having trouble breathing because of her mother's insinuations. "Mama! Please, we do not wish to hear or speak of this."

Jane and Georgiana tried steering the conversation toward Jane and Bingley's wedding. Mrs. Bennet fell silent, but she continued to watch Elizabeth, a frown on her face. Her eyes narrowed and remained focused exclusively on Elizabeth.

Jane stood and asked whether the ladies would care to walk in the gardens. "Oh, yes," cried Georgiana, her expression showing relief.

Sarah had been sitting quietly in a corner, listening to Mrs. Bennet. She grew alarmed by what she heard, and knew she would have to be extra vigilant so no harm came to her mistress. She believed Mrs. Bennet was dangerous and, given the opportunity, would harm Elizabeth, for her imaginings were too close to the truth.

SARAH STAYED BEHIND, DETERMINED TO speak with Mrs. Bennet. As soon as the three ladies were out of sight, Sarah confronted Jane's mother.

"I am Sarah, Mrs. Bennet, and I have taken care of Mrs. Darcy since she was born. Be warned, madam, I will protect my mistress, even if I have to harm the person threatening her. Mrs. Darcy is not your child! She belonged to Jonathan and Margaret Worthington, and now she is Mr. Darcy's wife. Neither he, nor I, will allow you to harm her."

Mrs. Bennet's eyes grew wide as she listened to Sarah. Whispering, she said, "You are the demon child's emissary. She is here to harm me or have me harmed."

"No one is here to harm you, Mrs. Bennet, unless you harm my mistress. As long as you do no wrong, you are safe. However, harm even one hair on her head and you will answer to me. Do not make me angry, madam. You do not want to witness my wrath!" Having given her warning, Sarah turned and hurried away.

Mrs. Bennet watched her rush to catch up with Mrs. Darcy, and she was afraid.

Unfortunately, obsession can sometimes overcome fear.

As they walked away from Longbourn, Jane apologized, saying that her mother had never recovered from the loss of her twins, and that loss had caused her to act eccentrically at times. "She means no harm, truly. We are all used to her moods, but I am aware that strangers think she is very odd."

"Do not be concerned, Jane," Elizabeth assured her friend. "Now, where shall we walk?"

The path that Jane showed them went past the church and cemetery, and they stopped at the grave site of Jane's siblings. Elizabeth noted that the date of their birth and death was, indeed, May ninth, two days before she and Andrew were born. Feeling a sense of doom pervade her thoughts, she shivered, and Georgiana requested their return to Netherfield.

SARAH STOOD IN SILENCE AS she looked at the grave where her own poor child lay buried under another's name. She had no feeling left for the child. It had been forced on her by her father, and she had not had time to grow to love it. That part of her life was over. Elizabeth was her child, and she had been since the night Mr. Bennet had laid the child in her arms. She was happy to share her with the Worthingtons and with Darcy, but Elizabeth would always be her child.

MR. BENNET WAS OUTSIDE AS the ladies approached the Darcy carriage, and Jane ran to him, taking his arm. "Papa, come and greet Mrs. Darcy and

Miss Darcy."

As they chatted, they heard the sound of horses' hooves on the driveway. Darcy and Bingley had come to call at Longbourn. Darcy noticed Elizabeth's agitation, but when he raised his eyebrow in question, she smiled and shook her head, indicating she would speak with him later.

"Ah, Jane, your young man is here, but perhaps the gentlemen would like to join me in a glass of port first before visiting." Both men nodded their agreement, and Mr. Bennet led the two men into his study while the ladies walked in the east garden. A half-hour later, the men concluded their visit, and Darcy and Bingley met the ladies outdoors.

Smiling, Bingley went straight to Jane, ignoring everyone else. "Miss Bennet, you are looking well today — very well indeed."

Jane Bennet blushed and looked down at the ground. "Thank you, sir. It is good to see you again."

"Your mother has invited us to dine at Longbourn this evening. It will be a pleasure to see you again...this evening...again...will it not, Darcy?"

Darcy rolled his eyes. "Yes, Bingley."

Elizabeth and Georgiana stifled a giggle. Poor Bingley was so in love, he could hardly speak two words of sense together.

Instead of returning to Netherfield with the Darcys, Bingley decided he would stay at Longbourn a while longer. The Darcys left the couple in the garden, engrossed only in each other.

Upon their return to Netherfield, the Darcys were relieved not to encounter the sisters as they made their way upstairs. Darcy closed and locked the door to their chambers before asking, "Are you unwell, Elizabeth? You looked agitated when I first saw you at Longbourn."

"I am well. It is only that Mrs. Bennet is so odd. She makes me extremely uncomfortable."

Darcy insisted that she tell him everything that had happened, so she recounted the questions Mrs. Bennet asked and the manner in which she asked them.

"We walked past the graves of those two unfortunate babes, and they were born and died two days before Andrew and me. The Bennet baby girl's name was also Elizabeth Anne. The entire visit made me uncomfortable...restless."

"We have already accepted the invitation to dine at Longbourn tonight, but after this evening, you should stay away from Mrs. Bennet unless you are with me or Sarah. From what you just told me, I believe her to be unbalanced, and you should not be in her company alone. I only hope that Bingley knows what he is doing, marrying into that family."

"You are right, dearest. I will ask Mr. Bingley to invite Miss Bennet to Netherfield for our next visit."

"That would be wise. Perhaps all will be well, and Bingley will not stay at Netherfield past a year. He is still looking for an estate to buy in the North. That would not be an easy journey for Mrs. Bennet to make frequently."

Elizabeth frowned. "What disturbs me most is that Mrs. Bennet seems to be trying to link me with her dead child. It is almost as if she thinks I am that child."

"We know that to be nonsense, so I would think on it no more," Darcy said, as he took his wife into his arms and comforted her in the way he knew best.

BINGLEY ARRIVED BACK AT NETHERFIELD in time to change clothes before returning to Longbourn. Because Miss Bingley and her sister had refused the invitation to tea at Longbourn that morning, Bingley insisted they join the Bennets for dinner.

"It would be rude of you not to go. You have both declined the last two social invitations." Fixing his best imitation of the Darcy glare, he decreed, "You cannot avoid this dinner."

The expression on Miss Bingley's face told her brother that she was not pleased. "It is bad enough that you have dragged us to the edge of civilization; must you insist that we socialize with the likes of Mrs. Bennet? I cannot abide her! Jane is a sweet girl, but her mother..." Miss Bingley shuddered.

"Caroline, you are going, you will be polite, and I do not want to hear another word out of you. Is that understood?" Miss Bingley grumbled all the way to Longbourn.

As the Bingley party was shown into the drawing room at Longbourn, Mrs. Bennet rushed to Mr. Bingley. "Oh, Mr. Bingley, you and your sisters do us great honor tonight. Sit here by my Jane. Does she not look beautiful? And such a sweet disposition! Why, everyone in Hertfordshire swears that Jane Bennet is the most beautiful and the sweetest girl they have ever known. And your sisters — welcome, my dears! Please sit here, for they are the most comfortable chairs in the room."

Mrs. Bennet looked beyond Miss Bingley. "Mr. and Mrs. Darcy, Miss Darcy, sit wherever you like," she said and with a dismissive wave of her hand, Mrs.

Bennet turned her full attention back to the Bingleys.

Elizabeth and Darcy looked at each other. Although Elizabeth suppressed a smile, Darcy was not pleased that he, and especially his wife and sister, were treated in such a cavalier manner. If nothing else, the woman had to be the rudest person he had ever met.

For the rest of the evening, Darcy's body was rigid, and he had a scowl on his face. Jane Bennet noticed his displeasure and tried to include him and Elizabeth in the conversation, but Mrs. Bennet always turned it back to the Bingleys.

Toward the end of dinner, Mrs. Bennet locked eyes with Darcy, and she asked, "Mr. Darcy, what do you think of demons?"

Startled, Darcy said, "I have no thoughts on them, madam."

"That is strange, sir. Do you not know the damage demons can do? They can possess a person's body and cause that person to do all manner of evil."

"No, that is not something I have ever heard. Mrs. Bennet, I am the wrong person to speak with on this subject, as I know nothing about it."

"Hmm," Mrs. Bennet said. Then, with a sly look at Elizabeth, she continued. "Do you not know, sir, that demons have violet eyes?"

"Mama!"

"That is enough, Mrs. Bennet! Our guests are not interested in the subject." Mr. Bennet's voice was harsh, and the eyes he turned on his wife would allow no argument.

Mrs. Bennet had overstepped the bounds of propriety, even beyond what her amiable husband would normally allow.

"Forgive me, please. I tend to become over-excited on some subjects." Thereafter, she remained silent, and the evening ended early.

Mr. Bennet and Jane walked their guests outside, and in a low voice, Mr. Bennet apologized. "Please forgive my wife. Everyone in Hertfordshire remembers her as a sweet woman with a loving disposition before our tragedy, and they overlook her eccentric ways now."

Darcy said nothing, but Elizabeth smiled at Mr. Bennet. "Think nothing of it, sir. Perhaps she is merely tired and needs to rest."

"Yes, yes. Perhaps you are right." But when Mr. Bennet turned toward his house, his shoulders were slumped, and there was an air of resignation about him.

Chapter 21

After their guests left, Jane turned to her mother with tears in her eyes. "Mama, how could you be so rude to the Darcys, especially after the kindness they showed me in London, and the way they welcomed Aunt, Uncle, and me to their home in Derbyshire? I cannot believe you would insinuate that Mrs. Darcy is a demon because of her eyes. Papa, this is too much!" Jane turned and ran upstairs.

"Keep this up, Fanny, and Jane can say goodbye to Mr. Bingley. They are in love, but if you continue insulting his friends, you may drive Mr. Bingley away. Then what would you do after my death? Jane must marry well so that you will be taken care of when you are a widow. I hope your behavior this evening has not already made him change his mind."

Mrs. Bennet stood wringing her hands. "Perhaps that would be for the best. Mr. Bingley is friends with the Darcys, and I do not want Jane around them. I am sure Mrs. Darcy is the child that killed my son. Her father's name was Worthington, and you knew a Jonathan Worthington at Cambridge. I am certain you gave him that demon child to save her. And another thing — that servant of hers threatened me today, Thomas, and said she would harm me. My poor nerves! What am I to do?"

Mr. Bennet felt his heart begin to pound. How had she remembered Jonathan? She had met him only once!

"First, you can forget your delusion about Mr. Worthington, for I have not been in contact with him since I left Cambridge. Second, you can stop your nonsense about Mrs. Darcy. She is a woman we never met before she came to Hertfordshire, and she has been kind to our Jane. Your own brother and sister think highly of her and her husband. So let me hear no more about Mrs. Darcy, and the next time you meet her, you will be polite."

A gleam appeared in Mrs. Bennet's eyes. "I know what we shall do, Thomas. When the Gardiners come for Christmas, we will send Jane back to London with them. Surely they know someone wealthy enough to be a suitable husband for her, one that does not socialize with the Darcys."

"No more, Mrs. Bennet, no more, I beg of you! Jane is engaged to Mr. Bingley, and when she goes back to London after Christmas, it will be to buy her trousseau. She has no reason to look for another husband. She loves Bingley!" Mr. Bennet turned and walked to his study, slamming the door behind him.

No one spoke in the carriage returning to Netherfield, but as soon as they were inside the house, Miss Bingley could not resist commenting.

"So, Eliza, you have the eyes of a demon! And to think you consider her eyes to be so fine, Mr. Darcy. You see, not everyone agrees with you, sir. Perhaps your wife has merely bewitched you into thinking her eyes are so enticing."

Angry, Darcy stepped toward Miss Bingley, but her brother's expression said that he had had as much as he would take that night.

"Caroline, that is enough! I will listen to no more from you. You are consistently rude to Mrs. Darcy, and I will not have it! Kindly remember she is a guest in our home."

Darcy put his hand on Elizabeth's arm. "Come, dearest, let us retire." As he turned to his wife, Bingley stopped him.

"Darcy, I am appalled at Mrs. Bennet's behavior. What in heaven's name is wrong with the woman? She began to insult you, Mrs. Darcy, and Miss Darcy from the moment you came into the room."

Caroline laughed. "I am beginning to like Mrs. Bennet."

Bingley whirled around and faced his sister. "Caroline, go to your room, now! I am fast losing patience with you, and I begin to wonder if it would be best for me to send you to Scotland to my aunt and uncle's farm."

Miss Bingley narrowed her eyes at her brother. "You would not dare send me there."

"Do not try me," Mr. Bingley threatened.

Caroline huffed her way out of the room, mumbling that she would go to London instead. At least she would be back in civilization.

Mr. Bingley stood in front of his friends. "I am so sorry. Between Mrs. Bennet and Caroline, the evening could not have been worse. Poor Jane must be mortified, as am I. I cannot apologize enough for the behavior to which you have been subjected. I just do not understand the provocation."

"Miss Bennet is a lovely girl," Darcy said, "but I agree that something is not right with her mother. I have already told Elizabeth that I do not want her at Longbourn after tonight."

Elizabeth had remained quiet during this discussion, but now she spoke. "Mr. Bingley, are you not planning to buy an estate close to Pemberley? I believe Mr. Darcy said you would stay here a year, but perhaps it would be wise to give up Netherfield sooner. You and Jane could live in London until you find another estate."

"I have thought the very same thing. I dread even thinking of being around Mrs. Bennet another year."

Darcy had been pacing up and down the room, but he stopped in front of Bingley. "After you marry, you both could stay at Pemberley while you are looking. I would be glad to go with you to view the different estates."

"Thank you, my friend, we may do that. I have already spoken with Jane about moving from Hertfordshire, and she does not object. She loves her mother, but she does not want to live close to her."

"Charles, I need to speak with you about another matter. Miss Bingley is rapidly losing control, especially where Elizabeth is concerned. But we are all tired tonight, so let us talk about this tomorrow."

Bingley's expression showed that he was also worried about his sister. "Yes, I think it is time for us to talk. I must make some decisions about Caroline. She is as much a problem as Mrs. Bennet."

"Shall we meet in your study tomorrow morning after breaking our fast?"

Bingley agreed and the men retired to their chambers.

WHEN THEIR PARTY HAD RETURNED to Netherfield, Sarah had been the first out of the carriage. She moved rapidly to a darkened corner, where she heard Miss Bingley's remarks to Darcy and Elizabeth. She decided then that she would confront Miss Bingley.

As soon as Miss Bingley reached the top of the stairs, Sarah looked to make certain that Darcy and her mistress had lingered downstairs; then she went directly to Miss Bingley's room.

At the knock on her door, Caroline called out, "Who is there?" Miss Bingley heard nothing but mumbling, so she jerked the door open. Before she had a chance to say anything, Sarah was inside, and had shut and locked the door.

"What are you doing?" Miss Bingley cried. "Leave my room this minute! I will complain to Mr. Darcy about this and have you thrown out immediately."

"I do not think so," Sarah smirked. "I have come to warn you to stop your nonsense with my mistress and her husband. You cannot make trouble between them, but I can make trouble for you, and I will if you do not heed me.

"I know how you question the servants about my mistress, trying to learn anything you can to use against her. I see the way you try to interrupt them when they want to be alone and the way you shamelessly flirt with Mr. Darcy. I also know how you trapped him in the library. You accomplish nothing with your mischief except to show yourself to be the fool that you are. And you have made an enemy of me. Trust me, Miss Bingley, you do not want me for your enemy, for you cannot win against me."

In truth, Miss Bingley had always been afraid of Sarah. Charles had told her of the special training Mr. Worthington had provided, and she had heard of the damage she had wrought on Mr. Wickham. She was determined, however, not to give in to her too quickly. Sneering, Miss Bingley said, "I am not afraid of you."

Suddenly, Sarah grabbed the front of Miss Bingley's gown and pushed her against the wall. Caroline felt the blood drain from her face, and for a moment, she thought she would faint.

"I tell you this: Be afraid of me. Do not incur my wrath. Cease your trouble-making or else! And you do not want to see the 'or else.' Do you understand me?"

Miss Bingley could only nod her head. Sarah turned and unlocked the door, slipped out into the hallway, and faded into the shadows. She knew that eventually she would also have to deal with Mrs. Bennet.

In Miss Bingley's room, the lady discovered that she had soiled herself.

Chapter 22

"What a night!" Darcy remarked as he closed and locked their chamber door. "I tell you, Elizabeth, Miss Bingley will never be allowed in either of our homes again. I am out of patience with her."

"I am unable to tolerate her either. No longer is she merely disagreeable and unpleasant, she is cruel and vicious. Her hatred of me is well beyond the pale. I am sorry that Jane has to suffer Miss Bingley for a relation and a mother such as Mrs. Bennet. Jane and her father may have convinced themselves that she is eccentric, but she is more than that. Why does she imagine that demons have violet-colored eyes?"

Darcy sat on the side of the bed and removed his boots. "Sir William told Bingley and me that when the Bennet twins were born, the boy was stillborn. The girl lived for a few hours before she died. Mrs. Bennet has always insisted that the female child killed the boy. She decided that the girl was a demon and refused to hold or feed her. Apparently, the girl's eyes were violet, and that is why she thinks the way she does. Insane, I know, but there you have it."

Elizabeth sat silent for a few minutes, biting her bottom lip, as she took the pins out of her hair. "Poor Jane! You and I were so blessed to have our loving parents. I cannot imagine what life must be for her, having that wretched Mrs. Bennet for a mother."

Darcy embraced his wife. "And someday, you will be the same wonderful mother to our children that your mother was to you."

Elizabeth smiled up at him. "Our own little babe that we have made together — I look forward to seeing him someday."

"Ah, so you concede that our first babe will be a boy," Darcy smirked.

"I do nothing of the sort. I simply will have to call the child *something* and *he* is as good as *she*."

"Mrs. Darcy, shall we desist this talking and proceed to the more urgent matters that claim our attention?"

Elizabeth laughed and arched an eyebrow. "Why, sir, what can be so urgent at this time of night? I do not feel an urgency about anything."

"Well, I do, and one of the urgent matters concerns your having on too many clothes." Darcy pulled her gown over her head and then threw it over his shoulders. "There," he said, "that is much better. Let us remove the remainder as quickly as possible."

"What of your clothing? You are still completely dressed. Here, let me help you remove this." As she spoke, Elizabeth untied his cravat and unfastened his shirt. Darcy threw them on the floor and quickly removed his trousers. "How is that, madam?" he growled.

"Wonderful," she cooed.

ELIZABETH AWOKE THE NEXT MORNING to find that Darcy had left her a letter.

Dearest,

Forgive me for leaving you, but Bingley wanted me to ride over the estate. We should be back by early afternoon. I thought this would be a good time to speak with him about Miss Bingley.

I miss you already!
Fitzwilliam

Elizabeth smiled. Her husband was so thoughtful, and she considered herself the most fortunate woman on earth to be able to share his life — to know his love.

As a child growing up at Rosehaven, she had felt loved and safe. Her parents were kind and loving people whom she and Andrew adored. She wanted them to be proud of her, so she tried not to give them any trouble beyond childish mischief.

The Worthingtons had encouraged their children to be independent and to think for themselves while setting guidelines for the siblings to follow. Her parents urged them to marry only for love and respect as they had. With

Fitzwilliam, she had fulfilled her parent's hopes, and someday Andrew would find his true love just as she had with Fitzwilliam.

"Mistress, your bath is ready."

"Oh, Sarah, thank you. While I am bathing, please ask Georgiana if she would like to ride out with me this morning. It is such a beautiful day. Will you come with us?"

She smiled. "A ride sounds wonderful, lovey. I will go now and speak with Miss Georgiana."

After breakfast, the three set out at an easy pace, delighting in the beauties of the countryside. They saw the figure of a woman walking toward Meryton, and soon realized it was Jane Bennet. When they came upon her, Elizabeth dismounted to walk with her.

"Good morning, Jane. If you are walking to Meryton, may we accompany you?"

She looked up at the three ladies and greeted them with a smile. "Yes, I am on an errand for my mother, and I would be delighted to have your company."

After chatting for a short time, Jane turned to Elizabeth. "I am so sorry for the way my mother treated you, your husband, and Georgiana last night. I hope you can forgive her rudeness."

Tears appeared in Jane's eyes, and Elizabeth immediately took her hands. "Please do not let it upset you, my friend."

Blinking her tears back, Jane said, "I talked with Papa this morning, and he thinks it would be best for me to see you at Netherfield. I hope Mr. Bingley is not upset with me over this."

"No, Jane, he is not, but he is speaking with Mr. Darcy about looking for another estate close to Pemberley after you are married."

"Yes, we have discussed moving away. Papa thinks it would not be wise for us to remain in Hertfordshire. He believes Mama would not leave us alone — that she would be at our house day and night."

Elizabeth thought a change of conversation was needed. "I understand Mr. Bingley is hosting a ball soon, and he has invited the neighborhood."

"Yes, he spoke of that. Everyone is excited about a formal ball." Jane continued walking. "How was Mr. Bingley this morning? I hope he is well."

Elizabeth laughed. "I do not know, for he and Fitzwilliam left after breaking their fast to ride over the estate, and I have not seen them."

The ladies had reached Meryton by this time, and they arranged to meet at the dressmaker's shop after Jane's errand was completed. Georgiana and Sarah followed Elizabeth as she stepped inside the shop to look over their selection of ribbons and fabrics.

They were pleased to find suitable material to make a gown for Sarah to wear to church and light blue muslin for Georgiana. As a surprise for her, Elizabeth also bought lace for Sarah's dress and ribbons to wear in her hair. Happy with their purchases, they walked outside just as Jane came toward them.

"Ah, Jane, there you are. We are finished with our shopping if you are."

Affirming that she was through, they began their walk home. Sarah suddenly put out her hand to restrain them. Lifting a finger to her lips to indicate they should be quiet, she pointed toward the blacksmith shop where they saw George Wickham.

Moving quietly, Sarah walked up behind him, tapped him on the shoulder, and yelled, "WICKHAM!"

The soldier was so startled his feet left the ground as he turned to see who was behind him. Sarah laughed so hard she doubled over. Straightening up, she looked him in the eyes.

"Hate me all you want, Wickham, but make sure your fear is greater. Only your fear will keep you alive. If there is a next time, I will finish the job I started at Pemberley and leave you to bleed to death." Then she rejoined the others, and they continued walking back to Longbourn.

Mr. Wickham immediately decided to leave Hertfordshire that night. He had no wish ever to see Sarah again.

DURING THEIR WALK BACK, JANE asked why the Darcys disliked Mr. Wickham. He seemed a pleasant enough man to her.

"He is not to be trusted, Jane. His father, a good man, was the steward at Pemberley. George Wickham's behavior was always bad. Perhaps he was jealous of our wealth — I do not know. Everywhere he goes, he leaves debts at all the shops. Fitzwilliam paid off the ones he left in Lambton, but I wonder how many he has run up here in Hertfordshire.

"He has ruined several young girls, and Pemberley supports two of them and their children. Fitzwilliam's father tried to help in many ways, but Wickham took advantage of him, and now goes about telling lies about the Darcy family." Elizabeth sighed as she thought of all the ways Wickham had brought dishonor to his father and to the Darcys as well.

"I call him 'Sticky Wicky,' because he stole things from our house. Everything he touched stuck to his hands. He was eventually barred from entering Pemberley."

Georgiana laughed as she told how Elizabeth had fought him and won when she was but nine years old. "He was cruel to those younger and a coward with those his age or older."

"I am sorry to hear that, but do you think he has changed now? Perhaps he is ashamed of his former ways and is trying to change."

"Think that if it gives you pleasure, Jane. If anything, he is worse. Just make sure you are never alone with him, and please warn your friends about him."

Jane replied that she would and then mentioned that she would be staying with her Aunt and Uncle Gardiner in London after Christmas.

"Oh, how long will you be there? We are spending Christmas at Pemberley but plan to return to London in February. Perhaps we can meet if you are still there."

"I will be having my wedding dress made as well as the rest of my trousseau. Our wedding is to be the first day of May, so I will return home sometime in March. I would not want to leave my mother to make all of the wedding arrangements. It would be too hard a burden on her."

"Very well, Georgiana and I will send you a message when we return from Pemberley. Will Mr. Bingley be in London at that time?"

"Yes, he will accompany his sisters and me back to Hertfordshire when it is time for me to return home."

"Then we shall look forward to seeing you in London."

WHILE ELIZABETH, GEORGIANA, AND SARAH were away from Netherfield, Miss Bingley decided she would visit Mrs. Bennet. She was still afraid of Sarah, but she thought she would be safe this one time. If she was caught, she could always say that she was only being a good neighbor and had come to ask the Bennet ladies to tea. After all, Mrs. Bennet would soon be family. Caroline did not think she was in any danger of being exposed, so calling for the carriage, she set out for Longbourn.

Mrs. Bennet was happy to see Miss Bingley and rang for Hill to bring tea and light refreshments. After several minutes of pleasant conversation, Caroline approached the topic of her obsession: Elizabeth Darcy.

Leaning forward in a confidential manner, Miss Bingley said, "I wish to speak with you of an important and personal matter regarding Mrs. Darcy. I would not wish this to be discussed among anyone but ourselves."

Mrs. Bennet's attention was caught immediately. "Yes, Miss Bingley?"

"Madam, you seemed to insinuate last evening that you think Mrs. Darcy is a demon. Am I correct?"

"Yes, yes, you are."

"I quite agree with your assessment of her. I have known her for some time and have always been suspicious of her. Did you know that Mr. Darcy and I were once engaged?"

"No, I did not. Tell me, my dear, what did that demon do to you? She must have taken Mr. Darcy from you since they are now married."

"Sadly, yes." Caroline held her handkerchief to her eyes in a show of emotion. "We were so happy in our love for each other until Mrs. Darcy decided she wanted him. I have long suspected that she used the black arts to engage his attention. Before she decided on Mr. Darcy, she was responsible for ending several happy marriages and parted at least two engaged couples. She is quite brazen! Although her father was wealthy and she is supposed to be a lady, in truth, she is no better than a common trollop."

"I am not at all surprised. I knew the minute I saw her that she was no lady." Mrs. Bennet reached for Miss Bingley's hand. "My dear, how can I help you? She must be stopped! I confess that I believe she is either my own evil child, or she has been taken over by the evil spirit of that child. I know that is shocking to a lady such as yourself, but, alas, I fear it is the truth."

"I am certain you are correct." Miss Bingley gripped Mrs. Bennet's hand while trying to squeeze tears from her own eyes. Making her voice very small like a child's, Caroline asked, "Is it possible? Do you suppose? Is there a way for you to remedy this situation before she does you harm? I am not afraid for myself, you understand, for she has done her worst to me. She has taken all my strength, and I am helpless against her. No, it is you, dear lady, for whom I fear."

Mrs. Bennet patted Miss Bingley's hand. "You poor, dear woman, do not be concerned. Someday you will have your Mr. Darcy back again, but we must have patience. Jane and Mr. Bingley must be married first, and then I will think of a way to defeat this evil being that torments us. Leave everything to me."

Miss Bingley smiled to herself. Mrs. Bennet had responded the way she had hoped, and she would not have to lift a finger against Eliza. All blame would fall on Mrs. Bennet.

However, while Mrs. Bennet and Miss Bingley were talking, Mr. Bennet was standing just outside the door. He had heard the entire conversation, and his one thought was that the Darcys had to be warned. Never would he allow harm to come to his Elizabeth! Knowing that his wife would not seek to harm Elizabeth until after Jane's wedding, he decided to wait and speak with the Darcys on the night of the ball.

Chapter 23

Excitement charged the air on the night of the Netherfield ball. Georgiana had obtained permission from Darcy to attend with the understanding that Sarah would stay by her side. She would not be allowed to dance as she was only fifteen and not yet out, and she would have to return to her room after supper.

Bingley had included the Yorkshire militia in his invitation, and they were all relieved when Wickham did not appear. Later, they heard he had deserted and was nowhere to be found. Sarah snorted when Darcy informed her.

Netherfield had never looked better. Miss Bingley had outdone herself. There were flowers everywhere, and beautiful chandeliers, each sporting many candles, cast a lovely glow over the room. The food was like none the neighborhood had ever tasted, and everyone was impressed with Netherfield's splendor.

Caroline considered herself exquisitely turned out, appearing, as usual, in an orange gown trimmed with yards of intricately woven lace, her hair adorned with brilliantly colored feathers, her neck draped with necklaces of gold and topaz.

As she observed Elizabeth, Caroline thought Mrs. Darcy, despite her great wealth, looked quite plain, for her teal-colored gown was simple with very little lace — no doubt a consequence of her poor taste coupled with her lack of style. She wore no feathers in her hair, only fresh flowers and ribbons that matched the color of her gown. While Caroline secretly rejoiced in the simple state of Mrs. Darcy's ensemble, Mr. Darcy said he thought she looked beautiful.

THE BENNETS WERE ONE OF the first families to arrive at Netherfield, and Mrs. Bennet watched Elizabeth carefully.

She had played her conversation with Miss Bingley over and over in her mind, and she knew she had to be careful and plan well. She knew what had to be done, but it would not do to move against Mrs. Darcy too quickly. Jane was leaving for London after Christmas, and her prolonged absence would leave Mrs. Bennet time to make her plans. After carefully thinking through her options, she thought that the time to strike against Mrs. Darcy would be immediately after Jane's wedding. Miss Bingley might be helpless to act, but she was not.

MR. BENNET WATCHED HIS WIFE to make sure she did not cause a scene. While Mrs. Bennet talked with Lady Lucas and Mrs. Long, he sought out the Darcys.

"Might I have a word in private with you both? I wish to speak of a matter of some importance to us all."

Darcy and Elizabeth were surprised at his strange request, but they agreed to meet with him. It was decided that the Darcys would go to the library and that Mr. Bennet would join them a few moments later.

Upon entering the library, Darcy looked at Elizabeth and raised an eyebrow in question, but she could only shrug her shoulders. Soon, Mr. Bennet appeared in the room, closing and locking the door behind him.

"I hope you do not mind my locking this door. I would not want anyone to come in during our conversation."

Darcy nodded his consent and requested that Mr. Bennet continue, his curiosity now fully engaged.

"Mrs. Darcy, you and my daughter, Jane, seem to have formed a close friendship?"

"Yes, sir. Jane is a lovely person, and I enjoy her company."

"I hope you will forgive me if I presume too much, but I would ask a favor of you and your husband."

"How can we help you, sir?"

"Jane is returning to London after Christmas. I would appreciate if you, Mrs. Darcy, continued your friendship with her. Perhaps you could go with her when she and Mrs. Gardiner shop for her trousseau."

"I will be happy to do so. I have already spoken with Jane and told her I will send a message to her and Mrs. Gardiner when we return to London."

"That is generous of you. Now, Mr. Darcy, what do I ask of you? I am sure you recognize that my wife is not merely eccentric. She is a different woman than the girl I married. Since the death of our twin babies, she has become quite mad. She believes Mrs. Darcy is our daughter, based primarily on the color of her eyes, and that her name is Elizabeth Anne. I fear she could be a danger to you, Mrs. Darcy, for she thinks you are here to harm her."

Elizabeth gasped, "Sir, I assure you—"

Mr. Bennet held up his hand, "I know that you would never harm her. When our daughter died, I placed her in the casket with our son and then sealed it. My mistake was in not letting her see them. My wife was too ill to come downstairs, and I did not realize the trouble my actions would later cause."

Darcy's concern showed in his troubled countenance. "Other than keeping my wife away from yours — and I assure you I will — what else do you wish me to do? You have obviously thought about this a great deal."

"Please convince Mr. Bingley to give up Netherfield and move Jane far away. They will never have a moment's peace, for she will visit them every day, and she will try to convince Mr. Bingley to give up his friendship with you. She will make their lives miserable."

"I am surprised Bingley has not discussed his plans in full with you. I hesitate speaking of this with you, but I do not think Bingley would mind in light of your concerns. After the wedding, Bingley will take Miss Bennet to London, and then they will travel to Derbyshire and stay with us at Pemberley. While there, he plans to look for an estate to purchase. So, you see, sir, you need not be anxious."

"I see that my future son is an intelligent man with excellent intuition. I cannot tell you how this calms me. But there is another, graver matter of which I wish to warn you. While Jane was away one day, Miss Bingley visited my wife and told her things about Mrs. Darcy that, were they true, would be grave indeed."

Darcy and Elizabeth were shocked, and Darcy felt the heat of anger come over him. "What lies did she tell your wife? If Miss Bingley spoke ill of my wife in any way, I can assure you that she lied."

"She stated that she had been engaged to you and that Mrs. Darcy stole you from her, using the black arts to do so. In addition, she said that Mrs. Darcy had ruined several marriages and at least two engagements. I must warn you, Miss Bingley did her best to plant a seed in my wife's mind to harm Mrs. Darcy so that she might have you for herself. I need not tell you that Miss Bingley was overwhelmingly successful in further poisoning my wife's mind against Mrs. Darcy. I have overheard my wife talking to herself about the various ways she might harm Mrs. Darcy and how she might carry out her plans."

Elizabeth put a restraining hand on Darcy's arm. "I beg of you, do nothing foolish, Fitzwilliam. We must discuss this first when we are calm, when we can examine this information from every aspect."

Darcy shuddered, and when he spoke, rage still consumed him. "Lies, all lies, Mr. Bennet! If you think your wife will listen to reason, please speak with her. Elizabeth and I will discuss this and make plans to keep her safe from the hands of Mrs. Bennet or her accomplices."

"Yes, that would be wise, although I have never known my wife to listen to reason. I can promise you, however, to keep a closer watch over her. I understand you and your wife leave Hertfordshire the first of December for your home in Derbyshire and that you will return to London in February."

"That is correct. At least, those are our plans at this time."

"Then I wish you a safe journey and a Happy Christmas. Please know how sorry I am to have had to impart this information to you." Mr. Bennet bowed and left the library.

The Darcys followed him a few minutes later. As they stepped back into the ballroom, Darcy gasped. "What is he doing here?"

Elizabeth looked out over the ballroom. There was Colonel Fitzwilliam, and he and Miss Bingley looked very cozy together.

Chapter 24

Darcy grabbed Elizabeth's hand and led her to where Richard and Miss Bingley stood. "Richard, what are you doing here?"

"Ah, Cousin! I have surprised you! Miss Bingley was kind enough to send me an invitation, and here I am. I was just telling the lady how beautiful everything looks, including herself."

Miss Bingley giggled, and Darcy thought he would be ill. It was obvious she had consumed too much of her fine wine. The music began and the colonel said, "Excuse us. I promised this dance to the lovely Miss Bingley." Taking her hand he said, "Come, my beauty."

Darcy and Elizabeth looked at each other. "What the devil is he up to?" Darcy asked. "Whatever it is, it cannot be good."

"Well, she did invite him, my love. Perhaps he is simply being polite, although he does seem to be overdoing the flattery."

"He certainly is! I suppose we will have to wait and see. At least Miss Bingley is leaving me alone for the moment."

"And for that, you should thank your cousin," Elizabeth laughed.

Georgiana and Sarah joined them, and Georgiana asked her brother if he would dance the next one with her. "Please, Brother. I do so want to dance just once."

"Oh, very well, but only one! Elizabeth, do you mind sitting out the supper dance?"

"Not at all. Sarah will keep me company."

ELIZABETH AND SARAH MOVED TO a corner of the room away from everyone, and she told Sarah of their conversation with Mr. Bennet.

"I believe that she is mad, lovey. Thank goodness we need not be in Hertfordshire much longer. I will be glad to leave this place."

"As will I." Elizabeth sighed. "Returning to Pemberley sounds like heaven, and I will be so relieved to be home."

"Until we leave, you must avoid both Miss Bingley and Mrs. Bennet. I have already had one conversation with Miss Bingley, and I plan to have another."

Elizabeth looked at her and Sarah patted her hand as she said, "Never you mind, lovey. I will tell you all later. For the present, it is only important that we keep you from harm."

AFTER ALL THE BALL GUESTS had departed, Netherfield's overnight guests sat in the drawing room discussing the events of the evening — that is, everyone but the colonel and Miss Bingley. They sat apart, and everyone became aware of the colonel's laughter and Miss Bingley's giggles. Her brother looked at them incredulously.

Finally, Darcy stood and held out his hand to Elizabeth. He would wait until tomorrow to speak with his cousin. He was tired, and there seemed to be no way to pry Richard away from Miss Bingley's side without causing a scene.

In their chambers, Darcy yawned and began changing his clothes, while Elizabeth slipped on her nightgown. When she began brushing her hair, Darcy came up behind her and took the brush. "Let me do that for you, my love."

They were silent for a while until Darcy remarked, "Will you be as glad as I to be home again? This has been a stressful time. Now Richard is here and behaving as though he is courting Miss Bingley."

"It is all very strange. Mr. Bingley did not look pleased at the sight of them so intimately engaged."

"He knows his sister is capable of anything, and Richard is known to be a terrible flirt. Bingley's plans do not include letting Miss Bingley live with him and Miss Bennet in London. She will have to either live with the Hursts or make other arrangements. He does not want his wife and sister living in the same house."

"That is wise of him. Miss Bingley would run roughshod over poor Jane, and after what we heard tonight, I would fear for Jane's safety."

"As would I! What are your thoughts on what Mr. Bennet told us?"

"In truth, Fitzwilliam, I am afraid of Mrs. Bennet and Miss Bingley. While I understand Miss Bingley's motives very well, I do not understand how Mrs. Bennet can think I am her daughter."

"I am taking Mr. Bennet's warning very seriously. You do not know how difficult it is for me not to physically harm Miss Bingley, but that is not in my character. I have never disliked anyone as much as I do her. I know I will need to speak with Charles about what Mr. Bennet said, but I dread telling him."

She put her head back against his chest and closed her eyes as he continued speaking. "It is for your own safety that I must insist you not ride or walk out unless someone is with you." Darcy pulled her up and held her close to him. "Elizabeth, promise me you will be careful. I could not bear it if anything happened to you."

"Nothing will happen to me, dearest," she assured him, "as long as I have you."

"You have me forever."

THE FOLLOWING MORNING, DARCY WAS breaking his fast when the colonel came into the breakfast room.

"Good morning, Cousin. Good party last night, aye?"

Darcy laid down his fork, "What are you up to, Richard, acting as though you are courting Miss Bingley?"

"Jealous, old man?"

"Do not be ridiculous."

The colonel buttered a piece of toast before he spoke. "What if I am courting her? I have to marry someone. She has 20,000 pounds, she is willing to give me a son, and my mistress is of no interest to her. I would have the best of all worlds."

"You disgust me, Richard! Miss Bingley is a cruel, vicious woman who would make your life miserable. Do you honestly think your parents would approve of your marrying her? You would be cutting yourself off from all your family, including Elizabeth and myself. I have told Bingley that she is no longer welcomed in my home. Marriage to you would make no difference. It would only mean that you would not be welcomed either."

"Are you serious? I would not be welcomed at Pemberley?"

"Yes, by God, I am! Richard, I beg of you; listen to me. You do not know Miss Bingley as I do. I fear for your life if you attach yourself to her. Elizabeth and I were warned last night that she means to harm Elizabeth through Mrs. Bennet, Jane's unbalanced mother."

Richard stopped eating and looked at Darcy. "Truthfully, Cousin, I never intended marrying Miss Bingley, and I am glad of an excuse to leave. I have enjoyed discomfiting you, Darcy, but I know you are not prone to histrionics. Very well, I will leave for London immediately and have nothing more to do with Miss Bingley. Thank you for warning me." The colonel stood and hurried from the room.

"Was that your cousin I saw rushing out just now?" Bingley asked as he came into the breakfast room. "He pushed past me and did not bother speaking. Is something going on that I should know about?"

Darcy snorted. "You would do better to ask your sister than me."

"As if she would tell me!"

"Bingley, you will be a much happier man when you remove your sister from your home and take Miss Bennet away from her mother as soon as you marry."

Bingley put his head in his hands. "I know," he groaned. "Between Caroline and Mrs. Bennet, I am going mad. Why does everything have to be so complicated? I am a peace-loving man, Darcy. I do not like all this pressure!"

"Have you thought about marrying before May? That would remove you from Mrs. Bennet and your sister. I do not understand why you are waiting so long to marry. It is a long time to wait."

"I will speak to Jane today about hastening our wedding date, but I do not think she will wish to change it. I only want to be rid of all this nonsense. Lord knows we do not need any more insane people around here."

Darcy and Bingley were laughing when, suddenly, Caroline Bingley marched into the breakfast room in a rage.

"Mr. Darcy, what did you say to the colonel? I am certain he was going to ask for my hand in marriage until he spoke with you, and now he had the gall to say he was leaving for London. I know it is all because of whatever you said to him."

"Where is Richard?"

Miss Bingley stamped her foot. "He is gone, you stupid man! Gone! You do not want me, so why on earth would you try to persuade him not to marry me? I want an answer, and I want it now."

Darcy looked at Bingley, who shrugged. "You might as well tell her the truth, Darcy."

"I would rather not."

"Well, someone had better tell me something, now!"

Bingley held out his hands to his sister. "Caroline, calm down! You will make yourself ill!"

"Silence, Charles! Mr. Darcy, are you a coward, or will you be a man for once and tell me the truth? I want to know what you told Richard."

Barely capable of curbing his rage, Darcy rose from his chair and faced Miss Bingley. "Very well, madam, I will! I advised my cousin that you would make his life miserable, that if he married you he would be cutting himself off from all of his family, including Elizabeth and myself."

"What makes you think I would not be welcomed in his parents' home?" Caroline spat.

"I do not *think* that, Miss Bingley, I am certain of it!" Darcy hissed. "Elizabeth is Lady Matlock's godchild, and they are very close. Do you think they would welcome a woman who hated their godchild? You have already incurred my aunt's wrath by your rude behavior toward Elizabeth in London."

Miss Bingley growled and then slapped Darcy. Before he or Bingley could react, she raised her hand as though to slap him again. "This is what I think of you, Mr. Darcy! You deserve that little chit you married!"

Before Miss Bingley could strike Darcy again, Sarah, who had come into the room unnoticed, grabbed her wrist and looked at her squarely.

Her voice was eerily calm as she instructed Caroline. "Go to your room, Miss Bingley, and do not leave it. I will have your meals sent up until Mr. Bingley decides what he will do with you."

Miss Bingley trembled in rage as she attempted to match Sarah's steely gaze. Slowly, her strength faded as Sarah's increased. Caroline was foolish in many things, but she was wise enough to do as Sarah told her. It was not a request; it was an order.

Chapter 25

On December first, Darcy, Elizabeth, and Georgiana waved goodbye to Bingley and the Hursts and left for Pemberley.

Miss Bingley had been sent to Scotland to stay with her aunt and uncle. She did not go quietly! She was escorted by two large men as well as a female companion. Bingley had arranged for them to stay with her during her visit, which promised to be of long duration. Their uncle's farm was isolated, and Miss Bingley would be expected to help with the chores. Her brother hoped rather than expected that this visit would help her to see reason, at which time he would allow her to return to London.

Darcy had spoken with Bingley about Miss Bingley's visit with Mrs. Bennet. Charles had demanded that his sister tell Mrs. Bennet the truth, but Caroline flatly refused.

Before her departure, Miss Bingley expressed her rage by hurling every breakable object she could take in hand towards the walls of her chamber. The sounds of shattering glass and porcelain echoed throughout the house. Later, as she calmly entered the carriage, she stopped and turned to speak to Darcy and her brother. "Do not think that I will forget this great injustice you have done to me. Be forewarned that I will at some point in time have my revenge!" Bingley sadly realized he would most likely have to commit his sister to an asylum.

Bingley and the Hursts were staying at Netherfield through Christmas, after which, together with Jane Bennet, they would travel to town. The Darcys planned to meet them in London in February.

GEORGIANA LET OUT A SIGH of relief as she settled back in the carriage. "I am very glad to be leaving Netherfield for Pemberley. It will be good to spend a quiet Christmas with family."

"I agree," Darcy said. "I have had enough nonsense from Mrs. Bennet and Miss Bingley to last a lifetime."

"I am glad Sarah took charge after Miss Bingley slapped you, my love. She remained calm and in control while you and Charles were stunned. Sarah told me at the ball that she had already warned Miss Bingley about her behavior. I am very sorry she did not heed Sarah's warning."

"Richard is fortunate to be rid of her, although, before he left, he confessed he had never intended to marry Miss Bingley."

"Fitzwilliam, your cousin must cease his reckless ways. He has made a bad situation much worse with regards to Miss Bingley. It was cruel of him to encourage her. Can you not speak with him about this?"

Darcy ran his hands through his hair. "I am willing, but I do not believe it will discourage him. Richard has always done what he wanted, and I have never had much influence with him."

"I suppose not," Elizabeth agreed, and she grew silent.

Darcy soon took out a book and began reading while Georgiana and Elizabeth looked out the window, commenting on the passing scenery.

After they had ridden for several hours, Georgiana asked Elizabeth, "How long has Sarah been with you, Lizzy?"

"She was there the night Andrew and I were born. My father hired her as our wet nurse and nanny. Papa was so afraid something would happen to us that he had Sarah trained as our guard. She has always been more a member of our family than a servant. I trust her with my life."

"She was very young when your father hired her, was she not?"

"Yes, dearest, she was only fourteen years old. She came from a very poor family, and her father was a drunkard who beat her regularly. She adored my parents because they rescued her from a life of horror."

Elizabeth yawned and laid her head on Darcy's shoulder. He put his arm around her, drawing her close. "Are you warm enough, dearest? What about you, Georgiana? Do either of you need another blanket?" They both declined, and soon Elizabeth was lulled to sleep by the steady rhythm of her husband's heartbeat.

THE DARCY'S ARRIVAL AT PEMBERLEY two days later was a relief for them all. Mrs. Reynolds greeted them with the welcoming news that hot tea awaited them.

They settled in for the winter, and the day after they arrived home, Mrs.

Reynolds, Elizabeth, and Georgiana made plans to decorate the house with extra care that Christmas. Andrew and Henry Worthington would arrive a week before Christmas, and on the twenty-third, Mr. Worthington's special friend, a Miss Rose Garnon, and her parents, Mr. and Mrs. Edward Garnon would arrive. The ladies were excited about their guests, and they wanted Pemberley to look festive.

They greatly anticipated meeting Miss Garnon. Lady Matlock had invited the Garnon family to Elizabeth's coming out at the request of Henry Worthington, but the Darcys did not know them. Mr. Worthington had written to Darcy and Elizabeth while they were still at Netherfield, requesting the Garnon's presence at Pemberley for Christmas. Elizabeth sat down at once and sent them an invitation, which was happily accepted.

On the day Andrew and his uncle arrived at Pemberley, a light snow was falling. Elizabeth and Georgiana had decorated the house with fragrant garlands and wreaths. They had also woven holly with red berries throughout their decorations to create a merry atmosphere for the family and their guests.

Elizabeth flung herself into her brother's arms, and hugged and kissed him, for she had not seen him since her wedding. Andrew held her away from him and exclaimed, "Let me look at you, Lizzy. You look quite happy and content. I believe I can safely say that Darcy is treating you well."

"Oh, yes, he is." Elizabeth looked lovingly at Darcy, who was smiling at his wife and her brother.

"I must treat her well, Andrew. You know only too well what Sarah would do to me if I did not."

Everyone laughed and, while Darcy greeted Andrew, Elizabeth hugged her uncle.

"You must tell us all about Miss Garnon. Where did you meet her, Uncle Henry? How old is she?

"Now, now, Lizzy, there will be time for that later," Henry laughed as he returned her hug.

"Miss Darcy," Andrew greeted her, "how lovely you look! You are all grown up. Mr. Darcy will soon have to chase away your many suitors."

Georgiana blushed and immediately excused herself to return upstairs.

"Andrew," Elizabeth scolded, "do not tease Georgiana. She becomes a little shy when suitors are mentioned. Remember, she is only fifteen, and it is yet three years before her coming out."

Darcy had noticed his sister's response to Andrew, and he recalled the attention Andrew had paid to Georgiana before he and Elizabeth married. Although he knew that Andrew was a gentleman and could be trusted, Darcy would keep an eye on them nonetheless.

After dinner, when everyone had gathered in the drawing room, Mr. Worthington called for everyone's attention.

"I know you are all curious about the Garnons, in particular Miss Garnon, so I shall keep you in suspense no longer. Mr. Garnon is a wealthy tradesman, and the Garnons are lovely and gracious people. I met Miss Garnon at her father's home when I visited for a business meeting and, afterwards, they invited me to stay for supper. I was impressed with their manners and intelligence and, over time, I asked for, and was granted, the honor of courting Miss Garnon.

"She is ten years my junior, but we are in love, and she is all that I could hope for in a wife. I will ask Miss Garnon for her hand in marriage and make a request to Mr. Garnon for his blessing while they are visiting here at Pemberley. If all goes as I hope, we will travel to my estate at the first of the year so that she can determine what changes need to be made to the house. I am aware that some in the *ton* may not accept her since she is the daughter of a tradesman, but that does not concern me, for she makes me very happy."

The others were quiet for a few moments, but then Elizabeth spoke. "Uncle, I want only your happiness, and if Miss Garnon makes you happy, that is all that concerns me. I will do whatever is necessary to help ease her way into society, and I am sure Lady Matlock will also help."

Andrew spoke, "I agree with Elizabeth."

Worthington then turned to Darcy. "What are your thoughts and feelings on this matter? How do you feel about Mr. Garnon being a tradesman?"

"Henry, your niece has taught me to look at a man's character and not how he makes his living. She has made me a better man, and now I would never presume to try and tell anyone how to live his life. If you, Elizabeth, and Andrew are happy with your decision, that is all that matters. Miss Garnon and her parents are very welcome at Pemberley."

A BLIZZARD ACCOMPANIED MISS GARNON and her parents upon their arrival. Mrs. Reynolds and Elizabeth led them to their rooms where trays of tea and other refreshments awaited by well-stoked fires.

After assuring them that hot water for baths to warm them were being readied, the housekeeper and Elizabeth left — Mrs. Reynolds to the kitchen and Elizabeth to the blue drawing room, where she joined her family for tea.

The Garnon party met their hosts in the drawing room before dinner. When they were shown in, Elizabeth hurried to make them comfortable. "Miss Garnon, allow me to welcome you and your parents to our home." She led them closer to the fire and bade them to sit. "I trust you have found your rooms acceptable?"

"Oh yes, Mrs. Darcy. They are very comfortable, indeed." Mr. and Mrs. Garnon agreed and smiled at everyone before Mrs. Garnon spoke. "Thank you for seeing that we had hot baths upon our arrival. We had grown quite chilled before reaching Pemberley."

After dinner, while the men were having their brandy and cigars, the ladies became better acquainted. Miss Garnon and her mother were pleasant companions, and before the men joined them, Georgiana, Elizabeth, and Miss Garnon were calling each other by their Christian names.

"WHAT DO YOU THINK OF Miss Garnon and her mother, my love?" Darcy asked as he and Elizabeth prepared for bed. "I will admit to being most impressed with Mr. Garnon. He appears to be a clever and honest man. His father was a vicar, and he built his business from nothing with no help from anyone. He told me that they had some lean and hard years; however, I understand he is now a very wealthy man.

"Your uncle had him thoroughly investigated upon meeting him and found not one hint of scandal or dishonesty attached to him. Henry invested in his company and has been rewarded with excellent returns."

"Georgiana and I like Rose and her mother very much. I especially liked the way they included Georgiana in our conversation. Rose admitted she plays the pianoforte, so I plan on the three of us entertaining you gentlemen after dinner tomorrow night."

Darcy smiled and kissed her nose. "That is excellent news, my love. I look forward to being entertained." His voice grew husky as he enfolded her into his arms. "What say you to some other entertainment?"

With a soft laugh, Elizabeth led her husband to their bed. He could never have enough of her, and from her responses to his caresses, she felt the same. How he loved her! Darcy buried himself deep within her, and they began their mating dance.

She whispered, "Fitzwilliam, I love you so," causing his heart to overflow with happiness. He responded in a husky voice. "You are my love, Elizabeth, my only love." Their release was intense and all the warmth they needed on a snowy night.

Chapter 26

Christmas Eve morning found Pemberley snowed in. Elizabeth glanced out the window as she came into the breakfast room and discovered Andrew and Georgiana outside having a snowball fight. She laughed aloud, and the others left the table and hurried to the window to see what amused her.

"I believe Georgiana has the better of Andrew. Look, she must have planned her attack in advance, for she has a pile of snowballs all ready to use." Elizabeth pointed to Georgiana's pile of ammunition. The others laughed and then returned to their food.

"Fitzwilliam, do you think we could take the sleigh out today?"

"I am afraid it is too cold, my love, and the snow is very deep. We would do better to stay inside and entertain ourselves."

They heard voices in the hall as Andrew and Georgiana burst inside laughing, their cheeks red from the cold. Mrs. Reynolds followed close behind, scolding them for tracking in snow. Noting that they stood in a pool of water, Mrs. Reynolds insisted they remove their coats, gloves, and boots.

After that was accomplished, she pushed them toward the stairs and demanded they go to their rooms and change into dry clothes. Still laughing, Georgiana hugged Mrs. Reynolds and then ran upstairs, leaving the housekeeper in the breakfast room, smiling and shaking her head at the young girl's antics.

An hour later, Darcy was in his study with the door open when he saw Andrew passing by and called out to him. Andrew stopped and stepped inside.

"Did you wish to speak with me, sir?"

"Yes, Andrew. Close the door, please."

Darcy's face had a scowl on it. He pointed to the chair next to his desk. "Sit down, please."

"Is anything wrong?"

"No, nothing is wrong. I only wish to speak with you about Georgiana."

Darcy cleared his throat before speaking. He was nervous. "I would appreciate if you kept this talk between the two of us for now. You are aware that Georgiana is only fifteen, and she will not be out for three more years."

"Yes, I am aware of that."

"I have noticed that you and Georgiana seem to be very friendly with each other."

Andrew jumped up, his face suddenly red with anger. "Darcy, if you are implying there is anything improper between us, you are—"

"No, no, Andrew. Sit down. I am not implying anything of the kind. I know you are a gentleman, and you would never intentionally injure her sensibilities; however, she is still young and has no experience with men. I am afraid she has developed a fancy for you, and I do not want her hurt."

"I must be honest with you. I care for Miss Darcy more than I should at her young age, but I swear to you that I had intended waiting until she was out before declaring my feelings for her. She should have the opportunity to enjoy her coming out."

Darcy smiled. "I am glad to hear it. I was once in much the same situation with your sister. I wanted to declare myself long before I did, but I knew it would not be proper, so I waited. All I am asking is that you do the same. You do not have to distance yourself from Georgiana to the point of being unfriendly, but do not tell her of your intent and do not allow yourself to be in a situation where you are tempted to go beyond what is proper."

"As a gentleman, I vow to you that I will never do anything to hurt Miss Darcy. I care too much for her."

"Yes, well, I am glad we had this talk, and I want you to know that I consider you to be a fine young man. I would be proud to have you court Georgiana when the time is right. I am glad, however, that you will be at Cambridge for the next three years. You cannot, of course, write directly to her, but messages can be sent through Elizabeth's letters."

"Thank you, sir. I strive always for your high opinion of me."

"I feel certain that you will not betray my trust in you."

CHRISTMAS DINNER WAS FESTIVE, AND all agreed it was the best meal they had ever eaten. Half-way through, Henry Worthington stood to make an announcement.

"Christmas this year is a very special time for me. Although my dear brother and his wife are not with us, I am happy to be spending it with my niece and nephew, Elizabeth and Andrew, and with my new nephew, Fitzwilliam." Mr. Worthington lifted his glass to each of them. "What has made this day even more delightful is that Miss Garnon has agreed to become my wife, and her father has given his consent and blessing. I would like to propose a toast to my future bride, Miss Rose Garnon!"

As soon as everyone's excitement had calmed, Darcy stood. "I believe I can speak for my wife when I say that she and I wish the very best for our uncle and Miss Garnon. May you both be as happy as Elizabeth and I."

Nothing would do then but for Andrew to stand and welcome his future aunt into the family. Then Mr. Garnon stood. "My daughter could not have found a better or more worthy man than Henry Worthington. Let us drink to the happy couple!"

After the women withdrew to the drawing room, Elizabeth approached Rose and her mother with an offer to host an engagement ball for the couple. "Please allow us to do this for you, Rose. Have you and my uncle decided on a date?"

"We plan for the first of April. Father will publish the announcement in the paper when we return to town. After we leave Pemberley, we will travel to Henry's estate. I am very excited to see my future home. We plan to stay several nights before returning to London."

"Perfect," Elizabeth declared. "Now, let us begin compiling a list of all those we wish to invite."

The men were not surprised to see the ladies with their heads together, making plans and giggling. At last, they were able to prevail upon Miss Garnon to favor them at the pianoforte. It was evident that she had the benefit of a good teacher and that she practiced often. Mr. Worthington watched her with a tender look in his eyes.

Afterwards, Georgiana played while Elizabeth sang, and as usual, Darcy positioned himself where he could watch his wife. He had always loved to hear her sing, and tonight she sang directly to her husband, never taking her eyes off him.

What no one noticed was Andrew's eyes as he watched Georgiana. She had always been his favorite, and he knew that he loved her. He was suddenly very glad that he would be at Cambridge and out of the way of temptation for the next three years. His studies would give him something to think about besides Georgiana and her sweet blue eyes.

Chapter 27

The Darcys traveled back to London in February, and Elizabeth began to set her plans in motion. The engagement ball for her uncle and his intended would be the largest social event she had arranged as Mrs. Darcy.

Elizabeth invited tradesmen as well as gentlemen. She was excited about bringing them together. Of course, she suspected that some of the *ton* would not attend because of Miss Garnon's background, but she did not care. The distinction between gentlemen and tradesmen was ridiculous as far as she was concerned. She decided she would enlist the help of her godmother, Lady Matlock, to help pave Miss Garnon's way into society.

Her immediate plan was to send an invitation for tea to Jane Bennet and Mrs. Gardner. Elizabeth received an answer the same day, and she and Georgiana looked forward to seeing the two ladies.

The following day, Jane and Mrs. Gardiner were shown into a small sitting room already occupied by Elizabeth and Georgiana. Elizabeth hurried to greet them.

"It is so good to see you both. Please make yourselves comfortable while I ring for tea."

"Thank you for inviting us, Elizabeth. My aunt and I have looked forward to seeing you again."

"Now, you must tell us what you have been doing since coming back to London."

Mrs. Bowers chose that moment to enter with a tray of tea and refreshments. After tea was served, Elizabeth focused her attention back to Jane. "Do not keep us in suspense, Jane. We insist on knowing all your activities."

Jane Bennet smiled, and Elizabeth saw the happiness in her eyes. "While you were at Pemberley, Mr. Bingley took us all to the theater and to the opera. Then, one of my uncle's business associates held an engagement dinner for us. We have also been quite busy at the dressmakers."

"Jane, may we honor you and Mr. Bingley with a dinner party soon? You may let me know the best date for you."

"Oh, Elizabeth, that is so kind of you! I will speak with Mr. Bingley about the date."

"There is another happy event I wish to announce. My uncle, Henry Worthington, is soon to be married to Miss Rose Garnon, and Mr. Darcy and I will host an engagement ball for them. Her father is Edward Garnon. Do you happen to know them?"

"Oh, yes," replied Mrs. Gardiner. "My husband and Mr. Garnon are business associates. He also knows Mr. Worthington and has done business with him as well."

"Wonderful! An invitation will be sent to you this week. In addition, we are having a dinner party for the couple on Friday evening. Will you do us the honor of attending?"

"The honor will be ours, Elizabeth." Mrs. Gardiner paused for a moment and then continued. "Jane's father wrote to tell us that he had spoken with you and your husband before you left Netherfield, and we thank you for your continued friendship with Jane. We also know about the conversation between Miss Bingley and my sister. We are saddened by my sister's foolish ideas and that you have been singled out in her delusions."

Mrs. Gardiner smiled. "Oh, I wish you could have known her before the twins died. She was such a happy woman with a sunny disposition. Everyone liked her, but now she was so different. Mr. Bennet's estate is entailed to the male line, and they so hoped to have a son. It was when the twins died that we first sensed her illness. Mr. Bennet took her to a number of doctors, but no one was able to help."

Jane spoke. "When I was young, I thought of her as a kind and loving mother, but lately…" Jane's voice trailed off, and a look of pain appeared in her eyes.

Mrs. Gardiner knew that Mrs. Bennet had not been the kind of mother Jane deserved, but she did not wish to cause any more pain to her niece by saying otherwise.

FRIDAY NIGHT CAME, AND WHEN the Gardiners and Jane arrived, they were surprised to see such a large gathering. Mr. Gardiner was happy to see the familiar faces of Mr. Garnon and Mr. Worthington, and Elizabeth took care to introduce Mrs. Gardiner and Jane to the other ladies present.

Earlier, Elizabeth had spoken to Lady Matlock about Jane Bennet and Rose Garnon. She had received assurance that her godmother would include both engaged couples in every event the Darcys were to attend. In addition, she would do whatever was necessary to ease Miss Garnon's acceptance into London society.

BINGLEY AND THE HURSTS ARRIVED shortly after the Gardiner party, and Charles Bingley was happy to see his betrothed. She was speaking with Darcy's cousin, Colonel Fitzwilliam, and a friend of Darcy's from Cambridge, Clive Barrows, as well as Elizabeth's brother Andrew. Charles could not help but feel a bit jealous to see her enjoying the company of other men. He quickly hurried toward her, and a joyous look came over Jane's face when she saw him.

"MISS BENNET, HAVE YOU SEEN the beautiful painting of Darcy's estate, Pemberley?" the colonel asked.

When she answered that she had not, he guided her past Bingley, making sure he saw them, and led her to the painting. While the two stood talking, the colonel stole a glance at Bingley and noted that he looked jealous. *Excellent,* the colonel thought, chuckling to himself. *This should be an entertaining evening.*

As they went into dinner, the colonel was delighted to discover that Elizabeth had placed him across from Miss Bennet and Mr. Bingley. However, all of the colonel's flirting was for naught, for Miss Bennet noticed only Mr. Bingley.

AFTER ALL THE GUESTS WERE gone, the Darcys and Andrew agreed that Elizabeth's first dinner party had been a success. As they sat sipping a last glass of wine and talking about the dinner, Darcy took Elizabeth's hand and brought it to his lips.

"You are a little imp, seating Miss Bennet across from Richard. It was fortunate for Bingley that Miss Bennet is so in love with him that she ignored Richard's flirting."

"I did not arrange it that way deliberately." Elizabeth laughed.

Andrew yawned and then stood. "Good night, everyone. I have to be up early tomorrow, so I had better return home." Shortly after he left, Georgiana kissed her brother and Elizabeth, and retired to her chambers.

Darcy pulled his wife onto his lap, nuzzled her neck, and nipped at her earlobes. "My love, I have hungered for you all evening. I could hardly wait until everyone left."

He captured her mouth in a fiery kiss and breathlessly spoke of how much he loved and wanted her. Then he picked her up and carried her to their chamber.

Chapter 28

The dinner party for Jane Bennet and Charles Bingley was another success for Mrs. Darcy. Lady Matlock had suggested Elizabeth invite a select few from within the *ton*, and then she made sure that those selected knew that she approved of Jane and Charles. Charles Bingley's introduction to society was relatively new, so the approval of Elizabeth's godmother was important and understood for the favoritism it implied. Jane's status as a gentleman's daughter, coupled with her dowry of 20,000 pounds, made her acceptable to London society.

On the night of the engagement ball for Henry Worthington and Rose Garnon, Bingley filled in his name for all of Jane's dances so no one else would dance with her. Jane was stunning in a gown of light blue silk, and the other men attending the ball were very disappointed to find her card was full.

Elizabeth noted that Bingley would not leave Jane's side, and his eyes showed jealous sparks when other men paid her attention. He was not the only man watching her either. The colonel followed her every move.

"Good Lord, Elizabeth," Darcy whispered, "Richard and Bingley are acting like two dogs in heat. I am sure I never behaved in such a ridiculous manner."

"Indeed you did not, my love." She smirked. "You were very proper and dignified at all times."

"You are teasing me, Elizabeth," he said, feigning a scowl.

Before she could answer, Georgiana and Sarah appeared before them. "Brother, I know you do not want me to dance tonight, but would it not be proper for me to dance with you and Richard? Please say yes, please."

Darcy stood looking at her and then glanced at Elizabeth.

"I do not see what harm it would do, Fitzwilliam. This is a special night for all of us. And she will be going upstairs with Sarah after supper."

"Very well, Georgiana. You may have one dance with me and one with Richard. Does this satisfy?"

Georgiana flung her arms around her brother and squealed, "Oh yes! That makes me very happy. Now go tell Richard that he must dance with me."

When the first dance began, Mr. Worthington and Miss Garnon led off, with Darcy and Elizabeth following them to the dance floor. Bingley and Jane soon followed, while the colonel looked very unhappy.

"I hope Richard behaves himself tonight. I do not want anyone ruining this evening for my uncle and Rose."

"I will alert Andrew, and we will keep an eye on him, but I do not think you have cause to worry. His parents are here, and he would not embarrass them before this assembly."

Darcy was correct, and there were no problems. When the ball was over, Henry Worthington and Rose Garnon's faces glowed with happiness. The ball was a great success, and attendance had been excellent. Mr. Worthington was highly respected, and Mr. Garnon was extremely wealthy — both good ingredients likely to sway the argument for acceptance.

In addition to that, Lord and Lady Matlock as well as the Darcys had accepted Rose Garnon into their elite social circle. As Mrs. Henry Worthington, Miss Garnon would unquestionably be accepted by the *ton*.

During the ball, Louisa Hurst had taken the opportunity to talk to Elizabeth and Darcy about Miss Bingley. "I do not believe I have said how sorry I am about the way my sister behaved at Netherfield. She is unhappy in Scotland, but I am convinced she would be unhappy regardless of her living accommodations." Mrs. Hurst sighed. "I do love my sister, but I cannot approve of her behavior. She makes herself unhappy, and she will not listen to reason."

The Worthington-Garnon wedding was the social event of the year, thanks to the Darcys and Lady Matlock. Andrew was chosen as his uncle's witness, and Rose chose a friend she had known since childhood.

The wedding breakfast was hosted by Mrs. Garnon with Elizabeth's help, and it was held at Matlock Mansion. To no one's surprise, the couple left early, giving the excuse that they had to catch a ship for their honeymoon trip to Italy.

The day after the Worthingtons' wedding, Elizabeth awoke wrapped in the arms of her husband. Feeling content, she snuggled closer to him. "Are you awake, my love?" she whispered in his ear.

"Hmmm, a little, but I am not yet ready to leave our bed. I cannot get enough of my wife," he said in a husky voice, as his hands caressed her body.

Suddenly, Elizabeth felt as though she was going to be ill, and she struggled to escape her husband's arms. "Let me go, Fitzwilliam!" she pleaded, as she pushed against his chest.

Confused, Darcy let go of her, and she hurried to the chamber pot and emptied her stomach. Sinking to the floor, she felt herself covered in a cold sweat and was certain the room was spinning.

After her retching had past, he wiped her face with a damp cloth and carried her back to bed. He grabbed his robe and rang for Sarah, then covered Elizabeth with a blanket.

As soon as Sarah appeared, Darcy relayed what had happened and drew her toward the bed. "We must send for the doctor immediately!" he cried in a panic.

"Master, calm yourself, and let me speak with my mistress first." Sarah bent down and whispered into Elizabeth's ear, and Elizabeth answered her, also in a whisper.

"Please, Mr. Darcy, bring me another damp cloth. I will attend to my mistress."

"Sarah, should we not send for a doctor? Elizabeth is very ill."

"She will be well, sir. Please dress while I attend to her. You are only in the way."

Darcy exhaled, trying to calm himself. He was not happy to have his concerns dismissed, but he left as Sarah had requested, trusting her to alert him if all was not well.

Sarah helped Elizabeth rinse her mouth and get back into bed before she rang for a maid and requested that a tray with weak tea and dry toast be sent to Mrs. Darcy's chamber.

Darcy knocked lightly on the door and stepped back inside, hurrying to his wife. "My love," he said, as he put his hand on her forehead, "are you still unwell?"

Elizabeth assured him that she felt well enough to dress. "Oh, no, lovey," Sarah protested. "You must stay in bed until we are sure your stomach is settled."

As she spoke, the tray appeared, and Darcy took it from the servant and placed it on a table by the bed.

After pouring her a cup of tea, he reached for the toast, but only stared at it. "Sarah, there is nothing on this toast."

Sarah laughed as she took it from his hands and handed it to Elizabeth. Both women glanced at each other with smug looks on their faces.

"What? What is going on?" Darcy demanded.

"I will leave now and let my mistress speak with you." Sarah gave another laugh as she left the room.

Darcy took the cup and toast out of Elizabeth's hands and laid them on the tray. He stood by the bed with his hands on his hips, his concern now tinged with irritation.

"Tell me what is going on this minute, or I shall send for the doctor."

She held out her arms to him and when he sat down on the bed, she pulled him close to her and spoke softly. "It is far too soon to be certain, and I want you to promise me that you will not be disappointed if it turns out Sarah is wrong."

"Elizabeth, are you trying to drive me mad?" he groaned. "You have me very worried."

"Sarah thinks we might be expecting the next heir to Pemberley, my love."

Darcy sat up straight and looked at her, his mouth moving but with no sound coming out. Finally, he licked his dry lips and stammered, "A b-b-baby? We are h-h-having a son?"

"Or a daughter!"

"No, no," he exclaimed. "Remember? Darcy men have sons first and then daughters. This one will be a son." He ran his hands through his hair, a huge grin covering his face. "Oh, Elizabeth, I am so happy! I cannot even speak it in words. Thank you, my dearest, most wonderful wife!" He pulled her close and covered her face with kisses.

"I am the most blessed man on earth. There is nothing more I could wish for, except that my most beautiful wife be safely delivered and my son be born healthy."

"Do not be too hopeful just yet. I have missed only one of my monthly courses, but Sarah thinks that evidence, along with my being sick, is a fair indication that I am with child. My breasts are tender, which is another sign. But we cannot be certain until the child quickens and, according to Sarah, that could take another three months to happen."

"I am sure now, my love, I am very sure that we are going to have a son," Darcy said, while Elizabeth laughed at the smug grin covering his face.

In the days following, Elizabeth continued to experience sickness in the morning, as well as changes to her breasts. "Oh drat, Sarah," she complained, "my clothes will soon have to be altered, or I will have to buy new ones. My bosom looks like two big melons, and they are so sore that even wearing my clothes hurts them."

Elizabeth wondered if all women became more passionate when carrying a child. She wanted Darcy all the time, and he was more than happy to accommodate her.

She became obsessed with pleasing him, to the point of waking him in the middle of the night. The first time she woke him she whispered, "Surprise!" and laughed. Needless to say, he immensely enjoyed each of her little surprises.

They never went to sleep without first making love, regardless of how tired they were; the act relaxed them. From their wedding night when they first joined and shared their passion, they were as one. A glance spoke volumes. One night after making love, Darcy clung to her and whispered fervently, "You are in my soul, Elizabeth. You are breath to me."

Darcy wanted her with him at all times, so he brought a small desk into his study where Elizabeth could write her letters or go over her household accounts while he worked on business matters. They were happiest when they were alone together.

Chapter 29

The Darcys planned their return to Netherfield on the fifteenth of April. Elizabeth looked forward to being with Jane during that exciting time of her life, but she dreaded being thrown, once again, into Mrs. Bennet's company.

"I shall have to make the best of it and never be alone with her," she sighed to Darcy. Although she understood the importance of their decision, Elizabeth was not happy at being so restricted. She was used to coming and going as she pleased.

Before Jane returned to Longbourn after the Worthingtons' wedding, Elizabeth had asked her to tea. Mrs. Gardiner, also invited, was unable to attend. Elizabeth, Jane, and Georgiana sat chatting about Jane's wedding and her pending return home.

"Jane, I understand that you will make the trip to Hertfordshire with Mr. Bingley and the Hursts."

"Yes, Charles does not wish for me to travel alone by coach."

Elizabeth smiled as she teased Jane. "I would say instead that he does not wish to be without you."

Jane laughed. "Well, he did mention that. He said he was very lonely while I was away in March."

"Lonely is not the word, Jane. He sat inconsolable with those sad, puppy dog eyes, sighing. Fitzwilliam was ready to bar him from the house! He said he could not tolerate hearing another sigh."

Everyone laughed, but then Jane said, "Elizabeth, I am concerned about Miss Bingley."

"Why? Has she contacted you?"

"No, but she writes to Louisa. She still vows to exact revenge against Charles, Mr. Darcy, and you. Do you think she could find the means to carry out her threat?"

"I do not think so, Jane. The two guards that went with her are men that served under Colonel Fitzwilliam. They are trained for combat, and Mr. Bingley is paying them well to keep her in Scotland."

Darcy chose that time to join the ladies. "Miss Bennet, it is good to see you again. I hope your family is well."

"Yes, sir, I thank you."

Elizabeth handed her husband a cup of tea, and they talked another half-hour before Jane Bennet left.

When the family had gathered in the sitting room, Darcy asked, "What do my two favorite girls think of attending the theater on Friday evening? The production is *Much Ado about Nothing*. I understand Bingley is going to invite Miss Bennet and join us. Shall we invite them to a late supper after the play?"

Both ladies agreed that the theater sounded lovely, and Elizabeth said she would discuss the menu with Mrs. Bowers for that night.

Later, in their chambers, Darcy remarked that he was glad the colonel had reported for duty and they would not see him at the theater.

"Richard seems determined to flirt with Miss Bennet whenever they meet. After the fiasco at Netherfield with his sister, Bingley is in no humor to put up with my cousin's tomfoolery. Thank heaven we are married and I do not have to chase other men away from you. Now, everyone knows you are mine, and I would fight any man who dared look at you in an improper manner."

"You do not need to worry, dearest. You have always had my heart."

Darcy pulled Elizabeth to him and kissed her. She slipped her hands under his shirt and ran her nails up and down his back.

He shuddered, as that simple act always aroused him, but he remained in control while he finished undressing her and then discarded the rest of his clothes.

Elizabeth could feel him hard against her stomach, and it sent her desire soaring. He placed his hands on her bottom and lifted her so she could catch him around his hips with her legs.

"How I need you, my beloved!" he moaned, as he carried her to their bed. His legs were trembling as he laid her down and slipped in beside her.

When she was close to fulfillment, Elizabeth slid her mouth down to his shoulder and bit him gently. Losing control, Darcy thrust harder and they reached their release together. Panting, they tried to calm their breathing.

They lay in each other's arms, kissing and speaking softly, until Elizabeth turned her back to him so they could sleep in their favorite position. Nestled in his arms, his warm breath blowing gently on her neck, Elizabeth felt content and deeply loved.

As she was dropping off to sleep, Darcy asked, "Do you think there will come a time when we will not be so eager for each other, my love? I confess I cannot imagine my ardor for you ever cooling."

"Perhaps when I am seventy, and you are eight and seventy?" she teased.

"Mmmm, regardless of our ages, I hope when I die that I will have just finished making love to you."

The last thing Darcy heard before falling to sleep was Elizabeth's soft agreement.

Chapter 30

Sarah, being a great lover of Shakespeare, was invited by Darcy to attend the theater with them. "You can be the chaperone for Mr. Bingley and Miss Bennet," he teased.

Once the play began, Sarah pulled out of her reticule the opera glasses Darcy had bought her for Christmas and settled back to enjoy herself. She loved Mr. Darcy, and she was proud that he did not treat her as an ignorant servant. He was always kind to her, even when he was a child. They were her family, and it was up to her to protect them. In her mind, it was as simple as that.

Their late dinner was a cozy affair until the colonel walked in. "Richard!" Darcy exclaimed, "What are you doing here? I thought you had reported for duty."

"I had, but the general sent me back to town on a mission, and I thought I might stay with you and Elizabeth. I will be here for the next three days."

He looked around the table and spoke to Georgiana; then he spied Jane and Bingley. Looking flustered for a moment for he knew Bingley was unhappy about what had happened between him and Caroline, he soon recovered and went directly to Jane, requesting that a servant place a chair for him next to hers.

Ignoring Bingley, the colonel lifted Jane's hand and brought it to his lips. "Miss Bennet, it is lovely seeing you tonight. You look absolutely stunning as always." He then set about dominating all conversation with her.

Bingley was no longer smiling. He looked at Darcy, but he saw no rescue coming. No one knew what to do or say without causing problems. Elizabeth and Georgiana were upset with Richard, but neither said a word. In fact, no one said anything at all except for the colonel, and he ignored everyone but Jane.

JANE WAS VERY UNCOMFORTABLE WITH her companion's behavior. After all, she was Mr. Bingley's intended. She decided it was up to her to handle the situation, so in a kind but firm voice, Jane addressed Colonel Fitzwilliam.

"Colonel, perhaps you do not know that Mr. Bingley and I are engaged to be married."

Wondering what she was leading up to, Richard answered, "Why, yes, I do remember someone informing me of that."

Smiling, Jane continued. "Then perhaps you will understand when I say I am uncomfortable that you are sitting so close and flirting with me."

The colonel's face turned red, and for a moment, he did not know what to say. Georgiana could not contain herself, and she laughed out loud. "Oh, Richard, if only you could see your face! It is high time someone put you in your place."

Darcy and Elizabeth chuckled and looked at Bingley. He was laughing, and he had Jane's hand in his own.

Colonel Fitzwilliam began sputtering, "Why…why…I was not! Oh, very well, I was flirting! I cannot help myself when I see a pretty lady."

He turned toward Jane and Bingley. "Please forgive me, Miss Bennet. I did not intend to cause offense." He paused and then remarked, "I may as well be truthful. I wanted a reaction out of you, Charles, but I give you my word never to do it again. Will you forgive me?"

Bingley kissed Jane's hand. "Certainly I forgive you, Richard, but make sure you keep your word or I will…I will set Miss Bennet upon you!"

Charles could hardly get that last bit out before he began laughing again. Everyone else, including Richard, laughed with him, and the mood turned lighthearted.

Later, after they were in bed, Darcy and Elizabeth remarked about the incident. "I do not believe Sarah could have done a more effective job, Fitzwilliam. Miss Bennet has more steel in her than I suspected."

"Yes, she surprised me as well." Darcy chuckled. "Her voice was so gentle, yet she certainly put Richard in his place. I think he will leave her alone now."

SATURDAY MORNING CAME, AND MR. Bingley's carriage pulled in front of the Gardiners' house. Jane stood outside with her aunt and uncle, saying their goodbyes as her trunks were loaded.

Mr. and Mrs. Hurst stepped down from the carriage for a moment so they could offer their own greetings to the Gardiners. Jane's aunt and uncle assured her they would arrive at Longbourn several days before her wedding.

"Take care of our dear girl, Mr. Bingley."

"I will, Mrs. Gardiner; do not be concerned."

Jane embraced and kissed her aunt and uncle, and then Bingley helped her into the carriage. As they watched it roll out of sight, Mrs. Gardiner wiped away a tear. She and her husband went back inside their home, already missing their dear Jane and knowing that the next time she returned it would be as Mrs. Charles Bingley.

Chapter 31

At Longbourn, Mrs. Bennet went among her friends and neighbors, acting for all like a happy mother. She bragged to everyone how her Jane was soon to be wed to a rich and handsome man and how the even wealthier Darcys were close friends. What more could a mother want for her daughter!

At home alone, however, she was very different. With Jane, Mrs. Bennet was careful not to let her daughter see her true feelings. Instead, she bedeviled Mr. Bennet at length in his study where Jane could not hear.

"Something must be done about that Mrs. Darcy. You surely see that, do you not, Thomas?"

"No, Fanny, I do not! Please, while Mrs. Darcy is at Netherfield, do not bother her. When you encounter her before the wedding, try to be pleasant. She and her family will return to Derbyshire after the wedding, and you will never have to see her again."

While Jane had been in London attending Mr. Worthington's wedding, Mrs. Bennet decided it would be to her advantage to stop speaking ill of Mrs. Darcy and appear to accept her. She did not want her family to suspect what she had planned.

Mrs. Bennet continued working on Jane's wedding, but she spent her days muttering and mumbling to herself when Mr. Bennet was not around. The servants heard her, however, and they began shaking their heads at her increasingly erratic behavior.

Upon Jane's return home, Mrs. Bennet invited Bingley and the Hursts to supper. "There is no reason you cannot stay. You are tired, and Hill has been cooking all day. She will be disappointed if you do not dine with us."

Mrs. Bennet was so friendly and pleasant that Bingley accepted the invitation. Having ridden outside the carriage on their return to Longbourn, he was anxious to spend time with his betrothed.

Mrs. Hurst, who had grown quite fond of Jane Bennet, was happy she did not have to deal with servants and supper so soon after their return. She was impressed with Mrs. Bennet's calm behavior and was happy to stay for supper. Mr. Hurst did not care where they ate, as long as the food was good and the wine was plentiful. Since Mrs. Bennet was known to set a good table, the gentleman was happy to accept the invitation.

Dinner was relaxed and conversation flowed easily. Mr. Bennet's expression showed that he was surprised and pleased with the events of the evening.

After their guests left, Mrs. Bennet followed Jane to her bedchamber, seemingly eager to talk. They chatted about Jane's activities in London, and she thought how pleasant her mother was being. When Mrs. Bennet left, Jane prepared for bed, feeling as though everything was going to be all right. Her mother had not said one unkind word about her friend.

Mrs. Bennet returned to her chambers where she paced the floor, wringing her hands and muttering to herself. She had to do something about Mrs. Darcy before she left for Derbyshire! But how was she to manage it? She did not want to do anything to ruin Jane's wedding. She needed Mr. Bingley as a son when Mr. Bennet died, otherwise, she would be thrown into poverty. If only her son had not died, he could have taken over Longbourn after Mr. Bennet's death.

A knock at Mrs. Bennet's door filled her with apprehension. Had Mr. Bennet or Jane heard her mutterings and come to censure her? She had to continue to appear to have put her objections about Mrs. Darcy to rest, otherwise, the protection around her would tighten, and Mrs. Bennet's plans would be foiled. She knew her behavior that night had impressed her guests and family, and she could not afford to fail with whoever was at her door.

Mrs. Bennet opened her door, and her husband smiled at her. "Come in, Thomas." She smiled in return.

Mr. Bennet stepped inside, and taking his wife's hands in his, he spoke in a kind voice. "Thank you for an enjoyable evening, Fanny. I stopped by Jane's room just now, and she told me you two had a wonderful talk after our guests left. She is very happy about your changed demeanor."

"Oh, Thomas, while Jane was away, I thought about this sad business, and realized how foolish I have been. Jane's happiness must come first, and if she likes Mrs. Darcy, so be it. I must accept her too."

Mr. Bennet was greatly relieved and kissed his wife on her cheek. "Thank you again, my dear. You have set my mind at ease and made Jane very happy."

After her husband left, Mrs. Bennet sighed with relief. Her plans were working! She had fooled her husband and daughter, now she must fool the Darcys.

THE DARCYS LEFT LONDON ON the fifteenth of April as planned, and this time, Andrew joined them. He had decided to take time away while his uncle was on his honeymoon. It was only for a few weeks, and their steward was capable of handling both estates. He looked forward to spending this time with all the Darcys, especially his sister. They had always been close, and he had missed Elizabeth after she married. The fact that he would be with Georgiana was an added bonus not to be overlooked.

The two men rode their horses, which gave them time to talk. Andrew had the highest regard for Darcy, and he looked forward to speaking with him about their mutual interests.

ON THEIR ARRIVAL AT NETHERFIELD, Bingley met them on the portico. He had delayed going to Longbourn so he could welcome his friends. Inside, Mrs. Hurst greeted them with enthusiasm. She had gone through a great change in attitude since her sister had been banished to Scotland. Life was much more pleasant without Caroline, and Mrs. Hurst found herself telling Bingley, rather guiltily, that she hoped her sister would never return home.

Bingley soon left for Longbourn, and the Darcy party went to their chambers. Elizabeth planned to rest until dinner.

After changing from his traveling clothes, Darcy returned to his wife's chamber, and lay on the bed beside her. "Are you well, my love? You seem unusually tired."

"I am well, dearest. Sarah says it is normal for me to tire easily now that I am with child. I am looking forward to returning to Pemberley, however, where I shall grow fat until the child is born."

Darcy chuckled. "I do not care how fat you become. You will always be beautiful to me, no matter your size."

"I was surprised to hear Mr. Bingley and Mrs. Hurst say that Mrs. Bennet has been so pleasant and friendly since they returned. Perhaps we will not have any problems with her while we are here."

"We can only hope that is so, but I do not want us to let down our guard. I still do not trust her."

As they lay in each other's arms, Darcy kissed and caressed his wife. She had changed into a nightgown, and he found it was hard to resist her.

"Are you too tired for me, my love?"

"Mmm, not at all, Fitzwilliam. I feel very relaxed."

Darcy's excitement grew as he watched her desire for him blaze in her eyes. He was concerned that he would hurt her now that she was carrying their child, so he tried to be gentle. Darcy was pleased that she was even more passionate now that she was with child, and he delighted in her moans of pleasure.

How had he lived before marrying her? Darcy could hardly believe how happy she made him, and he felt pity for men with wives who looked on the marriage bed as their duty. His wife sought his pleasure as much as he sought hers and, as he entered her, his joy and love for his wife soared until he thought he would surely die from happiness.

Chapter 32

*J*ane and Bingley's wedding day dawned bright and beautiful. Elizabeth, Georgiana, and Sarah met Jane and her mother in a room off the vicar's study to help her finish dressing. Sarah had styled Jane's hair beautifully, using fresh flowers and ribbons. Elizabeth had loaned Jane her bonnet, which matched her wedding gown perfectly.

Elizabeth sank down in a chair, feelings of fatigue and nausea overcoming her. The Darcys and Bingleys had dined with the Bennets the previous evening, and she had excused herself and retired for the night as soon as they returned to Netherfield, wanting to be rested for today. However, she had felt ill at breakfast and was unable to eat except for sips of tea and small bites of dry toast. Even that was beginning to trouble her stomach. Sarah watched her mistress, a concerned look on her face.

Mrs. Bennet had tea waiting for them when they arrived. She had put peppermint in it to calm their nerves, and she was especially solicitous of Elizabeth's health. Sarah was suspicious, but since they were all drinking the tea, she allowed Elizabeth to drink a cup.

Although Elizabeth pretended to be well, Sarah knew that her mistress should have stayed in bed. When she had a moment alone with her, Sarah asked, "Are you not feeling any better, lovey?"

Elizabeth replied that she was well, but Sarah did not believe her. "Mr. Darcy and Andrew are concerned for you, and Mr. Darcy has decided to accept Mr. Bingley's offer for you to rest at Netherfield after the wedding. Perhaps a few days in bed will make you better able to withstand the trip to Pemberley."

Tears sprang to Elizabeth's eyes. "Oh, Sarah, all I want is to be home. Everything will be all right once we are back at Pemberley."

It had taken every ounce of strength Elizabeth possessed to remain through the wedding and the celebration afterwards. She was relieved when Jane and Bingley waved goodbye and headed for London, where they would spend their honeymoon. From London, the Bingleys would travel to Pemberley, and Charles and Darcy could look at estates with the hope that one would be suitable for Bingley to purchase.

Although she missed her home, Elizabeth did not argue when Darcy told her they would stay at Netherfield until she felt well enough to travel. They would send the Bingleys a message when they reached Pemberley.

AFTER RESTING ABED FOR TWO days, Elizabeth felt well enough to grow restless with her confinement to the indoors. She longed to walk in the gardens. The day was beautiful, and the fresh air was beckoning her to the outdoors. Andrew and Darcy had taken the opportunity to ride out, and Elizabeth decided a walk was what she needed. If she continued to feel well, they would leave for Pemberley in two days.

Elizabeth was secretly glad that Darcy had gone riding, because she knew he would have objected to her walking alone. She believed there would be no harm so long as she stayed on Netherfield property and did not venture near Longbourn. When she thought about it, Mrs. Bennet no longer seemed to be a danger. Elizabeth had begun to feel more comfortable in her presence.

Georgiana was in the music room practicing on the pianoforte, and Sarah was busy working upstairs. Fearing that Sarah would be displeased and not let her go, Elizabeth decided not to tell anyone where she was going.

She started down one of the many pleasant trails on the Netherfield property. After walking a good distance from the house, she thought she heard footsteps behind her. Certain that someone had discovered her missing and had come looking for her, Elizabeth stopped and turned around to call out to them. "Sarah? Fitzwilliam? Is that you?"

Not hearing or seeing anyone, she resumed walking. Twenty minutes later, she began to tire and decided to turn around and walk back to the house. After a few moments, Elizabeth once again heard a noise behind her. As she started to turn around, there was a searing pain to her head, everything went black, and she fell to the ground.

SARAH HAD BEGUN LOOKING FOR her mistress after finishing her chores, and when she could not find her, she became anxious. It appeared that no one had seen Elizabeth until a stable hand reported that he had seen Mrs. Darcy walking about the garden paths.

"She went toward the pond, but that was some time ago, and I have not seen her since."

Sarah then asked if he knew where Darcy and Andrew could be found, and urged him to ride out immediately and find them.

"Hurry now! Tell Mr. Darcy that his wife is missing, and he must come immediately! If he cannot find Mrs. Darcy on Netherfield property, he must ride to Longbourn at once."

Sarah was feeling more and more desperate. She had searched but could not find Elizabeth on any of the trails, and she did not answer Sarah's frantic calls. Finally, she ran back toward Netherfield with the intention of saddling a horse, when she saw Darcy and Andrew riding toward her.

Running to them, she cried, "Master, Elizabeth left the house without telling me, and now I cannot find her. I am very afraid for her."

Darcy held his hand down for Sarah to take, and pulled her up to ride in front of him. "Do not worry, Sarah, we will find her," he reassured her, but his voice was trembling, and his face was pale as they rode toward Longbourn.

Upon their arrival, they were shown into Mr. Bennet's study, but he had not realized his wife was also missing until he made inquiries of Mrs. Hill.

"We need to make a plan and decide where each of us will look." Then Mr. Bennet voiced aloud his greatest fear. "I believe we should go to the cemetery first, and if they are not there, then we will split up."

Mr. Bennet had his stable hand make ready his horse, and they set off for the cemetery.

When they arrived, they saw a scene that filled them with horror. Elizabeth was bound and gagged, with blood running down her face. Mrs. Bennet had opened the grave of her dead twins. She was on her knees bringing up the tiny casket, which had rotted in many places and threatened to fall apart in her hands.

Mr. Bennet quickly dismounted and ran to her, shouting, "What have you done, Fanny?"

She stood and snarled, her eyes wild with madness. Nearby was the heavy shovel she had used to dig up the grave, and she seized it to use against anyone who would stop her. "I will prove, once and for all, that the demon child is not in this casket. If she is not, then I will know that Mrs. Darcy is that demon, and I will rid the world of her. Do not come near me, Thomas, for you cannot stop me."

In an anguished voice, Andrew cried out for his sister and started to dismount, but Darcy held out his arm to restrain him. He froze where he was, afraid that any movement would endanger his wife. All he could think of was how to rescue Elizabeth safely from the demented Mrs. Bennet.

Sarah slipped from Darcy's horse and hurriedly made her way beside Mr. Bennet. She spoke quietly to him. "Let her open the casket, sir. When she sees two bodies, she will realize how wrong she is."

Mr. Bennet stared at his wife for a moment and then nodded his head. "Very well, Fanny, open the casket, but when you see you were wrong, you must let Mrs. Darcy go." As he spoke, he walked slowly toward her.

"Stay back, Thomas," she hissed. "I know there is only my poor boy in that casket." She reached down and pulled the lid off, and it fell apart in her hands. Looking down, her eyes beheld what little remained of the bodies of the two tiny babes, and she fell to her knees, wailing and beating the ground.

"No!" she screamed. "It cannot be!" Mrs. Bennet began to keen in a way that sent chills through everyone gathered.

Darcy used that moment of distraction to dismount and run to his wife. Taking her in his arms, he made his way quickly back to his horse. He took the gag from Elizabeth's mouth, and he and Andrew quickly untied the ropes from her hands and feet. When she was free, she clung to Darcy, sobbing while he tried to soothe her, whispering words of comfort and holding her tight.

Before anyone could stop her, Mrs. Bennet jumped up and disappeared into the thick woods.

Chapter 33

Sarah ran after Mrs. Bennet and, a moment later, Mr. Bennet followed her. Darcy noticed no one but his wife, and calling to Mr. Hill to go for the doctor, he and Andrew rode to Netherfield with Elizabeth clutched tightly against his chest. When they arrived, Darcy told Andrew to wait downstairs for the doctor while he carried Elizabeth to their chamber, laying her on their bed in her room. He rang for one of the maids and told her to bring hot water for the basin.

Attending to Elizabeth himself, he placed a clean nightgown on her, while she sobbed and trembled. The cut on her forehead was near her hairline, and it was still bleeding. Darcy held a cloth tightly against it to stop the bleeding.

Soon there was a knock on the door, and the physician who attended the people of Meryton rushed into the bedchamber and asked Darcy to ring for the housekeeper so that he could examine his patient. Darcy did as he asked, but Elizabeth clutched his hands, begging him not to leave. The doctor reluctantly gave his consent saying, "Do not get in my way, and do not speak until I am finished."

Elizabeth was given a draught to calm her before the doctor began his examination. The bump on the back of her head that had rendered her unconscious was deemed not to be dangerous. He then cleaned and treated the cut on her forehead.

"This looks worse than it is. Head wounds bleed freely," the doctor informed them.

Elizabeth had a slight concussion and would certainly have a headache. There was bruising, especially at the wrists and ankles, and from the cuts and scratches on her legs, it appeared that she had been dragged through the woods by her arms. Those were cleaned and treated with a salve.

Darcy informed the doctor that they believed Elizabeth was with child, and they wished to be reassured that the babe she carried was not harmed. The doctor replied that since there was no bleeding, he thought she was in no danger of losing it. He ordered her to stay in bed, however, and rest for several days. He stated he would return the next day to see her.

Elizabeth had grown sleepy from the draught the doctor had given her, and Andrew was called to stay with her while Darcy escorted the doctor to the front door.

"Please go to Longbourn and see to the Bennets. If they have found Mrs. Bennet, she will need you." He did not go into detail but requested that he speak with Mr. Bennet when he arrived.

Darcy then returned to their chambers to stay with Elizabeth until Sarah returned. Andrew insisted on staying with his sister as well.

Much later, Sarah returned from Longbourn. After making certain that her mistress's injuries had been dressed properly by the doctor and that she was sleeping soundly, she told those assembled the news that Mrs. Bennet was dead. All were stunned, and Sarah explained what happened.

"She was running, looking back over her shoulder and not watching where she was going. We reached her at the top of a hill, and she turned to run away from us, lost her balance and fell down a steep embankment. Her neck was broken during the fall."

"What of Mr. Bennet?" Darcy asked.

Sarah sat down, leaning her head against the back of the chair. "The doctor is helping Mr. Bennet make arrangements for his wife. We had to procure another casket and rebury the bodies of the children before it became dark."

Andrew went to Sarah and gathered her into his arms. Leaning his lips close to her ear he whispered, "Sarah, did you...?"

Sarah put her fingers against Andrew's lips and whispered back, "My dear, sweet boy, I will tell all after things settle down." Andrew nodded and looked at her. Sarah's eyes were cold as steel, and he wondered if they told him what he needed to know.

Darcy nodded his head, for he guessed what Andrew had asked, and he had seen Sarah's eyes. He suggested they leave as there was nothing further they could do for Elizabeth. He would keep a close watch over his wife that night and would send a message if there was any change in her condition.

After Sarah and Andrew left, Darcy stripped to his shirt and trousers and lay down beside his wife. When he took her in his arms, she whimpered and he kissed her. "All is well, my love; you are safe."

Later, he heard a soft knock at their door. Darcy donned his robe, and upon opening it, saw Mrs. Hurst and Andrew standing in the hall, concerned expressions on their faces.

"I am sorry, but I cannot eat or sleep for worrying about Lizzy. Is she feeling any better?" Andrew asked anxiously.

Darcy stepped outside the room so as not to disturb Elizabeth. "She is asleep and seems to be resting well."

Mr. Hurst appeared and asked him to have a maid stay with Elizabeth while they had a drink in the library. Darcy, who desperately needed a glass of brandy, agreed and rang for a maid.

When the maid arrived, Darcy gave her instructions. "I will be in the library with Mr. and Mrs. Hurst and Mr. Worthington. Please stay with Mrs. Darcy while I am gone. I will not be long. If she should awake, send for me at once." The maid bobbed a curtsey and assured him she would.

In the library, Mr. Hurst poured glasses of brandy for himself, Andrew, and Darcy and a glass of wine for his wife. The Hursts then begged Darcy to tell them what had happened.

"The servants said Mrs. Bennet kidnapped Mrs. Darcy, but that is all we know. What is to be done with Mrs. Bennet?"

Before Darcy could respond, there was light knocking on the door. He opened it and Georgiana came in looking anxious. Hugging her brother, she told him that her maid had said that Elizabeth had been involved in an accident. She wanted to know what had happened and if Elizabeth would be well.

Darcy pulled up a chair next to his and asked her to sit down. Pouring her a glass of wine, he gently shared with her and the Hursts everything that had happened.

Georgiana was shocked and wanted to go to her sister, but Darcy told her that Elizabeth was asleep and asked her to wait until she was awake in the morning before visiting. "I know she will be glad to see you, but let her rest for now. It is what her body needs to heal."

Georgiana glanced at Andrew. He was pale and his hands trembled, but he assured her he would be all right.

In an angry tone of voice, Andrew exclaimed, "It is hard to believe that anyone would treat my sister, who has never harmed anyone in her life, in such a cruel manner! I am not sorry that Mrs. Bennet is dead."

Darcy decided to send for Sarah so she could give them an account of what happened after Mrs. Bennet died. Sarah looked pale when she walked into the library, and Darcy immediately felt guilty for sending for her.

In a tired voice, Sarah began to relate what had happened after they returned to Longbourn. "Mr. Bennet sent an express to Mr. and Mrs. Gardiner as well as to Mr. and Mrs. Bingley. Then he notified Mrs. Bennet's sister, Mrs. Philips. He also had a message delivered to the undertaker, who is now preparing Mrs. Bennet's body for burial. After seeing her sister's body, Mrs. Philips became hysterical, and the doctor was required to give her a draught to calm her nerves. Her husband took her back home.

"I stayed with Mr. Bennet for a good while. He wanted to speak of the events that had changed his wife, and I felt the need to listen to the man as he poured out his heart." Sarah looked at everyone through red-rimmed eyes. "It has been an exhausting day. I told Mr. Bennet that I would return to Longbourn tomorrow, if I am able, and help in any way I can, but my main concern is Elizabeth." Sarah's voice was dull and strained, so Darcy sent her back to her room.

After Sarah left, Darcy suggested that trays be brought to the sitting room adjacent to his chambers, so that Andrew, Georgiana, and he could have their supper there.

Darcy rubbed his hands over his eyes. "I would like to go to bed early, for I believe tomorrow will be another long day. I feel certain the Bingleys will arrive by the afternoon."

After they had eaten, Darcy's valet prepared a hot bath, and he soaked until the water was cold. Putting on his nightshirt and robe, he hurried back to Elizabeth's room and dismissed the maid. He slipped in next to his wife and drew her close. Looking at her precious face, he shuddered to think what might have happened had they not arrived in time.

With his hand lightly caressing Elizabeth's stomach, he lay awake for a long time, wondering what the following days would bring, but soon he, too, succumbed to sleep.

Chapter 34

Elizabeth woke late the next morning enfolded in Darcy's arms, his eyes fixed on her face. Not remembering at first what had happened the previous day, she smiled and caressed his cheek with her hand. "You look very tired, my love. Are you unwell?"

He drew her closer and buried his face in her neck, unable to speak for a few moments. He could only hold her, feel her, smell her scent, and rejoice that she was safe with him.

In a voice husky with emotion, he said, "I should be angry with you for leaving yesterday and not telling anyone where you were going, but I am so thankful that you are well and here with me that I cannot be angry. Promise me from now on that you will always take Sarah or someone else with you when you walk. It is very important for you to abide by my wishes, especially now that you are with child. If I should lose you, dearest, I would not wish to live. Life would have no meaning for me without you."

Suddenly, memories of the preceding day came flooding back to Elizabeth, and she began to cry and tremble. She clung to her husband, and he held her tightly, one hand caressing her hair. In a soft voice, he murmured words of love and comfort, assuring her that she was safe.

"I promise, my love, and I am so sorry to have worried you. I truly believed it would be safe for me as long as I stayed on Netherfield property. Mrs. Bennet had been so solicitous that I no longer thought I was in danger from her. Do you know what became of her?"

"Sarah said Mrs. Bennet fell from a precipice and broke her neck. All that matters is that she is dead and cannot harm you ever again."

"I hesitate to ask, but did Sarah—"

"I do not know with certainty, Elizabeth. Sarah said Mrs. Bennet was enraged and distracted and did not watch where she stepped. She fell down a steep embankment and broke her neck. Mr. Bennet witnessed her fall."

Elizabeth sighed. "Poor Jane! Poor Mr. Bennet — for he must have once loved her. Has anyone notified the Bingleys?"

"Mr. Bennet sent them an express last night, and we expect them by the afternoon."

"I must be with Jane to comfort her after she arrives. Let us go to Longbourn when she comes and see if we can be of any help to them."

"Elizabeth, the doctor ordered you to stay in bed — at least for a few days. If I had my way, we would leave for Pemberley this very morning. I know you would be safe there."

"I am safe here now, Fitzwilliam. Those poor babies! Mrs. Bennet was such a horrible woman, but I cannot help but feel some pity for her. Her life must have been miserable, haunted by the delusions that plagued her."

Elizabeth shuddered and tears welled up in her eyes. "I am very glad my mother was Margaret Worthington."

Elizabeth's voice was trembling, and her hands clenched into fists as her agitation rose.

Darcy sought to calm her. "I was only eight at the time, but I remember when you were born and how happy my mother was that your parents had twin babes. I held you when you were but a few days old."

Elizabeth looked into the eyes of the only man she had ever loved. "Make love to me husband, please. I need your love to wipe away the memory of that horrible woman."

Darcy was concerned about making love to her so soon after her ordeal. "Dearest, perhaps it would be best if I do not." With a smile, he added, "At least not today. We must do nothing to harm you or the babe."

Her disappointment was evident in her voice. "Very well."

Elizabeth sounded so forlorn that Darcy embraced her tighter, placing soft kisses to her face and neck. Anxiety for his wife and their babe would not allow him to make love to her, but they could still hold and kiss each other.

Later, Darcy called for a tray to be brought to their chamber, and they broke their fast. Again, Elizabeth began speaking of going to Longbourn so she could be with Jane, but Darcy would not hear of it.

"The doctor insists that you follow his instructions," he stated firmly.

"But Fitzwilliam, I am feeling well now. It would not hurt me to be there when Jane arrives."

His face tightened, but he tried to keep his voice calm. "Elizabeth, do not be foolish! That vile woman struck you on your head and then dragged you through the woods. We cannot know yet whether the ordeal was too much for your body. I insist you stay in bed until the doctor examines you again and reassures us that all is well with you and our child."

Elizabeth made a move to leave her bed, a stubborn look on her face. "I know my body better than you, Fitzwilliam, and I say I am well enough to go to Longbourn. Jane will have need of me."

This was too much for Darcy! All the worry and tension he had been restraining overwhelmed him, and he yelled in a voice he had never before used with her.

"Your stubbornness almost killed you yesterday! Now you seem determined to harm our child! You will not leave this house until the doctor releases you! I cannot believe you would insist on taking an unnecessary chance!"

She was startled at his harsh tone and, when Elizabeth looked at him, his body was rigid and his hands were in tight fists. Never had her husband spoken or looked at her in that manner, and she was unable to speak. Instead, she broke into tears and began sobbing.

Darcy rushed to her and enfolded her in his arms, his anger forgotten. "My love, please forgive me for speaking so harshly to you. We are both under great pressure, and our nerves are raw. I will send Sarah to Longbourn and have her bring Jane back. Is that agreeable with you?"

She nodded her head, and he rang for Sarah. When she came into the room, he told her what they had decided and asked for her help in persuading Jane to come to Netherfield.

Sarah agreed and, shortly after, Darcy called for his carriage and Sarah made the trip to Longbourn. She encountered Mr. Bennet sitting on a bench at the side of his house. Going to him, Sarah put her hand on his shoulder and asked, "Have you heard from the Bingleys, sir? My master wishes me to bring Mrs. Bingley to Netherfield. Mrs. Darcy is anxious to see and speak with her."

Mr. Bennet stood, his face pale and his body slumping. "Thank you, Sarah. They have not arrived yet but, when they do, it would be best if Jane does not remain here at Longbourn. She should be with her friend although I fear she will believe that Mrs. Darcy is angry with her."

"No, Mr. Bennet. Neither Mr. Darcy nor my mistress is angry with you or Mrs. Bingley. They are only concerned for your well being."

At that moment, they heard the sound of a carriage and saw that the Bingleys had arrived. Jane went immediately to her father and clung to him.

"What happened, Papa?" Jane cried.

In a dull voice, Mr. Bennet told Jane what her mother had done and, consequently, how she had died.

"When may I see my mother?"

"Mr. Ross is attending her and must not be disturbed. You will be able to see her this evening. Sarah is here to take you to Mrs. Darcy. She is very concerned and anxious to see you."

"Oh, Papa, how she must hate us for what my mother did to her! I am so ashamed. How will I face her?"

Sarah put her arms around Jane. "No, my mistress does not hate you. She wishes to be with you, as she is concerned for you. She wanted to be here when you arrived, but Mr. Darcy insisted she heed the doctor's advice and stay in bed."

"As she should!" Turning to her husband, Jane asked, "Charles, will you come with me? It will not take long." Bingley nodded.

"Would you be so kind as to tell my mistress that I have stayed to help Mrs. Hill prepare for visits from family and friends, but I will return to her this evening?"

DARCY WAS WAITING OUTSIDE WHEN the Bingleys arrived, but Jane asked him if there was a room where she could speak with her husband privately before being taken to Elizabeth.

"Of course. No one is using the library, so you and Charles will have privacy there."

When they were alone, Bingley saw Jane was having difficulty speaking, so he held her in his arms and encouraged her. Jane could not bear to look at her husband as she told him that she released him from their marriage. She took off her wedding ring and placed it into his hand.

Bingley's face twisted in despair. "No, Jane! You cannot blame yourself for what your mother did! She was ill and could not help herself. You married me knowing about Caroline, and this is no different. I will not allow you to release me! I love you too much to lose you.

"Here, give me your hand so I can put this ring back on your finger, just as I did the day we were married. Remember that day, Jane? We promised to remain together for better or worse. We made that vow to each other before God. How can you ask me to forsake you now? Have I done anything to make you doubt my love for you?"

Charles held her hand as he slipped the ring onto her finger, and Jane began to sob and cling to him. He lifted her onto his lap, gently rubbing circles on her back, and he held her thus until her tears were spent. "Now, that is better. We will get through this together, my sweet angel."

JANE WAS STILL ANXIOUS ABOUT meeting with her friend, even though Sarah had assured her that Elizabeth was not angry. When she was shown into her chamber, Elizabeth smiled and held out her arms.

Jane rushed to her. "I am so sorry, Elizabeth. I hope my mother did not harm you or your child." Elizabeth took Jane into her arms and, once again, the older girl cried bitter tears of shame and sorrow.

At last Jane's tears subsided, and when she lifted her head, her expression was one of anguish as she looked into Elizabeth's eyes. "I am so sorry," she said again. "I hope someday you will be able to forgive my mother."

"My dearest friend, I have already forgiven her. She was not aware of what she was doing. Let us now concentrate on you and your father. You have difficult days ahead, and I want to be there to comfort you in any way I can."

"I feel so ashamed of my mother's actions. I do not believe I can bear to speak with the many people that I know will come. The only ones I wish to see are my Aunt and Uncle Gardiner."

"Stay here with me. Mr. Bingley can bring the Gardiners and your father back with him. It would not do for him to be alone tonight."

At that moment, there was a knock on the door. Darcy opened it to the doctor. Bingley and Darcy glanced at each other and then excused themselves. "We shall be in the library if you should need us," Darcy said to the doctor.

After the men left, the doctor examined Elizabeth and spoke with both ladies, assuring them and himself that they were both well. He left a draught for each, in case they had trouble sleeping that night and then left to speak with their husbands, knowing they were anxiously waiting downstairs.

THE GARDINERS ARRIVED EARLY THAT evening, having left their children in the care of their household staff in London. They were informed that Jane was at Netherfield, so Mrs. Gardiner made the short trip in order to see her niece. After Mrs. Gardiner assured herself that Jane was well, she went straight to Elizabeth, holding her arms out to her and inviting her into a motherly embrace.

Elizabeth could feel tears coming, and she laid her head on Mrs. Gardiner's shoulder while she cried. Finally, she began to relate the events of the previous day to the older woman.

"My dear Elizabeth, what a horrible experience!" Mrs. Gardiner exclaimed. "I knew my sister was obsessed, but I truly did not believe she would harm you. I left Mr. Gardiner at Longbourn to be with Mr. Bennet, and I will remain with you and Jane."

Mrs. Gardiner looked up at the sound of footsteps and saw Mr. Darcy standing in the doorway, looking very tired and anxious. "Make sure Elizabeth sleeps well tonight, Mr. Darcy. Tomorrow will be a trying day for us all, and she will need her rest." Saying goodnight to the Darcys, she left and returned to her niece.

A DINNER TRAY WAS REQUESTED and sent to the Darcy's chambers, and the couple dined in their bedroom.

Sarah had returned to Netherfield with Mr. Bennet and Mr. Gardiner and, while they had dinner, she made her way to Elizabeth's chamber. When she entered the room, Darcy asked her to have a bath prepared for his wife.

"Master, while the tub is being filled, I will be in the kitchen assisting Cook."

When the bath had been prepared, Darcy undressed Elizabeth and slowly lifted her into the tub, then undressing himself, slipped in behind her. Very gently, he bathed her, and then while she leaned against his chest, he bathed himself.

Stepping out of the tub, he dried them both, and after putting on their nightclothes, he rang for Sarah. She was soon there with their tea. After Sarah sat the tray down, she made sure the proper amount of the sleeping draught was put into her Elizabeth's tea. "Drink this now, lovey, and then get some rest." Turning to Darcy, she bade him goodnight and left the room.

Shortly after Sarah left, there was a knock on the door, and when Darcy answered it, Andrew and Georgiana stood there wanting to know about their sister.

"Come in," Elizabeth called.

They hurried to her bedside and Georgiana embraced her. Elizabeth smiled and told them that she was feeling a bit better and was only a little tired. "I shall be completely well by tomorrow."

Andrew embraced his sister. "Do not try too much too soon, Sister. You must take good care of yourself and my nephew."

"Oh, you men!" Elizabeth laughed softly. "All you can think of are boy babes. Would you not like a niece? A cute little girl that will wrap you around her finger?"

"Of course, next year, but this year I shall have a nephew." They all laughed, and Georgiana and Andrew said goodnight and took their leave.

When they were alone, Elizabeth declared she could drink no more tea. "All I want is sleep, my love. Hold me."

"Very well, dearest." He removed their robes and crawled into bed next to his wife. They fell into a deep sleep with their arms and legs entwined.

Chapter 35

The funeral was at eleven o'clock the following morning, and at the last minute, Mr. Hurst decided to attend with the other men.

While the gentlemen attended the funeral, the ladies stayed with Jane so she would not be alone. Darcy told Elizabeth afterwards that the church was full. Mr. Hurst, Darcy, and Andrew sat in the back, but Bingley and Mr. Gardiner sat up front with Mr. Bennet.

Elizabeth could not help but weep when Darcy told her of the vicar's message about forgiveness, but her tears were primarily for Jane. She remembered her own deep sorrow when her parents were killed, but how much worse it must be for Jane.

At *least*, Elizabeth thought, *my memories of my parents are happy ones.*

Mrs. Bennet was buried next to her twins, and the graveside service was mercifully short. Those who attended the funeral returned to Netherfield where a meal was provided. Everyone asked about Elizabeth and Jane, but neither lady appeared.

ON THE MORNING OF THE funeral, Darcy and Elizabeth had talked about inviting the Bingleys and Mr. Bennet to travel with them to Pemberley. They thought it might help them to be away from Longbourn and the reminders of what had happened. They had also spoken with Bingley at breakfast, and he agreed.

Consequently, Darcy requested a meeting with Mr. Bennet after the funeral, and he issued the invitation.

"Leave Longbourn in your steward's hands and stay with us as long as you like. We have no plans to return to town at this time. Elizabeth is with child, and we wish the babe to be born at Pemberley. Mr. and Mrs. Bingley have agreed to come, and I will also invite Mr. and Mrs. Hurst to go with us. With people there who care for you, perhaps it will be easier for you and Jane to heal."

Mr. Bennet was silent for a long time, and Darcy did not try to interrupt his thoughts. At last he spoke. "Thank you, Mr. Darcy. I see the wisdom of your words and accept your kind invitation. When do you plan to leave?"

"We leave in a week, sir. Will that give you sufficient time to settle your affairs here and have your staff pack for you?"

"Yes, that should be plenty of time. It will be best for Jane and me to be away from here."

Darcy left and went in search of Elizabeth and Bingley to give them the news.

A WEEK LATER, THREE CARRIAGES pulled away from Longbourn. Darcy, Elizabeth, Georgiana, and Mr. Bennet were in one. The Hursts and the Bingleys were in another, while the third carriage carried Sarah, Georgiana's maid, Heather, Darcy's valet, Williamson, and Mr. Bingley's valet, Jenkins. A maid for Jane and a valet for Mr. Bennet would be provided from the Pemberley staff. Darcy's horse was tied to the last carriage. Andrew had returned to Rosehaven earlier in the week, but he would be at Pemberley for Christmas.

Elizabeth and Darcy had agreed not to hurry their journey. Everyone was tired, and the carriages were comfortable, so they took their time, stopping each night at the best inns for a good night's rest. Darcy had sent an express message to Mrs. Reynolds so that rooms would be ready for their guests in the family wing.

WHEN THEY ARRIVED AT PEMBERLEY, Mr. and Mrs. Reynolds met everyone on the front steps of the great house, and the housekeeper announced that rooms were ready for them all. Trays of tea and other refreshments would be sent up to the guests as soon as they desired. To say that everyone was grateful for the opportunity to be pampered would be an understatement. It was with sighs of relief that each person went to change and rest from the journey.

Darcy and Elizabeth were more than happy to be home and to know that they would not have to leave again for quite some time. Mrs. Reynolds had been busy preparing the nursery, and the Darcys inspected it. Elizabeth leaned against her husband with a contented smile.

"This beautiful nursery makes me very anxious to see our child, my love."

Darcy kissed her forehead and grinned. "It is a fine room for our son."

"Or daughter," Elizabeth countered.

They both laughed and went back to their separate chambers. As soon as she entered, she called for Sarah. "When you bring up our tray, please put it in my room. Fitzwilliam will have tea with me."

Sarah grinned. "And after that, a quick nap, lovey?"

Elizabeth laughed. "You are far too impertinent, Miss Sarah. Now be gone! I wish to spend some time alone with my handsome husband."

Sarah left and had just returned with their tray when Darcy tapped on the connecting door. He was wearing a new maroon, silk robe, and Sarah called out in a sing-song voice when he stepped into the room.

"Oh, mistress, here is that handsome husband of yours, and I think he also desires a little nap."

Darcy laughed and pointed to the door. "Out Sarah, and do not disturb us until it is time to dress for dinner."

They sat in front of the fireplace and enjoyed their tea. After they were finished, Darcy stood and drew Elizabeth to him, untying her robe and letting it slip to the floor.

"I feel at peace for the first time in ages, my love. Just think, we can sleep in our own bed tonight." He nuzzled her neck and planted warm, moist kisses on it. With a mischievous grin, she reached down and stroked him lightly, causing him to startle.

"And what is my little spitfire up to now?"

"If you do not know, Husband, I am not going to tell you." She withdrew from him and ran clumsily to the other side of the bed, laughing at him.

"Oh, no, you little minx! Come to me," and he crooked his finger at her, beckoning.

"If you want me, you will have to catch me," she laughed as she ran to his bedchamber. He chased her, but she squealed and ducked behind a chair.

Every time he reached for her, she managed to run away from him. Finally, he caught her and, laughing, picked her up in his arms, taking her to his bed where he laid her down. Still laughing, she crawled away from him, but he was too quick for her. Turning her over on her back, he pinned her to the bed with his arms and legs. Leaning down, he put his mouth on her stomach and gently blew on it.

"Fitzwilliam, that tickles!" she cried, as she erupted with more laughter. He straddled his wife and then leaned down and kissed her, teasing her mouth with his tongue.

"I love to watch you run," he whispered. "Your breasts bounce and sway, and I want to take them in my mouth and eat them up."

"Well?" She smirked and raised her eyebrow. "Are you hungry, my love," she teased.

"Mmm, hmm," was all the sound he could make as he suckled first one and then the other breast. "Elizabeth," he cried, when she began stroking him. Their hands and mouths explored each other's bodies eagerly, and when he knelt between her legs and thrust deeply, Elizabeth's body exploded in release. He thrust once more and spilled his seed inside her.

"If you were not already with child, I believe we would have just made one," he panted, trying to catch his breath. "I love you, my sweet Elizabeth," he whispered as he lay beside her and wrapped his arms and legs around her.

Chapter 36

Everyone was rested and feeling refreshed at dinner, so conversation was lively. Bingley and Jane, however, spent more time speaking with each other in lowered tones than with anyone else.

After dinner, while the men lingered over brandy and cigars, the four ladies sat in the music room. Louisa Hurst was persuaded to play first, but soon Elizabeth and Georgiana were playing duets while Jane and Louisa looked through sheets of music.

"Do you play, Jane?" Georgiana inquired.

"Only a very little, but I do enjoy singing."

Jane had a beautiful soprano voice, and her singing enticed the men to the music room. Elizabeth was a strong alto, and the two women sang several duets, accompanied by Georgiana on the pianoforte. After much urging, the women convinced the men to sing with them.

"That was very enjoyable, and I am surprised we sounded as well as we did," Bingley bragged afterwards. "We need to do this more often."

"Only if the knowledge that I sing never leaves this room," Darcy warned. "I have kept this a secret for many years, and I want it to remain that way."

"What is wrong, Darcy? Afraid you will have to sing in concert?"

"No teasing from you, Bingley!"

They all laughed at the scowl that appeared on Darcy's face, and soon everyone but Mr. Bennet headed for bed.

"I believe I will take advantage of your excellent library, Mr. Darcy, and read for awhile."

"Of course, sir. It is there for your enjoyment. Please use it as you would your own."

AN HOUR OR SO LATER, Mr. Bennet looked up from his book, thinking how glad he was to be away from Longbourn. He was almost, but not quite, ashamed to admit how little he missed his wife. The years since his wife descended into madness had been a living hell for him, and because of her, he was doomed to live a lie. His Elizabeth would never know him as her father or Jane as her sister. He could not tell her how much he loved her or how proud he was of the woman she had become. He would never call Darcy his son, nor could he ever be a grandfather to the Darcy children.

There was so much he had missed, so much he would continue to miss, but Elizabeth was confident, witty, and most importantly, alive.

Mr. Bennet leaned his head back, his mind taking him back to that fateful day — Fanny's last day on earth. His wife had stood on the edge of that embankment, and he had heard Sarah say, "I warned you what would happen if you harmed my mistress, Mrs. Bennet, and I never make empty threats."

Fanny had snarled at her. "I will kill that demon the next time I have her in my hands. You cannot always protect her. I will find an opportunity."

Mr. Bennet shivered as he remembered Sarah's response. She laughed, slowly walked forward, and calmly said, "Goodbye, Mrs. Bennet. May you rest in hell!"

Then, to his surprise, Sarah suddenly stopped and turned away, a look of intense pain covering her face. "No, I cannot break my vow to Mr. Worthington. I promised him I would never kill another human except as a last resort."

What happened next was even more of a surprise to Mr. Bennet. He had expected to see his wife run away but, instead, she lost her footing and with a horrific scream, her arms flailing wildly, she tumbled down the steep precipice.

Sarah watched her fall, and when she turned to Mr. Bennet, she said in a voice so cold it had sent shivers down his spine, "Now Elizabeth is safe." He nodded his head, and together they walked back to Longbourn.

He was numb. Mr. Bennet could not mourn or hate his wife. She had killed any feelings for her the night he laid Elizabeth in Jonathan Worthington's arms and watched as she rode out of his life forever.

There was only that long-endured void left by the loss of Elizabeth, and he would continue to live with it just as he promised Jonathan. But at least, he now had the joy of being able to spend this time with her, and by God, he was going to enjoy every moment of it.

WEEKS AND THEN MONTHS PASSED by peacefully, and slowly, Jane Bingley healed. More and more often, a smile was seen on her face and her laughter was heard, especially when the women were horseback riding — everyone but Elizabeth. Darcy had declared she was not to ride, and she did not argue with him.

The friends took long walks, had picnics, and made a trip to Rosehaven where Andrew entertained them as though they were royalty. Shopping trips were made to Lambton by the women, and Darcy arranged for tours of surrounding estates. Pemberley was working its magic on them all.

Henry and Rose Worthington were the Darcys' frequent visitors. They had just learned that they were expecting their first child as well, and both couples were excited about becoming parents.

Andrew visited as often as he could, and Elizabeth watched as her brother grew taller and more handsome. She did not miss the glances that Andrew and Georgiana sent each other when they thought no one was watching. Elizabeth could not have been more pleased with the prospect that someday her brother and Georgiana would be married.

They celebrated Georgiana's sixteenth birthday, and Andrew kept his promise to Darcy, but he and Georgiana knew, without any words spoken, that they were destined to be together one day.

Out of respect, Andrew showed the birthday gift of a locket he had bought Georgiana to Darcy first, holding his breath that his brother would not look inside. He had had a very small picture of himself painted to fit in one side, and in the other, he put a lock of his hair. He was given approval to offer the gift without Darcy attempting to open it. Wisely, Georgiana did not open it either until she was alone in her room. It became her favorite piece of jewelry, and she wore it every day of her life.

As December approached, they all looked forward to Christmas at Pemberley. Lord and Lady Matlock, Richard, Lady Catherine, and the Garnons were expected the week before the holiday. Sadly, Anne de Bourgh had passed away in her sleep during the early part of September. Her death had left Lady Catherine quite despondent, and everyone hoped being around family would help ease her pain at losing her only child.

Elizabeth had been granted permission by her doctor to travel to Rosings during that sad time with the understanding that they would make frequent stops to allow her to stretch her legs. Upon arrival, Elizabeth went to Lady Catherine and took her in her arms. To the surprise of everyone there, Lady Catherine clung to Elizabeth and cried copious tears for the loss of her child.

After that experience, she would allow only Elizabeth to sit with her in her bedchamber before she went to sleep at night. The two women became very close, and Lady Catherine began to look forward to the birth of the Darcys' baby.

DARCY HAD INVITED THE GARDINERS and their children to join them for Christmas. He had received a letter saying they would arrive the twenty-first of December and would stay until the second of January.

The Bingleys and the Hursts made another trip to Lambton to buy gifts to send to Caroline, their aunt and uncle, and even the two guards and Caroline's companion. Their uncle was not wealthy, yet he stubbornly refused to accept money gifts, so the Bingleys included food items, such as sugar, flour, meal, rice, beans, nuts and candy, which he would accept. The packages were shipped in time to arrive by Christmas.

Darcy, Bingley, and Andrew went with some of the ladies to cut fir limbs and boxwood. Mistletoe and holly with red berries were gathered and used in decorating Pemberley.

Everyone set about making wreaths to hang on the doors and windows and over the fireplaces. Garland was draped across the mantles, and red berries and red bows decorated the wreaths and garland. Flowers from the greenhouse graced the breakfast and dining room tables.

Mistletoe hung in each doorway, and colorful candles were placed near the table where the gifts were laid. They would be lit on Christmas Eve and Christmas morning.

Elizabeth felt content, and she walked around Pemberley with a glow on her face, rubbing her tummy. At night, Darcy moved his hands over her stomach and talked to his son, sometimes crooning to him. He laughed with joy when the baby kicked at his touch.

"He is saying hello to his papa," a very proud Darcy declared to his amused wife.

The night before Boxing Day, Elizabeth directed the others to fill large boxes with clothing, blankets, toys, and sweets, along with other food items for all the tenants. Georgiana, Jane, Louisa, and Bingley spent a full day delivering them and came back with well wishes for the Darcys and the new babe.

Mr. Hurst was content to sit in a comfortable chair drinking wine, not moving except to go back and forth between his chair and the decanter.

ALTHOUGH EVERYONE WAS OCCUPIED WITH Christmas plans, Jane and Charles were anxious to buy an estate close to Pemberley. Bingley and Darcy had been in touch with various agents and made numerous trips to look at estates. Each had aspects that recommended its purchase.

One evening, Jane and Bingley spoke with Mr. Bennet about turning Long-bourn over to his cousin, William Collins, and coming to live with them. They would give him a suite of rooms with his own library.

He promised to think about their generous offer, knowing at once that he would live with them. There was nothing left for him at Longbourn — a few friends, perhaps, but he had never needed friends, only his books and his two daughters, although one would never acknowledge him as her father. He would be happy with his new life, especially if it afforded him the opportunity to see Elizabeth and his grandchildren, but he would wait to accept Jane and Bingley's invitation until they found their estate.

Chapter 37

The previous year had been especially trying, and Darcy now wished for a peaceful and joyous Christmas. He wanted gifts, good cheer, and friends and family to prevail over Pemberley. So it was that the house was bursting with all that Darcy wanted by Christmas Eve.

Lively conversation with laughter blended with the sound of the Gardiner children running throughout the house, which put everyone, including the staff, in a festive mood. They all agreed that children had been missed at Pemberley for too long. A generous bonus for the servants helped further their good mood.

Elizabeth and Darcy had exchanged their gifts in the privacy of their chambers. She presented him with a new riding crop and boots. His gift to her was a single strand of the most beautiful pearls she had ever seen. It had been securely fastened in a square box against purple fabric and shaped into a heart. Her excited squeals of delight and the kisses she placed all over Darcy's face left no doubt how much she loved her gift.

Family gifts were exchanged on Christmas Eve, but the next day was saved especially for the children. There was much noise and excitement that morning when the Gardiner children ran downstairs to see what Father Christmas had left for them.

Elizabeth was so large with child that she could barely walk down the stairs — and then only with Darcy's help. Once downstairs, she sank into a comfortable chair and enjoyed watching the children play with their gifts. She smiled as she thought of their next Christmas, imagining her own child playing happily at her feet.

Darcy interrupted her thoughts by proclaiming, "Come, little mother, it is time for both of you to eat." Laughing, he and Andrew pulled Elizabeth up so she could go into the dining room to break her fast.

"When is little Darcy supposed to arrive, Mrs. Darcy?" asked Bingley.

"Please, I think it is time you called me Elizabeth, and I will call you Charles," she said. "And when this little one will arrive is known only to him. The doctor said he is late, which is not uncommon with a first baby. I wish he would hurry and put in his appearance, so that I might walk on my own again." She laughed.

AFTER BREAKFAST, THEY ALL ADJOURNED to the drawing room where they witnessed an amazing sight. Lady Catherine was on the floor playing with Amanda Gardiner while her parents looked on, pleased with the attention Darcy's aunt was giving their daughter.

The Fitzwilliams and the Darcys looked at each other, their mouths agape. Lady Catherine laughed at the looks on their faces.

"Well, what is the good of Christmas if one cannot play with dolls and tea sets? Do you think I am too old for this?"

While they denied that she was too old, they still stole glances at her all morning as she went from playing house to playing war with the boys and their toy soldiers.

"Elizabeth, I now believe in miracles," Darcy whispered to his wife.

"Indeed," she replied, unable to utter another word.

The colonel pulled Darcy into the library, shaking his head as he exclaimed, "The old biddy seems almost human, does she not? I did not think I would ever see our aunt crawling around on the floor, playing like a child. And did you hear her laugh? I did not think she knew how."

Darcy chuckled and agreed it was an unusual but most welcomed sight.

ONCE CHRISTMAS DINNER WAS OVER, Darcy helped his wife upstairs to bed. She had complained of a backache since breakfast and felt the need to lie down.

"Should I send for the doctor and midwife, my love?"

"Perhaps you should. The pains have moved to my stomach now."

Darcy rang for Sarah, and they helped Elizabeth to bed. Darcy then rushed downstairs to send messages to Dr. Avery and the midwife, Mrs. Hampton. He alerted Mrs. Reynolds and their guests that the babe seemed to be on its way.

As Darcy realized he was about to become a father, he became very unsettled. He paced the room distractedly, running his hands through his hair, before rushing back upstairs to his wife. His guests looked at each other in amusement.

As soon as he entered his wife's room, Darcy was at her side, squeezing her hands. "Are you in much pain, dearest? What can I do to help? Here, do you need another pillow? Sarah, bring Elizabeth another pillow! What about water or some tea? For God's sake, Elizabeth," he cried in a panic, "what can I do?"

Elizabeth could not help but laugh as she looked up at the anxious face of her adored husband. Some of his hair was standing straight up, while some was falling down in his face. He was pale and then flushed. Striding about the room, he was the picture of a nervous father-to-be.

In a calm voice, Elizabeth said, "Dearest, come sit by me and hold my hand. Sarah, bring this wild man a chair."

Darcy sat down and took her hands in both of his. "Please, Elizabeth, do not tease me. I am so worried for you."

"Why should you be worried? Women go through childbirth every day."

"But none of them is my wife. I care only about you!" he protested.

"Please, my love, try to stay as calm as possible. We may have a long night ahead of us."

"How long?" he yelled.

Elizabeth rolled her eyes. "Sarah, please get Mr. Darcy a brandy."

Shaking her head and laughing under her breath, Sarah left the room.

Darcy buried his face in Elizabeth's neck. "I am sorry, my love. I will try to be calm. It is only that I had not thought about the actual birth until now. I am frantic with worry that something will happen to you."

"Nothing will happen to me, Fitzwilliam, for I am young and healthy. Besides, do you think I would be so foolish as to die and leave you to face all those matchmaking mothers and their daughters? Oh, no, they cannot have you! You are mine and only mine! So be calm and help me get through this."

"Please do not speak of dying, Elizabeth," he whispered, as though afraid to say it any louder.

She reached up and smoothed his wrinkled brow. "I will speak of it no more, but you must promise to remain calm while you are with me. When the doctor makes you leave, then you may behave as you wish."

"I am not leaving you. They cannot make me leave!" he declared. "This is my house, and you are my wife, having my child, and I will stay here if you and I desire it," he said, sounding like a petulant child.

Elizabeth put her arms around her husband and sighed. "Oh dear, I did not realize I would have to tend to two babies."

"Well, you do, so hush," he laughed softly.

Sarah walked in with a small brandy. "At least you are laughing, master.

Here is your brandy. Sip it slowly. It will help your nerves."

By the time the doctor and midwife arrived, Elizabeth's pains had sharpened, and she was digging her nails into Darcy's hands. It was painful, but he thought if she could go through childbirth, he could stand having his hands scarred for life.

"Mistress, scream if you need to," Sarah told her. "No one will think less of you."

"Oh, Sarah," she moaned, "I never expected such pain."

Mrs. Reynolds wrapped a cloth around a piece of wood and brought it to her. "Mrs. Darcy, bite on this." Elizabeth bit down hard and then she screamed.

The doctor said, "Mr. Darcy, it is time you left. You are not needed here any longer."

"I am not leaving my wife all alone!" Darcy cried.

"She is not alone, sir. Please leave."

Sarah put her arms around his shoulders. "Master, you are in the way. I will be here, and I promise nothing will happen to her. Please, sir, go out into the hall until we call you."

Darcy believed as long as he was there holding Elizabeth's hands, she would be all right, but Sarah kept urging him to leave, and finally, after kissing his wife, he left her chamber.

Sarah led him to the hall, where they found everyone but the children sitting and waiting.

"Master Andrew, please find the bottle of brandy, and bring it up here," Sarah asked, and he rushed downstairs to comply. Then fixing her eyes on Darcy she ordered, "Do not gulp down the brandy — only sip it. You will want to be conscious when the child arrives."

Darcy nodded his head and then began to pace up and down the hallway nervously.

"Nephew," said Lady Catherine, "I will not have you behaving in this manner. It shows a lack of confidence in Elizabeth. Women were formed to bear children. It is our lot in life, and all your pacing will not change that."

Darcy did not acknowledge her, but he sat down and held his head in his hands until Andrew returned with the brandy. Each time Elizabeth screamed, he took a drink, and when she began calling for her mother, he took several long drinks. Finally, Mr. Bennet took the bottle away.

"That is enough, sir. You cannot be drunk when your child arrives. You need to be sober to greet him."

In an effort to distract Darcy, Mr. Bennet asked him about Elizabeth's parents, especially the mother she was calling.

"They were wonderful people," Darcy said. "Elizabeth was especially close to her mother, but she loved her father, too." He laughed as he recalled his wife as a young girl. "She had him wrapped around her little finger, and he loved both his children very much.

Yes, Mr. Bennet thought, *I chose well.*

Just as Darcy thought he could stand no more, there was silence in Elizabeth's room, and then they heard a lusty cry from the babe.

Shortly thereafter, Sarah opened the door and motioned Darcy back inside. "Go to your wife, sir. All is well. I will bring your babe to you in a few minutes."

Darcy hurried to Elizabeth. She looked tired, but she was smiling, glad it was over, and holding out her arms to him.

"What do we have, my love? A boy or girl?"

"I do not know. They would not tell me," Elizabeth frowned. "We will find out together."

Soon, Sarah brought them a wiggling, whimpering bundle. She was smiling as she laid the babe in Elizabeth's arms. Darcy quickly pulled back the blanket and looked carefully.

"I told you, my love! Darcy men always have sons first. The next will be a girl. May I carry him out so the others can see him? I promise to bring him right back."

Elizabeth knew how proud and excited he was, and though she was anxious to hold her son, she consented. "See that you do, Fitzwilliam! I long to hold my son."

Proudly, he carried his child out into the hall, holding him up so that everyone could see. Georgiana rushed to them with tears in her eyes, followed by Andrew. The baby stopped whimpering and looked at everyone.

Andrew was almost giddy with relief that his sister was safely delivered and very proud to be an uncle. He insisted that he be allowed to hold his nephew, and he held the babe close to his heart, gently kissing him on his head. His eyes met Georgiana's, and they smiled at each other.

Lady Catherine sniffed, but there was a smile on her face. "He is a Darcy in looks, but I would have expected nothing less."

Jane and Bingley were thrilled that Darcy had his son and that Elizabeth was well. Both hoped that the horrors of the past could finally be left behind, and that a bright future for them all lay ahead.

Mr. Bennet feared he would cry, but he managed to hold back his tears. Everyone, including the colonel, was in awe of this tiny little human who had a head full of dark, curly hair. After everyone had seen him, Darcy carried him back to his mother.

"Here, little mother, here is our son!" Darcy laid him in Elizabeth's arms. He leaned down and kissed her tenderly. "You have made me so very happy, my love. If I lost all my wealth today, I would still be the richest man on earth."

Sarah laid her hand on Darcy's shoulder. "Leave us now while we attend to your wife. I will call you back to your family very soon."

This time, Darcy did not argue with her. He walked back into the hall with a big grin on his face, feeling as though life could not be better.

THAT NIGHT, AFTER EVERYONE WAS asleep, Mr. Bennet heard a quiet knock on his door. When he opened it, Sarah was standing there, a candle in her hand. He was not surprised to see her. Earlier, Mr. Bennet had noticed her watching him, and he knew she recognized the pain he felt being unable to claim his first grandson.

"I have come to comfort you," she said in a low voice.

Motioning for her to come in, he closed and locked the door, then walked to the bed. Sarah sat down beside him and put her arms around his shoulders. Clinging to her, he leaned his head down on her breasts and wept. Silently, she gently rocked him back and forth until his tears were spent; then she lay back on the bed and pulled him to her.

Thomas Bennet poured out all his pain to Sarah that night while she lay holding him, saying not a word. At last, he was silent and still, and Sarah undressed herself and then him. He had not known a woman in many years, and he felt very awkward at first, but Sarah knew he needed to feel like a man again, and so she helped him.

Chapter 38

By the end of the first week in January, all their guests had departed with the exception of Andrew, Mr. Bennet, and the Bingleys. It was just as well, for Darcy and Elizabeth were completely enthralled with their new baby and had no time for anyone but him.

It was fortunate that the Bingleys still had eyes only for each other, and that Mr. Bennet preferred to stay in the library. Georgiana and Andrew were happy to spend extra time with each other unobserved by her brother, but Sarah kept a close eye on them as she had with Darcy and Elizabeth.

The Darcys named their baby Jonathan David Darcy, after their fathers, and called him Jonathan. In the early days after Elizabeth's delivery, they often broke their fast and sometimes had a mid-day snack in their chambers. Darcy did come downstairs for dinner, but all he talked about was Jonathan, not noticing the amused smiles of the other diners.

In truth, Andrew and Georgiana were just as enchanted as their brother and sister, and they spent a great deal of time in Elizabeth's room holding the baby when Darcy would release him to their care.

In the mornings and evenings, Darcy would disappear into the nursery and bring Jonathan back to bed with them. This was their time to cuddle and play with him, and both agreed he was the most perfect baby they had ever seen. His dark, curly hair reminded them of both parents, and his eyes were dark brown like his father's. He was a long baby and no doubt would be tall like his father. They both thought he more closely resembled Darcy, except for his lips, which were shaped like his mother's.

BINGLEY HAD RECEIVED A LETTER from his uncle in Scotland that told him

Caroline had settled down and was doing her chores without complaint. This was a great relief to them all, but Bingley vowed not to bring Caroline home until he was certain she no longer posed a threat to himself or the Darcys. He doubted it would be anytime soon.

CHARLES BINGLEY WAS WISE TO wait to bring his sister home. Miss Bingley knew her uncle had sent a good report to her brother, for she had read Bingley's reply. Things were going according to her plan. She had decided to put aside her plan to seek her revenge on her brother until later. First, she would kidnap the Darcy heir. Louisa had written and told her of the child's birth, and she was enraged by the news. Depriving the Darcys of their child would be the best revenge she could envision. If the babe should die before she found a place to leave him, then so be it.

She realized that she had to continue to deceive everyone at her uncle's farm in order to escape, so she began acting the part of the repentant niece. She was cooperative and pleasant. Her aunt and uncle, and even the guards and her companion, relaxed their vigilance of her.

Shortly after she arrived at the farm, Miss Bingley had begun to look around the house, and she had found a large bottle on a shelf in the closet of her aunt's chambers. At first, she thought it might be laudanum until she tasted it. Laudanum was known to have a very bitter taste, and this had little to none. With some careful questioning, she was able to learn that the bottle contained a draught that was used to help her aunt to sleep. Caroline hoped it was not too old to work effectively.

She had put it in the pocket of her dress, hiding it in her room when she went to bed that evening. She had known the bottle would not be missed, for it had been covered in dust and cobwebs and pushed to the back of the cabinet. Caroline had lifted the bottle very carefully and moved several items around to hide the spot where it had sat for so long.

Her uncle did not have servants, and one of Miss Bingley's duties was to prepare tea and serve it each morning and again in the evening before everyone retired for the night. Her plan was to put the sleeping draught in all the teacups, except hers, and pour the tea before leaving the kitchen. She had begun this practice as soon as she found the bottle, and no one thought anything of it.

Because the draught was old, she did not know how much to use for each person, so she experimented with the dosage on two different occasions. She did this in the evenings when everyone was tired and no one would be suspicious when they became drowsy and went to sleep. Using three tablespoons for each person would guarantee that they would sleep long and deeply enough to allow time for her to bind and gag them before making her escape.

She had hidden men's clothing and boots in the stable, and she planned to change into them before she left the farm. She would take one of the horses and ride it to the nearest town, where she would take a coach to Lambton.

On the morning of her escape, Miss Bingley was happily singing as she went about her chores, and everyone was pleased to see her good mood. She had decided to use the drug that morning so that she would have a full day of light in which to begin her journey. The medicine, ropes, and gags were hidden in the kitchen pantry.

"Here is tea, everyone," Miss Bingley trilled as she sashayed into the parlor. "Mmm, tea certainly will taste good on this cold day." Sitting her cup on a side table, she served each person, and then sat down to drink her own tea.

She had not long to wait. As they all lay sleeping, Miss Bingley ran to the kitchen for the ropes and gags. In no time, she had everyone bound and gagged on the floor of the parlor. On her way out the kitchen door, she took down a jar that contained the funds her aunt was saving for the purchase of additional farm animals, and she stole all the money. Caroline thought she had enough to secure her passage to Pemberley and then to London, where she had money hidden in her room.

In the stables, she quickly bound her small breasts and changed into the tattered clothing and well-worn boots. She pinned her hair tight against her scalp, and put on one of her uncle's old floppy hats. After she saddled one of the horses, she put on her uncle's thick work jacket and rode away.

THE NIGHT OF MISS BINGLEY'S arrival in Lambton, everyone at Pemberley was asleep. Even Mr. Bennet had gone to bed earlier than usual. All were asleep, that is, except for Sarah. She was uneasy and could not rest, so she sat reading a book in front of the fire. At intervals, she looked in on Jonathan. Finally, she sat down in a chair in his room and soon drifted off to sleep.

Sarah was not sure how long she slept or what woke her, but when she opened her eyes, she saw a figure going out of the room carrying a tiny bundle. Quickly, she checked Jonathan's bed. It was empty!

She flew out of his room and watched the figure going down the stairs. Sarah knew she had to be quiet and do nothing to cause the kidnapper to drop the baby or harm him in any way. Quietly, she crept down the stairs until she reached the bottom, where the baby had been laid in order for the person to put on a coat. At that moment, Sarah ran and wrestled the figure to the ground!

They both landed hard on the floor, and the person's hat flew off, revealing Caroline Bingley. Sarah was so enraged that she balled up her fist and hit Miss Bingley several times in the face, breaking her jaw and beating her unconscious.

Sarah scooped Jonathan up and ran for the Darcy's chamber, where she woke them by pounding on their door. Darcy opened it and Sarah rushed in, carrying the child to his mother.

"Mr. Darcy, come quickly. Miss Bingley tried to kidnap Jonathan, but I stopped her. She is lying on the floor by the front door. Please hurry!"

After warning Elizabeth to lock the door after them, Darcy ran out of the room in his robe, and he and Sarah rushed down the stairs. When they got there, however, the front door was wide open and Miss Bingley was gone.

"Where are the bloody servants?" Darcy cried.

Just then, they heard a groan and noticed two legs sticking out from one of the rooms. "Sarah, see to him and then alert the others while I dress," he yelled over his shoulder as he ran up the stairs, taking them two at a time.

In an instant, Darcy was back. He was relieved to see that Sarah had alerted Andrew and several other men and that they had lanterns lit, ready to depart.

"Clyde, you and Herman search all around the house. Bill, you and George search the back woods. Andrew, you and Mr. Reynolds come with me." Darcy turned to Sarah, "Please go back upstairs and stay with Elizabeth and Jonathan. Lock the door and let no one in except me. Hopefully, we will find Miss Bingley before she gets very far."

SARAH HAD INDEED STRUCK MISS Bingley hard enough to shatter her jaw. She lost consciousness for a short time, but soon she was on her feet and safely out the door. In a great deal of pain, she had forgotten where she left her horse and so continued her escape on foot. Her primary thought was to hide herself until she could make her way to London.

Snow began falling again, and her footsteps were soon obliterated. She ran as fast as she could manage without knowing where she was headed. Then an idea came to her. In the past, she had heard Mr. Darcy mention there were caves on Pemberley property, and in desperation, she now looked for one.

I must not be caught. I must not be caught, she repeated to herself as she lowered her head against the fierce wind and swirling snow.

Just as she thought she could run no longer, she spied a small opening against the side of a hill. There was brush close to the opening, and Miss Bingley hurriedly scooped it up and piled it at the front of the cave. After she had wedged herself inside, she pulled the brush over the opening, knowing that the falling snow would also help hide her.

She was in such pain that she could barely think. Too late, the magnitude of her actions overwhelmed her.

What have I done? Dear God, what have I done?

She had finally faced the truth. She would not escape, and she would have to face Mr. Darcy's wrath when he found her. He would never forgive her for trying to kidnap his child, and being Charles's sister would not save her from him. She knew she would never reach London; her dreams of being a leader in the *ton* were over. She would be shunned, and she had brought it all on herself.

Why, she asked herself, had she been so obsessed over Mr. Darcy? Why had she not moved on after he married? She had made a fool of herself and wasted her life by clinging to her dreams of being mistress of Pemberley. She had brought shame on the Bingley name and would be punished by ending her days in prison. She groaned out loud, then closed her eyes and prayed for death.

IT WAS DAWN WHEN THE men returned to the house without Caroline Bingley. Darcy hurried upstairs to let Elizabeth know he was home before returning downstairs to send a message to the constable in Lambton.

Sitting in his study, head in his hands, Darcy dreaded what he had to do next. Bingley had to be told about his sister. His heart breaking, he went upstairs and knocked on Bingley's door.

Chapter 39

Charles and Jane Bingley were stunned when Darcy informed them what had happened. Jane hurried to Elizabeth, and the two women cried with relief that Jonathan was safe. There were also tears of sorrow because it was Miss Bingley who had tried to kidnap him.

Mr. Bennet was greatly concerned when he heard knocking and hurriedly opened his door to find Jane standing there, tears flowing down her face as she explained what had happened during the night.

"The men have been out searching, but they have been unable to find Miss Bingley."

"Is Jonathan safe?" Mr. Bennet asked anxiously.

"Yes, he is well and with Elizabeth. Please dress and come downstairs to the breakfast room. Mrs. Reynolds is making breakfast so the men will have a hot meal when they return, but she has coffee ready now. I must wake Georgiana and take her to Elizabeth before she finds out from someone else."

"I will join you downstairs as soon as I dress."

Jane hugged her father and rushed to Georgiana's room, where the door was opened before she could knock.

"Jane, what has happened? The noise woke me."

"Dearest, I will explain while you dress." As Georgiana rang for her maid, Jane told her what she knew. As soon as Georgiana was ready, they made their way to Elizabeth's chambers where they found her and the babe with Sarah. Holding Jonathan tightly to her chest, Elizabeth led the other women downstairs so they could all be with Mrs. Reynolds and the other servants.

There was a grim look on Mrs. Reynolds's face, and it was clear that she was furious at what had happened.

"Pardon me, Mrs. Bingley, I know she is your sister, and I do not wish to hurt you by speaking ill of her, but I have never liked Caroline Bingley. And now she has tried to harm our little one, and I cannot find it in my heart to forgive her."

Elizabeth went immediately to Mrs. Reynolds, put her arms around the housekeeper, and then she showed her that Jonathan had not been harmed.

"No thanks to that she-devil!" Sarah exclaimed.

Mr. Bennet came into the room and asked where the men had gone. He wanted to help in the search for Miss Bingley, but Elizabeth and Jane begged him to stay with them, so they would have a man in the house to protect them. It was a duty he could not refuse and he relented.

Later that morning, the men returned to the house to change into dry clothes and to eat a hot meal. As soon as that was accomplished, they left to continue the search. It had snowed again and covered any tracks Miss Bingley might have left. The men determined that she was on foot, for none of the horses was missing, and the horse she had ridden was found nearby. One of the younger stable hands noticed him after the men left, and led him to the stables to wipe him down and feed him.

Darcy sent one of his servants to Lambton to inquire whether Caroline had caught the coach, but no one of her description had been seen.

Miss Bingley's whereabouts were still not discovered by the end of the first day, and the men came back to rest when the sun went down. Darcy and the constable, Mr. Merrick, were closed in his study for quite a while, but finally Mr. Merrick left, and Darcy managed to eat a small amount of food. Bingley stayed with him, but he was unable to eat anything.

Afterwards, the two men retired to Darcy's study where they stayed for several hours. When they left the room, Mr. Bingley's eyes were red. They walked to the drawing room where they collected their wives and retired for the evening.

That night, Darcy and Elizabeth slept with their door locked and Jonathan between them. However, they did not sleep well, waking frequently to make certain their baby was safe and had not been spirited away.

Chapter 40

Two days later, Andrew rode back to Pemberley shouting that they had found Miss Bingley's body. She was huddled in a small cave several miles from the house. The women had gathered in Elizabeth's sitting room to have tea and give support to Jane.

"Has Mr. Bingley returned to the house, Mr. Worthington?"

"No, ma'am. He has stayed to help remove her body, but he should be back soon."

Jane rose from her chair. "I shall wait for him downstairs," she said and quickly left the room.

After she had gone, Elizabeth asked Andrew what more he knew.

"It is doubtful that she survived the first night. She had pulled brush over the mouth of the cave, which is why we had trouble spotting her." Andrew looked at Sarah. "Miss Bingley's face is much bruised, and her jaw looks to be broken."

"Good," said Sarah vehemently. "She deserved to die for trying to harm Jonathan. I hope she died in great pain."

Andrew and Elizabeth looked at each other, and then Elizabeth pulled Sarah into her arms. "I understand your rage, dearest, but it is best that you keep such thoughts to yourself around Mr. and Mrs. Bingley. They feel guilty that it was their sister, and we do not wish to hurt them any further."

"I will keep silent, Elizabeth, but it is good that she is dead. Like Mrs. Bennet, now she can no longer harm anyone."

Andrew patted Sarah on the shoulder. "For a while, it seemed as though everyone had gone mad. I do not understand people such as Miss Bingley and Mrs. Bennet. What drives them to try and harm innocent people?" Andrew shook his head.

They heard the sound of boots pounding up the stairs and down the hallway. Moments later, Darcy burst into the room with word that Miss Bingley's body had been brought to Pemberley and the undertaker had been summoned.

At dinner that evening, no one had an appetite, and little was said. Bingley was pale, but he was trying to contain his emotions although Darcy could see that he was near collapsing. Everyone retired to their chambers early that night, but it was doubtful that anyone slept well.

ON THE DAY MISS BINGLEY's body was taken back to London, Darcy traveled with the Bingleys and Mr. Bennet only at Elizabeth's urging, even though he was fearful that something might happen while he was gone.

"Fitzwilliam, Charles needs you. You must go and lend him your support. If there is gossip, your presence will prevent it from spreading. Sarah will protect us while you are away."

At last, Darcy agreed and they set out for London. Before reaching town, they decided to say only that Miss Bingley had met with an accident. There was no reason for a scandal that could only hurt the Bingleys and the Hursts and, later, could possibly harm any children Bingley might have.

Since Mr. Bennet was traveling with them, Darcy insisted that Andrew stay at Pemberley until he returned home. Sarah knew she did not need Andrew. She was capable of caring for Elizabeth, Georgiana, and Jonathan, but she stayed silent on the matter. If Darcy felt more at ease having Andrew at Pemberley, she would not argue with him.

The women and the servants were still shaken by what had happened, but they were determined not to live the rest of their lives in fear.

Elizabeth received a message from Darcy after the funeral.

Dearest Wife,

I hope to be home by the end of this week although Bingley and Jane will stay longer to be with Mrs. Hurst as she is taking her sister's death very hard. She blames herself for indulging Miss Bingley all her life and not seeking help for her long ago. Bingley and Jane feel they need to remain with her.

Mr. Bennet plans to travel back to Pemberley with me. Miss Bingley's vengeful act and her death affected him greatly, and he is anxious to return to the peace and quiet of my library.

224

We have tried to prevent gossip and rumors by announcing Miss Bingley's death as an accident, and we have been successful. There has been only a small amount of talk among the ton. Thank you for urging me to come with Bingley as my presence helped more than the denials.

I miss you, my beloved, and long to be home with you and Jonathan. Give him a hug and kiss from his papa.

Your loving husband,
Fitzwilliam

THE DAY DARCY AND MR. Bennet arrived home, Darcy flew up the stairs and ran into Elizabeth's chambers. Handing Jonathan to Sarah, Elizabeth threw herself into Darcy's arms. They held each other for a long time, as if they never wanted to let the other go, each taking comfort from the other.

"Oh, Fitzwilliam, I have missed you desperately."

"I shall never leave you again," he vowed fervently. Then taking Jonathan from Sarah, he held his son tightly against his chest and kissed him. After several minutes, he handed Jonathan back to Sarah and said, "We wish to be alone. We will ring when we are ready for you to bring our son back." Sarah nodded and left the room.

Darcy pulled Elizabeth back into his arms and kissed her hungrily. "I know it is too soon to make love, but I crave your body close to mine."

"As do I," she replied eagerly.

Soon they were undressed and lay on the bed facing one another, enjoying the feel of their bare skin against each other. They embraced and kissed until their breathing became heavy. It was time to stop before they did something foolish.

Darcy left their bed and brought their robes. Laughing softly, they enjoyed another kiss before putting them on and ringing for Sarah.

When Sarah left again, the couple lay across the bed marveling over their son, thankful that they were still a family. Realizing that it could be swept away in the blink of an eye, they vowed never to take their happiness for granted. Their love, their child, and any future children they might have would be the most important gifts they could give to each other. This was a vow they never broke.

Epilogue

As soon as he discovered that Miss Bingley had escaped from Scotland, Mr. Darcy asked the constable in Lambton to send an express to the magistrate in the town nearest her uncle's farm. The occupants had spent more than a day bound and gagged and had suffered from the cold and from thirst, but all were expected to recover.

Darcy also sent a message to the guards to come to Pemberley, where he hired them to work on his estate. Miss Bingley's companion wished to stay with the elder Bingleys and help them on their farm. They had become close friends, and she did not wish to leave them.

FITZWILLIAM AND ELIZABETH DARCY HAD four more children — two sons, Andrew and Charles, and two daughters, Catherine and Sarah. Jonathan, as the eldest, became master of Pemberley. He married Lady Maria Compton, whose father, Lord Kingston, owned a great estate in Yorkshire.

Andrew was given one of the smaller estates that Darcy owned. He married Victoria Stapleton, the daughter of a wealthy tradesman.

Charles felt called to the church, and he became the vicar at Kympton. His wife, Nancy Reid, was the daughter of a bishop.

The girls, Sarah and Catherine, married fine young men. Catherine and her husband, Guy Robinson, a wealthy gentleman, made their home in London, but Sarah was happiest living in Staffordshire, the wife of James Worthington, eldest son of Henry and Rose Worthington.

Each marriage was a happy one. The Darcy children had vowed when they were young that they would marry only for love as their parents had done.

GEORGIANA AND ANDREW WORTHINGTON MARRIED when she turned nineteen. They had three children — a son named Alexander, who became Master of Rosehaven, and two daughters, Anna and Isabella. Anna became a world famous opera singer and never married. She was obsessed with her career and had no time or desire for a husband. Isabella, however, married Thomas Reed who was Master of Graywood, a large estate in Yorkshire, and she became the darling of the *ton*. She and her husband always traveled to London for the season.

JANE AND CHARLES BINGLEY BOUGHT Woodhaven, an estate near Pemberley. Mr. Bennet lived happily with them until his death. He had his beloved books and his port and was a regular visitor, along with Jane and Charles, to Pemberley. Elizabeth appreciated his wit and became very fond of him. The relationship between Elizabeth and Jane deepened and they became as sisters.

The Bingleys had a son named William, who was the heir to Woodhaven, and a daughter named Elizabeth. Both children married for love. William married Amanda Collins, the daughter of William and Charlotte Collins, and Elizabeth married Alex Birkshire, who owned a modest estate near Woodhaven.

COLONEL RICHARD FITZWILLIAM RESIGNED HIS commission two years after Jonathan's birth. He and his mistress, Olivia, married and immigrated to America, where they had one son named James. They lived happily in upstate New York for a number of years, then moved westward and bought a ranch where they lived for the rest of their lives. They never returned to England.

Richard's parents were devastated by his leaving, but Lord Matlock gave Richard his inheritance before he left, for he knew they would never see their son again. Before Richard and Olivia left England, they traveled to Pemberley at the invitation of the Darcys and spent two weeks with them before leaving for America.

SARAH DIED AT NINE AND eighty years of age after living a long and happy life, protecting her charge until her last breath.

Not long after Mrs. Bennet's death, Elizabeth confessed to Sarah that she wondered if she was, indeed, the daughter of Mr. and Mrs. Bennet. Sarah looked her straight in the eyes and said, "Elizabeth, you are the true daughter of Jonathan and Margaret Worthington. I was there from the beginning. They were your parents. Never doubt that!" Elizabeth breathed a sigh of relief, her fears put to rest.

Sarah knew that the truth would shatter Elizabeth's carefully structured life. She would be unable to live with the knowledge that the woman who gave birth to her had hated her and wished her dead. It was best that she knew her mother as the kind, loving woman that raised her. She had promised Mr. Worthington that she would never reveal the truth to Elizabeth, and she kept her promise. The secret died with her.

FINIS